THE HOUSE ON GALLOWS GREEN

An Inspector Jack Dawes Mystery

THE HOUSE ON GALLOWS GREEN

Frances Lloyd

ROBERT HALE · LONDON

ISBN 978-0-7198-0665-0

Robert Hale Limited
Clerkenwell House
Clerkenwell Green
London EC1R 0HT

www.halebooks.com

2 4 6 8 10 9 7 5 3 1

Typeset in 10½/14 Sabon
Printed in Great Britain by the MPG Books Group,
Bodmin and King's Lynn

CHAPTER ONE

GIBBET COTTAGE – GALLOWS GREEN, SOMERSET

A soft, balmy night with a light breeze shaking the trees. The man in the shadows was trembling. The palms of his hands were moist and warm sweat trickled down his neck and inside his shirt. He hoped he couldn't be seen, deep in the blackness of the moon shadow. The metal box he clutched to his chest was awkward and cumbersome. He searched desperately around the overgrown garden for a place to hide it; somewhere secure where he could return for it later when the heat had died down. He'd left it too late to store it away properly. Events had overtaken his usual careful planning and he couldn't take any chances. Only fools took chances in this game. The stakes were too high.

What was that?

He stood stock still, ears straining, his heartbeat pounding in the screaming silence. He could smell his own fear. Something was moving in the dense undergrowth. He tensed, ready to duck low and run zigzagging through the bushes. The sound came again. He took a long, deep breath to calm himself, then slid deeper into the shadows, his body taut; his ears tuned. A rustling, a snapping of twigs. Then a snuffling and grunting as something darted out of the thick shrubbery. It was small; an animal of some kind. A badger or maybe a fox. Gallows Green was running alive with filthy, flea-infested vermin. He relaxed a little and crept forward into the coppice that concealed a deep, stagnant pond; fetid and choked with weeds. It wasn't ideal but it would have to do.

He watched the heavy box sink slowly beneath the greasy surface, gurgling as it was sucked down into the sludge. His nose told him that the overflow from the septic tank probably emptied into this pond. So much the better. He didn't want some nosey neighbour poking around in it and there was nothing like raw sewage for keeping people away. He thought, not for the first time, that life in the English countryside was mostly stinking and crude and he didn't just mean the animals. The rural idyll of leafy tranquillity might fool some people but not him. This chocolate-box village with its superficial charm and sanctimonious morality hid corruption that would rival the most crime-ridden city. He smiled contemptuously, recalling how he had cashed in on that corruption; made these idiot yokels pay for their crass stupidity and lack of respect. But now the sky was lightening. Somewhere, not far off, a rooster crowed and a dog barked. Lights were starting to come on in some of the cottages. Lullington Barrow was waking up. It was time to leave, and fast.

He knew only too well that the Arabs were hot on his trail, maybe only minutes behind, and they didn't mess around. He'd got something they wanted; something valuable that belonged to them, and he planned to demand a great deal of money for it. But if they caught him now, he'd end up giving them everything, telling them all he knew. The Geneva Convention meant nothing to them and he'd witnessed some of their interrogation techniques. He still couldn't work out how they'd tracked him down. He'd been so vigilant, so careful to cover his tracks. He should have been safe here.

His ear caught another sound; the dry crackle of dead leaves on the garden path, crushed by quick, purposeful footsteps. He crouched in the bushes, feeling for the Caracal semi-automatic in his pocket. Then he smelt Chanel and glimpsed a flash of yellow hair in the moonlight. Saskia.

'Have you got the tickets?'

She held them out. 'We should be in Amsterdam by noon.'

'Let's get out of here.' He turned abruptly, grabbing her arm. The breeze snatched away the last whisper of her perfume as together, they crashed through the coppice. The track beyond would take them away from Gibbet Cottage and through the rear gate to safety. A Range Rover loaded with their luggage was already parked in the lane that ran along the back of Gallows Green. Three minutes after they roared away, a black Mercedes with tinted windows and Syrian plates drew up at the front of the house.

CHAPTER TWO

METROPOLITAN POLICE HEADQUARTERS, LONDON

It was official: the promised heatwave had arrived. The brass sun gonged down out of a cloudless sky and temperatures were forecast to reach the early thirties by midday. It was as if the pits of hell had opened up, spewing out heat and humidity that knocked everyone flat. And it wasn't even July, yet.

In the sweltering incident room, Detective Sergeant 'Bugsy' Malone of the murder investigation team was sucking an ice lolly to relieve the boredom of being stuck in an office with dodgy air-con and no action. The phones lay silent and the whiteboards, usually cluttered with photo-fits and angled shots of grisly corpses, were blank. For the Met, it looked like another tedious day of nicking drunks and drug dealers. Too hot for murder.

Dead on nine o'clock, Detective Inspector Jack Dawes swung his car into the car park. Gracefully for a tall man, he uncoiled his wiry six-foot-three frame from behind the wheel and clambered out, reluctant to leave the cool interior. His highly polished shoes left dents in the melting tarmac as he strode into the station.

Sergeant Malone chucked his lolly stick in the bin and lumbered to his feet. Blimey, it must be hot. It was rare to see the boss without a jacket, let alone in a short-sleeved shirt.

'Morning, Guv.'

Jack pulled out a handkerchief and mopped his forehead, already beaded with sweat. 'It's like a furnace in here, Bugsy. What's happened to the air-con?'

'On the blink again. The engineers are in Garwood's office, fixing up some fans.'

The MIT was one of the specialized homicide squads of the London Metropolitan Police Service and formed part of Scotland Yard's

Serious Crime Group. The Commands were split geographically, each unit led by a detective chief superintendent; in this case, DCS George Garwood. But this was only a stepping stone. Garwood was a career man, determined to rise to the top of his chosen profession. His sumptuous, oak-panelled office reflected this and he had commandeered the engineers to control the intolerable heat and humidity before it ruined the patina on his gleaming mahogany desk.

'Any suspicious deaths, Bugsy?' Jack asked, more in hope than expectation.

Malone shook his head. 'We nearly had one; late last night. Bloke found dead in the river. Because of his head injuries, the doc thought he'd been clobbered and pushed off the bridge, but then a witness came forward. Turns out the bloke staggered from a nearby pub, rat-arsed, climbed up on the parapet to do a wee and fell in, bashing his nut on the way down.'

'That's a terrible waste of a good corpse.'

'That's what I said. The poor devil's dead, whichever way you look at it. He could at least have had the decency to get himself topped and give us something to work on.'

'Yes, but if he'd had any decency, he wouldn't have been urinating in public.'

'Dead right, Guv. If I get caught short, I pee in a shop doorway. Much more genteel.'

'In the absence of anything more compelling, it's a good time to catch up on the paperwork.' Dawes headed for his office. 'I'll make a start on the Home Office Statistics before Garwood starts nagging.' He had barely fired up the computer when his phone rang.

'It's me, darling. Guess what's just arrived in the post.'

'Hello, Corrie. Don't tell me – it's one of your astronomical food bills.'

Jack's wife, Coriander, was a professional caterer, trading under the name of 'Coriander's Cuisine'. She had built the company from scratch and business was booming to the extent that she had recently moved to an industrial catering unit and taken on an assistant chef. Carlene was a laconic young woman with several studs through her eyebrows and tormented magenta hair. At the interview, Corrie had asked why she had applied for the job. The answer was honest and direct, like the girl.

'I wanted to work in caterin' but I never got enough GCSEs to deliver pizza, so it was either this or chopping giblets down the abattoir.'

For Corrie, this extra pair of hands had the added advantage of allowing her more time to help Jack with his murder investigations, although he insisted he could manage without her meddling, never mind the trouble it got her into. She seemed to be a magnet for danger. In the course of 'assisting' him, she had been poisoned by a psychotic professor, bashed unconscious with a ballroom dancing trophy and held hostage on the parapet of an eighty-foot tower. None of it had dampened her irrepressible enthusiasm. Right now, though, she was hoping to persuade Jack to take some time off.

'No, it isn't a bill; it's an invitation from my sister, Rosemary. She and Dick are having a house-warming barbecue at the weekend. Well, it's a cottage-warming to be entirely accurate.'

'I didn't know they'd moved.'

'Yes, you did; I told you last week. They've moved out of Bristol and bought a cottage in the country. Rosie said they wanted to break away from the gritty, drug-fuelled city and the spiralling gang violence, before it ensnares young Jeremy. Dick said rural life is much greener and more environmentally friendly and he's thinking of keeping free-range chickens.'

Jack snorted. His brother-in-law was a pompous, self-opinionated twerp. 'Well, he would, wouldn't he? Dick by name and dick by—'

'Jack! He can't help being tedious, he's a merchant banker.'

'You can say that again. And he's a short-arse. Barely five foot.'

'Sweetheart, he can't help that either and he's actually five feet six. I bet his feet don't stick out the bottom of the bed, like yours.'

Jack relented. 'Can we get there and back in a day?'

'Not really. Rosie wants me to help with the catering.' Out of the corner of her eye, Corrie could see Carlene hurling quiches into the oven. Under her whites, she wore low-slung jeans and a cropped, halter-neck top that exposed most of her middle portion. The colourful tattoo across her stomach reminded Corrie of a map of the London Underground with a belly bar through the Bakerloo Line. As a chef, Carlene would never give Nigella any sleepless nights, but she was clean, hardworking and reliable and above all, Corrie liked her. 'I thought we might take a little holiday. Carlene can manage here for a few days and you said things were quiet there. We both need a break and it'll be cooler in the country.'

Jack thought about it. 'I expect Sergeant Malone could cope. But we don't have to stay with Dick and Rosemary, do we?'

'No, I've booked us into the local hostelry. It's right in the heart of the village and it looks absolutely charming on the Internet. It has a thatched roof, oak beams and everything!'

'What's it called?'

Corrie hesitated. 'Hangman's Inn.'

Coriander had a twin brother, Basil, who was twenty minutes older; her sister, Rosemary, was born a year later. Their mother, a keen cook, had called her babies after her favourite herbs; fine for Basil and Rosemary but a little awkward for Coriander, especially when she married Jack and became Corrie Dawes. She had become accustomed to the sniggers when she introduced herself. On leaving school, Basil had qualified as a doctor and moved to New Zealand, Corrie had taken up catering and Rosemary had become a complementary therapist. Although not a close family, they kept in touch by phone and visited when work permitted.

Rosemary and Dick Brown started married life in a semi-detached town house on a tightly-packed estate. Dick had been a bank clerk then; now, ten years on, he headed up the merchant banking department. Rosemary had their son, Jeremy, within a year of marriage and temporarily gave up her job to look after him. Once he was old enough to go to school, she resumed her complementary therapy and set up her own practice from home. They both agreed that the time had come to move somewhere socially fashionable, more suited to their professional status; somewhere they could entertain important clients and impress their friends. Added to which, the police seemed powerless to control the gangs, drugs and mindless vandalism that were increasingly infesting the city and Jeremy needed to grow up in a safer, gentler environment. But deciding was one thing; finding the perfect house in the right location was another matter entirely.

If Rosemary hadn't bought a copy of the *Western Daily Press* while she was out shopping, they might never have discovered Gibbet Cottage. It had just come on the market and as she read the details, she became increasingly convinced she'd found their dream home.

'Gibbet Cottage is a delightful, Grade II listed property situated on the edge of Gallows Green in the attractive Somerset village of Lullington Barrow. Its deceptively rustic façade hides a large, elegant period house with a wealth of features and style. The mature garden reflects the charming character with a stream, coppice, pond and shrubs. To the rear, the garden extends to two acres of woodland, home to a wide variety of birds and wildlife. This much sought-after residence is within easy walking distance of the school, village shop and church.'

That evening, she thrust the paper under Dick's nose and he was equally impressed but for different reasons.

'For the keen golfer, there is a magnificent eighteen-hole links course built into the sand dunes, with excellent facilities and a warm, welcoming clubhouse. And for real-ale enthusiasts, the village boasts an historic hostelry dating back to the early eighteenth century when miscreants were hanged from a gibbet, a replica of which still stands on the summit of Gallows Green Hill. Hangman's Inn keeps a large range of ales and local cider, made in Lullington's very own cider mill. Access to the M5 is within four miles and there is a mainline railway station in the bustling town of Lowerbridge. Bristol airport is only twenty-five miles away.'

A decent pub, a golf club where both he and Rosie could play and easy access to his city office. What more could a man want? And the asking price for a quick sale was incredibly reasonable; a bargain, in fact, and being a banker, Dick loved a bargain. He immediately rang and made an appointment to view.

The Browns looked over the property next day and loved it. There were four thatched cottages grouped in a horseshoe around Gallows Green, each romantic and charming. Gibbet Cottage was the largest and most stylish, and the only one boasting two acres of woodland. Young Jeremy dashed about the wild garden, delighted to have a real 'jungle' to explore. Rosemary earmarked one of the bedrooms as a consulting room for her therapies and Dick gazed happily across the green at the pub and the golf links. A more observant couple might have noticed that the previous owners had left in a hurry. Abandoned pictures hung lopsided on the walls and there was still food in the kitchen cupboards and milk in the fridge; even clothes in a laundry basket. Something was not quite right about Gibbet Cottage and if the Browns failed to notice, it was because they were so beguiled by their new country paradise that nothing could be allowed to spoil it.

To Dick's amazement, his first, modest offer was accepted without haggling. The hastily departed owners played no role in either the negotiations or the final exchange of contracts; solicitors had been empowered to deal with everything. The legal paperwork was completed with record speed and the delighted Browns moved in very soon after. They immediately set about becoming part of the Lullington Barrow community by planning a summer barbeque to introduce themselves to the village. Rosemary issued an open invitation through Ted and Liz Boobyer, keepers of Hangman's Inn. Liz warned her that the whole village would turn up to inspect the 'incomers', which threw Rosemary into a panic. Everyone knew how important first impressions were, so the food and wine had to be perfect. Who better to manage the catering, suggested Dick, than Rosie's sister, Corrie? At least they could rely on her food to be edible. Privately, he reckoned she'd be a lot cheaper than hiring professionals. Rosemary had dashed off an invitation straight away.

On Friday, it seemed as if the whole of the UK had decided to take advantage of the heatwave and head down the M5 to the West Country. Corrie decided they should travel in her refrigerated delivery van which she had packed full of food for the Saturday barbecue. By the afternoon, they had joined the end of a convoy, which became longer and slower until it ground to a shuddering halt just short of the notorious Almondsbury Interchange.

'How much further?' Jack was munching one of Carlene's quiches while Corrie drove. He'd had no trouble taking a holiday. DCS Garwood had been on his way out for a round of golf with the commander when Jack requested leave and he simply dismissed him with an imperious wave of his hand. DS Malone promised to let him know instantly, if anybody had the courtesy to turn up suspiciously dead.

'We want exit twenty-two, south of Weston-super-Mare,' announced Corrie. 'I had hoped we'd be nearly there by now, but I doubt if we'll make it before evening. Then it'll be a big glass of chilled Sauvignon Blanc in the Hangman's Inn. Bliss!'

Jack glanced sideways at her as they chugged slowly along the choked motorway. 'Have you ever dreamt of swapping city life for a more peaceful existence in the country?'

Corrie glanced back, a look of shocked disgust on her face. 'Good Lord, no! What a ghastly suggestion. What made you ask?'

'Well, you know, clean air, beautiful sunsets, birdsong, a fox calling on a frosty winter's night, curling up in front of a log fire with scones cooked on a range with home-made jam . . .'

Corrie joined in, '. . . antiquated drains, smelly pig farms, bats, nosey neighbours, mud, smouldering pyres of foot and mouth carcasses, pollen, sheep farmers with unpleasant personal habits . . .'

'Yes, but apart from all that? Surely driving would be easier than in London?'

'. . . no street lights, no signposts, smoky diesel tractors with no exhausts doing ten miles an hour down the middle of the road, bridges so narrow you have to reverse back over them when the milk lorry approaches . . .'

'Okay, I get the message. You're not a closet outdoor-girl.'

'No, I'm blooming well not, and anyway, you can't have a closet outdoor-girl; it's an oxymoron – either that, or a compressed paradox. I think Rosie's nuts even to consider living in the sticks. Give 'em twelve months and they'll be back in Bristol; you wait and see.'

When Corrie walked into the bar of Hangman's Inn, it was humming with the rambling, haphazard type of pub-talk that is heard in any hostelry on a Friday evening. But here in Lullington Barrow, the noisy chat was softened somewhat by the slow country drawl of Somerset tongues. Corrie's first impression was of simple, rustic folk leading placid, happy lives. Ted and Liz Boobyer, the pub owners, chatted with their customers, who seemed more like friends and Danika, the very pretty young barmaid, had a charming foreign accent that Corrie guessed was Eastern European, probably Polish.

Plump, jolly Liz Boobyer, the stereotypical pub landlady whose name was over the door, bustled across to Corrie, an obvious visitor. 'Evenin', m'dear. What can I get you?' She looked puzzled, thinking she'd seen this stranger somewhere before.

Corrie smiled to herself. The family likeness between the sisters was strong but their shapes were completely opposite. Corrie had the cuddly figure of a caterer who enjoyed her own food and spent most of her life in leggings, a size eighteen overall and trainers. Rosemary was the skinny, highly strung type who travelled everywhere at a brisk trot, lived on her nerves and never went out without full make-up, high heels and a well-tailored jacket. Nevertheless, Liz Boobyer had spotted the resemblance. Corrie helped make the connection.

'Good evening. I'm Rosemary Brown's sister, Corrie, from London and I'd love a glass of very cold, very dry Sauvignon Blanc, please.'

'Well, bless me!' Liz called to her husband. 'Ted, come over 'ere and see! 'Tiz Mrs Brown's sister what does the posh cooking up London.'

The villagers turned to stare, smile and nod agreement to each other. Then came the salvo of questions. How long was she staying? Did she have children? Why not? How much did she make, cooking for rich folk? Was her hair really that colour? By the time Jack staggered through the door with the bags, everyone was on first-name terms and calling out to him, 'Cummin yer, Jack, an wet thee whistle.'

Ted pulled a pint of Lullington Gold and pushed it across the bar. 'First one's on the house.'

Jack picked up his glass, admired the pellucid liquid for some seconds, then took a long, appreciative slug.

'So what do you do for a living, Jack?' called someone.

Jack wiped the foam from his top lip. 'I'm a policeman. Detective inspector in the Metropolitan Police Murder Squad.'

The friendly hum ceased abruptly and people became absorbed in their games of darts and dominoes. Corrie glared at Jack and whispered, crossly.

'Why did you have to say that? Next to a funeral director or a tax collector, a copper has to be the worst possible conversation killer.'

'Only if you have something to hide,' Jack whispered back, calmly.

'Couldn't you have pretended to be a plumber or an electrician? Something less menacing?'

'Okay, and what would I have done if someone had asked me to mend a leaky tap or wire a plug?'

'What you always do; get me to fix it.' She emptied her glass. 'Come on, drink up. We'll book into our room, then go and find Gibbet Cottage.'

CHAPTER THREE

There was no doubt about it, thought Corrie, if you were looking for a swanky country retreat, simply oozing with what estate agents call 'period charm and character', Gibbet Cottage was definitely it. There were oak beams in every room, a magnificent inglenook fireplace and a farmhouse kitchen to die for. It was wasted on Rosie, of course, because she never actually *cooked* anything; most of their meals were delivered by specialist suppliers and she simply heated them up. 'What was the point,' she argued, 'of buying food that you had to fiddle with before you could eat it?' As a girl, Rosie had existed mainly on apples and Ryvita so Corrie suspected that half the time, she wasn't entirely sure what she *was* eating. The spectacular, dual-fuel range looked brand new and so did the giant chest freezer left behind by the previous owners. They couldn't have been keen cooks, either. What a terrible waste! Corrie could imagine herself and Carlene running 'Coriander's Cuisine' out of this huge kitchen without tripping over each other as they often did in Corrie's more modest premises in the catering unit she rented on the edge of the Kings Richington Industrial Estate.

Outside, in the overgrown garden, Jack and Dick were strolling by the stream, watching the dragonflies dart in the hazy evening heat. Dick thrust his hands deep in his pockets and looked smug. Until now, he'd always felt his brother-in-law had him at a disadvantage. Although Jack was always friendly and polite, he had an indefinable air of superiority that made Dick feel he was looking down his nose all the time, and that irritated him. But now Dick had the upper hand. There was no way a policeman could afford a house like this in such glorious surroundings. He reckoned Jack must be wondering how to regain the high ground.

In fact, Jack wasn't wondering anything of the sort. Far from feeling envious, he was trying to guess the cost of fire insurance on the place.

It must be astronomical with all that ancient timber and wonky floor-boards, never mind the whopping great thatched roof. And there were three others exactly like it on Gallows Green. If one of them caught fire, the whole lot would go up, including the outbuildings. It'd be Pudding Lane all over again. He reckoned Dick was crackers moving into this great barn of a house, miles away from civilization, but he was, after all, married to Corrie's sister and it was only good manners to show some interest.

'So how do you like living in Lullington Barrow after Bristol?'

'Fantastic, old man. Best thing Rosemary and I ever did, and it's so good for Jeremy, too. He's already found a best friend; young Aleksy, the barmaid's son. Nice well-mannered lad, not like the yobs Jeremy used to play with in Bristol. All that city filth and pollution that you and Coriander wallow about in every day can't be healthy, never mind the crime and violence in London. But I was forgetting . . .' he smote his brow, theatrically, '. . . that's what you do for a living, isn't it?'

'Not personally, no. If you believe the media, I'm one of the lazy, overpaid detectives who sit behind desks squandering taxpayers' money when they should be out catching rapists and murderers.'

'Hmm. Quite so.' Dick Brown never quite knew how to take Jack. It was hard to tell when he was being ironic and when he was deadly serious. 'Still, I suppose it's better than lying in wait with a revenue camera to catch some poor sod doing thirty-two on a deserted road at three in the morning. I shouldn't mind so much if these young coppers weren't so bloody rude. I blame those police documentaries on TV. Put 'em in a uniform and they swagger about like stormtroopers until it looks like things might turn nasty; then they disappear very rapidly till it's all over.' Dick was on his soapbox now. 'Wait till you meet our village bobby, Constable Chedzey. Now there's a policeman with a real sense of community. Been in the job for years but he hasn't forgotten he's a human being. Your Met lads could learn a lot from him. Old Gilbert knows how to treat decent people; he's diplomatic but gets results.'

Jack swatted a mosquito that had emerged from the stagnant pond and was feasting on his neck. 'I'll look forward to meeting him. Shall we go and find the girls?'

Rosemary had taken Corrie on a tour of the cottage. Corrie was amused to see that all the trendy Scandinavian furniture from her sister's Bristol town house had been replaced by stressed oak, antique mirrors, faded floral textiles and all things country vintage. In the bedrooms, there were dressing tables painted duck-egg blue, handmade needlepoint quilts and big bowls of pink and yellow roses.

'You've made a marvellous job of the interior design,' said Corrie, who felt like she'd strayed into one of Fay Weldon's novels. 'It really complements the character of the cottage.'

Rosie preened and toyed with her carefully tinted blonde curls. 'Yes, we're very pleased with it. Obviously I've had to ensure Feng Shui principles are observed.'

'Obviously,' said Corrie. Ever since she discovered Feng Shui was Chinese for 'wind and water', Corrie had regarded it as exactly that, but she knew it was important to Rosie. They were back downstairs in the main living room where Jack and Dick were sitting in matching rocking chairs, either side of the inglenook.

Rosie fussed around them. 'I'm trying to create calming, feminine *yin* in here and you two are positively teeming with aggressive, masculine *yang*.' She bustled around the room, lighting aromatherapy candles and adjusting her reed diffusers.

'Nightcap, old man?' Dick poured Jack a brandy in the tiniest glass he had ever seen and he knew there would be no refill when it was gone. No change there, then. His brother-in-law had never been renowned for his generosity, particularly when dispensing alcohol, and the legendary hospitality of country folk obviously hadn't rubbed off on him yet.

'Dick's been telling me about the previous occupants of Gibbet Cottage. Very mysterious.' Jack's detective curiosity kicked in. 'I wonder why they left so abruptly. There isn't a ghost, is there? Or skeletons under the flagstones?' Jack drained his thimble of brandy, ostentatiously turning his glass upside down and shaking it but Dick didn't take the hint.

Rosemary shuddered. 'Stop it, Jack, you'll give me nightmares. I'm sure there's nothing sinister about it; it's just that they left a lot of stuff behind. Papers in foreign languages, mostly. Some of it looks quite important. We'll ask the villagers tomorrow at the barbecue. They're bound to know something. They might even have a forwarding address.'

Judging by the third degree they'd given Corrie in the pub when she arrived, she wouldn't have been surprised if the villagers had taken fingerprints and DNA, never mind a forwarding address. It was true what they said about the country; everyone really *did* want to know your business.

Jack looked at his watch. 'Good heavens, it's gone midnight, Corrie. Doesn't time fly when you're having a good time?'

Corrie flashed him a warning glare. 'Yes, time we were on our way. See you tomorrow morning with the food and drink.'

'Are you sure you won't stay here with us?' asked Rosemary. 'We've plenty of room.'

No, really,' said Corrie, hastily. 'It's very kind of you to offer, but you're going to be very busy with your guests at the barbecue tomorrow; you don't want us getting under your feet.'

The two sisters did the 'mwah mwah' in the air beside each other's cheeks and the men shook hands. Jack and Corrie strolled back across Gallows Green to Hangman's Inn. From somewhere in the pitch darkness, an owl swooped on silent wings followed swiftly by the dying squeak of some hapless rodent.

Corrie shuddered. 'Hope it was a rat.'

Jack grinned. 'This is Somerset. More likely a dormouse. One of those tiny, furry jobs with whiskers and a long tail, like in Beatrix Potter.'

'Shut up!' Corrie stumbled and stopped to extricate her heel from a crack in the green, baked hard by the sun. 'Rosemary says Dick wants the barbecue food to be eco-friendly. She asked me if everything was organic.'

'And is it?'

''Course not! Dick wouldn't know an organic barbecue from a Hackney kebab stand. I'll do my lentil pâté and lots of beansprout salads. That should satisfy him, although goodness knows what the locals will make of it.'

The front door of Hangman's Inn was locked at midnight. Liz Boobyer had given Corrie a key and told her they should just let themselves in by the side door and help themselves to anything they wanted. There were no lights as they approached and Corrie stopped and rummaged in her bag for the key. Just as she found it, they heard scuffling noises coming from the outhouse where the empty cider barrels were stored, then the sound of a man, grunting. Suddenly, a figure emerged, running across the yard to the side door. The man called out, 'Come back here, you little bitch! I haven't finished with you yet.'

Head down and buttoning her blouse, the girl ran straight into Corrie. It was Dani, the barmaid, and when she looked up, her big blue eyes were brimming with tears. Before Corrie could speak, Dani shoved open the side door and quickly disappeared inside. Moments later, Ted Boobyer appeared, zipping up his trousers. Jack pulled Corrie back into the darkness. Boobyer passed them by and slipped furtively inside, locking the door behind him.

'Well,' said Corrie, after Ted had gone. 'What do you make of that?'

Jack shrugged. 'I guess he's not the first landlord to cheat on his wife with the barmaid. She is very attractive.'

'And very scared. He ought to be ashamed of himself, taking advantage of a young woman in a foreign country. I think Liz should be told; she'll soon put a stop to it! She'll chop off his privileges!'

'Yes, and sack Dani on the spot. She has a young son, Aleksy, he's Jeremy's best friend; she probably needs the job. Don't interfere, Corrie. It's none of our business and you'll only make things worse. Ted didn't see us and Dani's hardly likely to say anything. Stay out of it.'

'But he's a slimy old letch, old enough to be her father! Why let him get away with it?'

'Because we're in Somerset. Life's different in the country, living alongside the animals. The men are more in touch with . . . well, their baser instincts.'

Corrie sniffed. 'Sexist rubbish! If I had my way, Ted Boobyer would be in touch with a sharp knee in the goolies.' She unlocked the door and they went inside to help themselves to a cognac, somewhat larger than the one Dick had provided.

Saturday morning was another scorcher; clear blue sky and a white hot sun. At the same time, the distant threat of a storm hung in the air. Rosemary started to panic as soon as she woke. By the time Jack and Corrie arrived from Hangman's Inn, she was frantic.

'Suppose it rains,' she anguished to Corrie. 'What shall we do?'

Corrie glanced through the window at Dick who was struggling to erect a huge gazebo on the lawn, patches of which were surprisingly lush and green compared to the parched state of the surrounding grass. 'If it's just a shower, they'll be fine under the awning. I'll set out the food on some trestle tables that I brought in the van. If it's a thunder-storm, you'll just have to invite everyone inside; you've loads of room.'

Rosemary looked stricken. 'But I haven't hoovered!' She sprinted away, high heels clacking on the stripped wooden floorboards.

Jack grinned. 'I'll give Dick a hand,' he said and he pushed off outside leaving Corrie to unload the food and drink from the van single-handed.

The invitation was for twelve noon and at exactly one minute past, a couple wearing identical jeans, tee-shirts and trainers arrived at the oak front door, each holding a bottle of wine; one red, one white. Jack let them in.

'Hi! We're Giles and Edwina from next door.' They spoke in unison.

'Pleased to meet you,' replied Jack, amused.

The young man looked Dick and Rosemary up and down, taking in Rosie's designer afternoon dress and Dick's sports jacket, flannels and cravat. 'Great gear, Dickie. Are you going on somewhere posh afterwards?'

Dick was red-faced. 'Er – no. We usually dress for lunch.'

'Pompous twit,' thought Jack. 'He wondered what the Lullington folk really thought of Dick and Rosemary. Whatever it was, they'd probably be too polite to say it to their faces.

Rosemary blushed hotly. 'Do come through to the garden. We're so pleased you could come to our little barbecue.'

'I'm vegan and I'm allergic to fur and feathers,' announced Edwina to Corrie. 'Better to make things clear right from the get-go, don't you agree? Saves any embarrassment.' She had an authoritative, confident face but with a trace of wariness in her eyes. Her hair was cut very short and she wore two mobile phones clipped to her belt.

'So what do you two do for a living?' asked Jack, pouring the wine.

'I run my own business consultancy,' Edwina replied as if Giles wasn't there. 'I specialize in environmental issues and I've organized militant campaigns against quite a lot of things. Daddy was a diplomat but he advised me against a career in government. So frightfully exclu-sive, he said, especially if one is female and perpetually hitting one's head on the glass ceiling. So after Roedean, I took a degree in business studies. Terribly boring compared to Giles, though. He's a television producer. Worthy but rather pedestrian documentaries. I hardly see him these days; he's always abroad having fun with his media chums, aren't you darling?' Giles nodded but didn't elaborate as another couple appeared from around the side of the house. They were also bearing wine; champagne this time. 'Oh good,' squealed Rosemary, 'it's Marcus and Camilla,' and she shot off to greet them.

By 12.30, the party was buzzing. The whole village had turned out. As Corrie suspected, her steaks, burgers and sausages disappeared as fast as she could cook them but the bulgar wheat, pomegranate and beansprout salads proved too exotic for this entrenched country community where even pasta and rice were viewed with suspicion.

'Don't 'ee put me up nothin' continental.' The old man holding out his plate had the turnip-shaped head and excessively ruddy complexion that defined many of the locals. He wore grimy overalls, a milking cap that was almost welded to his head with grease and he stank of cider. 'I don't touch nothin' continental. 'Tiz filthy foreign muck!'

Corrie wondered what he regarded as 'continental'. Probably anything with garlic, tomatoes or olive oil. 'What can I get you, then?' she asked, unsure quite where she was supposed to 'put it up'. Must be a Somerset expression. You didn't serve food; you 'put it up'.

He looked disapprovingly at the magnificent spread and sneered. 'I only eats good plain Somerset grub. Crusty bread, bit o' tasty cheese and a pickled onion or two.'

'Well, you're easily pleased,' said Corrie. Her lips were starting to ache from smiling at this ill-mannered old man and as she handed over a length of crusty baguette, she knew exactly where she'd like to 'put it up'. She loaded his plate with cheese and onions and he snatched it ungraciously, then stomped off, grumbling under his breath.

'Charming,' muttered Corrie.

A pleasant, middle-aged man was helping himself to chicken drumsticks and corn on the cob. He leaned across. 'That's Thomas Tincknell, miserable old bugger. He owns Black Oak Farm. Mean as a snake but everyone reckons he's got a fortune stashed away somewhere.'

'Is he always that bad-tempered?'

'Yes, but don't take it personally; he hates anyone who hasn't lived in the village for at least fifty years and can't stand most of the folk who have. Isn't that right, Dani?' He offered a plate to the young barmaid who was hovering, waiting politely to be served.

'Yes. Mr Tincknell is really unpleasant man, I think.' The East

European accent was marked but hard to pin down exactly. 'He never bring wife to pub. Leave her on farm to work and look after horrid mother-in-law. Rude man and bully.' She smiled at Corrie then lowered her eyes, remembering their late-night encounter outside the pub. 'May I fetch my son, Aleksy? Bring him to taste your lovely food? Thank you.' She scurried off.

'Such nice manners,' observed the man eating the chicken drumsticks. 'But dear me, where are *my* manners? I'm scoffing your chicken and I haven't even introduced myself. I'm Peter. My wife, Jane, and I live on Gallows Green; next door to Marcus and Millie and opposite Giles and Edwina.'

'I'm Rosie's sister—' began Corrie.

'I know. Rosemary has told us all about you and Jack. He's a bobby and you're a cook.'

'More or less.' Trust Rosie to make them sound like characters in a Victorian melodrama. 'What's your line of business, Peter?'

'I used to be in tobacco. Of course, smoking isn't socially appropriate any more. I still keep the old pipe going, though.' He produced it, smouldering, from the scarred pocket of his shabby tweed jacket. 'Took early retirement five years ago, and Jane and I moved here to Lullington. Our son, Michael, is the real star of the family. He's a cabinet minister.' Peter leaned close and spoke conspiratorially. 'Tipped to become the next Home Secretary if all goes well.'

'That's splendid. You must be very proud of him.'

'We are. He's the apple of his mother's eye. Got her brains, you see.'

Jeremy and Aleksy bounded into the gazebo, full of boisterous energy. With the spontaneity of small boys, they had forged an instant friendship but Corrie was struck by the stark differences in their personalities. Jeremy was cheerful, outgoing and a bit scruffy from rolling about in the wild garden. Aleksy was strikingly handsome with a shock of blond hair and huge blue eyes but his manner was wary and withdrawn. He rarely smiled.

'Hello, Auntie Corrie. May we have some food, please? We're starving.'

'Of course.' Corrie handed them plates. 'Just help yourselves to whatever you fancy.' She winked and lowered her voice. 'But I wouldn't have the bulgar wheat salad, if I were you. It's like chewing your way through a donkey's nosebag.'

Jeremy giggled but Aleksy remained solemn, thanking her profusely for his lunch. Corrie thought Aleksy's excessive politeness was worrying in a youngster of only ten. Maybe it was the pressure of moving to a foreign country, going to a strange school and learning a new language. His mother, Dani, seemed always to be looking over her shoulder but possibly that was to avoid the unwelcome attentions of Ted Boobyer.

'Hello there, boys.' Father John, priest of St Mary's, had decided it was his pastoral duty to pop over, drink some wine and maybe even drum up a little business. He ruffled the lads' hair affectionately and smiled at Corrie. 'So good to see everyone enjoying themselves in God's sacred sunshine, don't you agree?'

'Yes, indeed, Father. I think the entire population of Lullington has turned out. I hope we don't run out of food.'

Father John squatted down until his face was level with Jeremy's. 'Tell me, young man, would you like to join the choir with Aleksy? He has such a beautiful voice. Who knows, with a little tuition, we might even make you an altar server, too.'

Corrie intervened. 'Actually, Father, Jeremy isn't a Catholic. He isn't even a Christian. None of our family attends church so I don't think it's a possibility, do you?'

Privately, Corrie believed that practising any religion was, at best, a manifestation of mental illness and at worst, a pernicious brain-washing that ultimately turned people against each other rather than uniting them. She lacked the immense capacity for self-delusion that it took to believe in a god. Rosie felt the same, having more faith in her Reiki powers than those of some spurious deity who was never around when you needed him . . . or her.

'Now, that's a pity.' Father John straightened up stiffly, his rheumatic joints creaking somewhat. 'Our little church of St Mary the Blessed Virgin welcomes all newcomers. Aleksy and his mother, Danika, are both very devout worshippers. Isn't that right?' He put an arm around Aleksy's shoulders and squeezed. The boy stiffened and his expression remained impassive until Jeremy shouted, 'Come on, Lex, we'll eat our lunch by the stream and look for kingfishers.' Aleksy smiled then and shot off after his friend.

Still intensely curious about the previous occupants of Gibbet Cottage, Corrie wondered if the old priest knew anything about them.

Priests usually stuck their noses into everything. She asked and was surprised by his curt, uncharitable response.

'They weren't liked in this village. Nobody was sorry when they left.'

'Come along now, Father, time for your rest before Mass.' A plump lady with a strong Irish accent had a pincer-like grip on his arm.

Angrily, he tried to shake her off. 'Don't be ridiculous, woman. There won't be anyone at Mass. People would rather have sausages from a barbecue than the blessed Sacrament dispensed by our Lord.'

'Will ye stop ye moaning, ye mouldy old spoilsport.' The woman acknowledged Corrie's presence with a brief nod. 'I'm Bridget O'Dowd, Father John's housekeeper. I hope you haven't fed him anything spicy or he'll fart like an old Labrador all through Mass.' She chivvied the priest away, ignoring his barrage of un-Christian remarks about her excessive girth and inadequate intelligence.

'You must be the fragrant Coriander.' Corrie had been chopping salad when the deep, old-Etonian voice flowed over her like warm custard over treacle pudding. She looked up into the impossibly handsome face of Marcus, who lived in the fourth cottage on Gallows Green. Corrie knew a smooth operator when she saw one and wondered where he'd left his wife, Camilla. According to Rosie, 'Millie' was glamorous, expensive and witless and spent her days shopping for things she didn't need. Marcus was a successful stockbroker but even so, he must find it hard to keep up with her extravagance. Dick described her as 'beautiful but tragic, like Marilyn Monroe'. Either way, she didn't sound like the sort of person Corrie could relate to. Her husband, on the other hand . . .

It was then that the first stormy raindrop fell, quickly followed by another until they were pounding on the canvas of the gazebo like rim beats on a snare drum. Most people ran back to their homes or to the Hangman's Inn for shelter. Dick and Rosemary herded their Gallows Green neighbours into their huge living room. Jack and Corrie were left to grab any food and drink that remained and sprint after them.

CHAPTER FOUR

In the kitchen, Corrie set out the remains of the canapés on a silver platter and carried it through to the living room in time to pick up snatches of pretentious conversation.

'. . . if I'd wanted to hear Rigoletto, I could have stayed in Milan. Not, of course, that I'm a fan of early Verdi. He didn't really reach his apogee until *Otello* – don't you agree, Jack?'

Jack was topping up wine glasses. 'I'll take your word for it, Edwina. I'm a Susan Boyle fan, myself.'

Corrie disguised a snort of laughter with a cough. 'I believe that's your mobile phone ringing again.'

Edwina snatched it from her belt, frowned at the screen and switched it off. 'Has anyone been to the Degas exhibition? Primitive Impressionism it may be, but for sheer, luminescent colour, he had no—'

Before Edwina could finish, Millie, more than a little drunk on champagne, emerged from the downstairs cloakroom swathed in loo paper like an Egyptian mummy. 'Look everyone! Rose-patterned bog roll; isn't it pretty?' Caught in the slipstream of flying tissue, a wood carving toppled from the wall niche and landed at Edwina's feet. She picked it up.

'Now, this is interesting. It's a *Maasai* donkey, if I'm not much mistaken. Probably the work of a *moran* warrior. Rough-hewn perhaps, but as a décor statement, it's very frank. It says what it is.'

'You're right, it does,' said Rosie, fed up with all the showing off. 'It's written on the bottom. *A present from Weston-super-Mare.* Jeremy bought it when he was on holiday.'

'Stockbroking must be a fairly high-powered job, Marcus,' Dick punctured the embarrassing silence. 'Good pickings, though, I've heard.'

'*Nihil est ab omni parte beatum,*' murmured Marcus in his deep, cultured voice.

'Pardon?'

'Nothing is all good, old sport. Ambition is a cruel taskmaster. It drives you on until you're caught in a downward spiral of stress management, emotional balance therapy and two bottles of vodka a day.'

So much for relaxed living, thought Jack. It made his job in the Met seem a doddle.

'Simon and Saskia used to have a Meissen shepherdess in that niche,' mused Millie. No one spoke and she looked anxiously around at the others. 'Sorry, sorry, slipped out.'

Is it my imagination, wondered Corrie, or has it gone very quiet all of a sudden? There was definitely an elephant in the room and a blooming big one at that.

Rosemary's curiosity overcame her attempt at dignified indifference. 'What were they like, Simon and Saskia? You see, we never met them. The house was already empty when we came to view. '

Peter pulled out his pipe and stuck it in his mouth without lighting it. Jane looked down at her shoes. Giles and Edwina stared at each other and Marcus and Millie took long sips at their champagne. Throats were cleared but still nobody spoke.

'Well, I don't know about the house being empty,' added Dick. 'They left a lot of stuff behind; there are tea chests full of it in the attic. We haven't had time to clear it out, yet. Do you suppose they'll want any of it? Only we don't have a forwarding address.'

It was Peter who answered. 'Don't worry about it, Dick. Simon and his wife weren't the kind of people to stay anywhere for long. They had a lot of business interests abroad, which meant they often needed to move on suddenly. I doubt if any of us will see them ever again.'

Tucked up in their pine bed under the eaves of Hangman's Inn, Corrie and Jack were exhausted but it was too hot and humid to sleep. Jack was mulling over the Simon and Saskia enigma and Corrie was trying not to listen to the scuttling noises in the thatch.

'What did you make of all that Simon and Saskia nonsense?' asked Jack.

Corrie threw off the bedspread. 'When Millie mentioned the ornament, there was definitely an elephant in the room.'

Jack looked puzzled. 'An elephant? I thought it was a donkey.'

'No, you dipstick. An elephant in the room means there's something dodgy that's going unaddressed; an obvious problem that no one wants to discuss. It's based on the idea that an elephant in a room would be impossible to ignore; so people who pretend the elephant isn't there are choosing to concern themselves with small, irrelevant issues rather than deal with the blooming big one.'

'Hence all that snobbish claptrap about Rigoletto and Degas.'

'Exactly. What could Simon and Saskia have done that made them so unpopular, do you suppose?'

'Probably not very much. To the casual observer, Lullington Barrow doesn't look like a village where you need to watch your back all the time but I sense a sinister underbelly.'

'Oh my God!' squealed Corrie, sitting bolt upright. 'You think Simon and Saskia are dead, don't you? Bumped off by someone. That's the trouble with the murder squad; you see death and destruction around every corner. Sometimes, I wish you really were a plumber or an electrician.'

'Calm down, Corrie. Most likely they just had to hurry away for some business deal.'

'But Peter said he was sure nobody would see them ever again. That's an odd thing to say, isn't it? What if their bodies are buried somewhere in Gibbet Cottage? Rosie would never get over it; her Feng Shui would be shot to pieces. Jack, you have to do something!'

He pondered. 'I suppose it wouldn't do any harm to carry out a few checks. I'll get Bugsy onto it, tomorrow. At the moment, MIT's pretty dead, excuse the pun; he'd welcome something to liven it up. I'll give him what we know and see what he comes up with. Don't say anything to Dick and Rosie; we don't want to cause panic and I don't want it to look like I'm interfering.' He pointed to the thermos on her bedside table. 'What's in there? Cocoa?'

'No fear. It's chilled Pinot Grigio. I'll pinch a couple of tooth mugs from the bathroom.'

In the room marked 'Private – Staff Only' along the corridor, Ted and Liz Boobyer were getting ready for bed after a quiet night in the pub. Most of the villagers had preferred to get their food and drinks free at Dick and Rosemary's barbecue. Ted pulled on his jacket.

'I'm just going down to check everything's safely locked up. You get on to bed, love, don't wait for me. I'll probably have a nightcap before I come up.'

'Ted, you're not up to anything, are you?' Liz was sitting at the dressing table, applying night cream to incipient wrinkles on her plump cheeks.

Ted feigned innocence. 'I don't know what you mean, love. What would I be up to?'

She turned and glared at him. 'You know exactly what I mean. The same thing you're always up to. If I find out you're playing around again, you're out of here. Do you understand?'

He tried to laugh it off. 'Don't be silly, Liz. Who could I possibly be playing around with? Bridget O'Dowd?'

'I've seen you, looking up Dani's skirt when she bends down; "accidentally" touching her breasts when you squeeze past her behind the bar. I'm telling you straight, Ted, this is your last warning. You may have forgotten but that's *my* name over the door and we both know why. Another spell in prison and you're finished. Do I make myself clear?'

Ted's face was sulky. 'Perfectly clear.' He took off his jacket and began to get undressed. If Liz knew about the cash he'd been stashing away she'd change her tune. But she wouldn't find out until after he'd split. Plenty of willing young women where he was going, and now he didn't have to worry about Simon and Saskia anymore, the future looked rosy – very rosy.

Next morning, Corrie decided to ring Carlene; partly to see how she was coping at Coriander's Cuisine but mostly for a quite different reason. She punched in the number and it rang for some moments. When it connected, there was a deafening clatter like scaffolding falling off the back of a lorry, followed by hoarse female cursing.

'Friggin' 'ell! That's the third time today!'

'Carlene, are you all right?' Corrie tried not to sound anxious.

'That you, Mrs D? You'll 'ave to shout up. The waste disposal's chewin' a fork.'

'How did it get hold of a fork?'

'Beggar only knows. How was the posh barbecue?'

'Great. What have you got planned for today?'

'I'm finishing off the party grub for that snotty cow what's married to Mr Jack's boss.'

Corrie smiled to herself. Cynthia was an old school chum who was now married to Chief Superintendent Garwood. 'Snotty cow' described her perfectly. 'Good. Now listen, Carlene, I need you to do a bit of sleuthing for me. Fire up my laptop and Google the Licensed Victuallers Association. I've a good chum on the federation board.' She spelled out the name and Carlene wrote it down. 'Ask her what she can find out about Ted Boobyer, landlord of Hangman's Inn.' Once a predator, always a predator, thought Corrie. There's sure to be some dirt on him. 'Oh, and if you should happen to speak to Mr Jack, don't mention it; I don't want him to think I'm interfering.'

Meanwhile, Jack was downstairs finishing a late breakfast and briefing Sergeant Malone on his mobile.

'Simon and Saskia de Kuiper; possibly not their real names. Last known address, Gibbet Cottage, Gallows Green, Lullington Barrow, Somerset. See what you can dig up on them.'

'Do we have a description?' Bugsy was scribbling furiously with one hand and eating a bacon roll with the other. Ketchup dripped, unchecked, down his tie as he wrote.

'Only a vague one; the villagers aren't very forthcoming. Seems the de Kuipers were *personae non gratae* in Lullington Barrow but I haven't found out why, yet.'

'Right, so we don't know their real names, where they've gone or what they look like. Gives 'em a bit of a head start, I'd say.'

'They might have form and if so, their faces will be on computer; maybe DNA too. I could get a sample from the cottage and we'd know if we'd traced the right people.'

'What have they been up to? Drugs? Diamonds? Prostitution?'

Jack scratched his head. 'No, my copper's nose tells me it's more than a bit of Amsterdam naughtiness. It's beginning to look like they left here in the middle of the night in a tearing hurry. I found lots of abandoned papers in the attic; mostly in Dutch, as you'd expect, but there's stuff in Arabic, French, Russian, Chinese and a language I think might be Urdu. It wouldn't raise any eyebrows in London but it's a bit cosmopolitan for a place like Lullington Barrow and they look like government documents to me. Of course, it could be nothing; just a business deal gone wrong and they owe some dangerous foreigners a lot of money.'

'I'd trust your bloodhound's nose any day. D'you want me to

contact the Avon and Somerset lads; see if they know anything?'

'Not yet. I know it's their manor and if it turns out there's been a local crime, we'll hand it over, but if I'm right and this is shaping up into something bigger, they'll do a hot-potato pass to the Met in any case. Normally, I wouldn't get involved but Corrie's worried for her sister so I said I'd do some checks.'

'Leave it with me, Guv. If there's anything to find, I'll find it.'

The sizzling heatwave erupted into a violent storm. Thunderclaps blitzed the South West and lightning knocked out Lullington's electricity. At Dick's bank in the city, computers crashed one after the other and the Internet went completely dead. Worried about customers' security, Dick leapt into his BMW and drove the twenty-odd miles at a speed that would have cost him his licence had he been caught. It was well past midnight before he was satisfied that nothing had gone too badly wrong and his bonus wasn't in peril.

As he approached Gallows Green, all was in darkness so the power hadn't yet been restored. Dick turned his key in the lock of Gibbet Cottage and crept in, hoping he wouldn't wake Rosie and Jeremy. Feeling for the hook, he hung up his raincoat and umbrella and carefully placed his briefcase by the hall stand as he always did. Loosening his gritty collar and tie, he stumbled through to the lounge, felt his way to the drinks cabinet and measured himself a double scotch by the simple expedient of sticking his thumb in the glass. Exhausted, he flopped into his favourite armchair. Or he would have done; except it wasn't there.

'Dick, why are you rolling about on the floor?' Rosie was standing in the doorway shining a flashlight on him. 'Do you have to make that racket? You'll wake Jeremy.'

'Never mind that, I've spilt whiskey all down my trousers,' he retorted crossly. 'I wish you'd tell me when you rearrange the furniture. I'd only just got used to the layout in daylight, never mind in the dark. For goodness' sake, woman, we've only been here five minutes; you can't have got fed up with it already.'

'No, of course not,' she snapped. 'Your armchair's over there, by the wall,' she shone her torch on it, 'but I certainly didn't put it there.'

'Rosie, you must have done.' He snatched the flashlight and tried to sponge his trousers with a tissue. He'd have to get them cleaned or he'd smell like a distillery and his staff would think he had a drink problem. 'We've had a storm, not an earthquake. The chair can't have moved on its own.'

She snorted. 'Don't be ridiculous. Nobody sane would put a chair there; it encourages the flow of bad chi. And someone's been upstairs and moved our bed. You know very well I can't sleep with my head pointing north; I toss and turn all night. I've had to cover the mirror to stop it bouncing energy all over the room. It's the worst possible Feng Shui.'

Dick stopped sponging; suddenly concerned. 'Is anything missing?'

'Not as far as I can tell but someone has definitely been in our house. I'm sensitive; I can feel these things. I've been waiting for you to come home so you can call the police.'

'But sweetheart, Bert Chedzey will be fast asleep by now.'

'Not that old fool! Go and fetch Jack from Hangman's Inn.'

'And just what exactly do I say to him? Sorry to get you out of bed at one o'clock in the morning, old man, but we've had a burglary. There's no sign of a break-in and nothing's been stolen but someone's disturbed Rosie's Feng Shui. I doubt if he'll mobilize his murder squad and a SOCO team for that, do you?'

Rosie snatched back the flashlight. 'Well, if you won't go, I will.' Moments later, the front door slammed.

Without a key, Rosemary couldn't get into Hangman's Inn and she didn't want to bang on the door so she picked up a handful of gravel and flung it at Corrie and Jack's window. When no one came, she hurled larger stones which reached their target just as the window opened.

'Ow!' yelped Corrie. 'Who is it? Who's chucking stones?' Blinded by the flashlight, she couldn't make out anything.

'It's me – Rosie. Sorry to wake you but could you and Jack come over? Something scary has happened.'

By the time they got back to Gibbet Cottage, Dick had lit some candles, changed into his dressing gown and made some tea on the gas hob. 'I'm sorry Rosie got you out of bed; it could have waited till morning.'

'No, it couldn't,' snapped Rosie, crossly. 'I shan't get a wink of sleep until Jack has investigated.'

Still bleary-eyed, Jack sipped his tea. 'What is it I'm to investigate?'

'We've been burgled,' said Rosemary, at once.

'Dear me, that's terrible,' said Corrie, squeezing her sister's hand. 'You don't expect that kind of thing in a pretty little village like Lullington.'

'How did they get in?' asked Jack.

'We don't know,' said Dick. 'In fact, we don't know for sure that anyone *has* been in. It's just that Rosie thinks some of our furniture was moved while we were out.'

'Is anything missing?' Jack walked about, shining his torch on the doors and windows.

'I don't think so but it's hard to tell. I'll check properly when the electricity's back on.'

Jack was still fuddled from lack of sleep. 'Sorry to be dim but can I just get this straight? The burglars got in without doing any damage, they didn't take anything and then they left again, possibly after moving a chair and your bed.'

'There's no 'possibly' about it,' said Rosie, getting upset. 'I can still sense the presence of hostile strangers in my home. I feel like we've been violated.'

'What you need is a good stiff brandy.' Corrie poured her one. 'Don't worry; Jack will get to the bottom of it, won't you Jack?'

'Is it possible that Simon and Saskia still have a key?' Jack wondered. 'In a place like Gallows Green, they could easily walk in and out without being seen, especially if they came via your woodland. Maybe they came to collect something valuable that they'd left behind; or perhaps to check it was still here. What about all that stuff in your loft?'

'It's possible,' said Dick, 'but why the cloak and dagger routine? Why not just knock on the door, introduce themselves and explain? It doesn't make sense.'

Jack could think of a number of reasons why the de Kuipers might not want to advertise their return to Lullington but thought he'd wait to see what Sergeant Malone came up with before suggesting any of them to Dick. 'With a Grade II listed cottage like this one, it's almost impossible to implement all the recommended security systems but if you're worried, you could install CCTV, outside lights and maybe have the locks changed, just to be safe.'

Dick was not convinced and as they were leaving to return to

Hangman's Inn, he drew Jack aside. 'Don't take this too seriously, old man. Rosie's always moving things then forgetting she's done it. The thunderstorm has unsettled her nerves, that's all. I'll get good old PC Chedzey to have a squint around tomorrow; he'll soon spot anything out of order.'

After the deluge, Lullington Barrow looked green and refreshed. Unfortunately, the rain had not drained effectively from the Browns' garden and the pond in the centre of their coppice became increasingly bog-like and smelly.

Now it was a little cooler, Corrie decided to walk to the village shop to see if they had a copy of her catering magazine. After the pub, the shop-cum-newsagents was the hub of all village gossip and the source of most of it. While she was browsing, the paperboy returned from his rounds. 'Paperboy' was something of a misnomer because he was seventy if he was a day. On that basis, Corrie thought he probably knew the village better than most and a little discreet investigation might be in order. After the customary pleasantries, she handed over the money for her magazine and asked, casually, 'Did you deliver newspapers to the people who lived in Gibbet Cottage before the Browns?'

'Ooh aarh. Mostly foreign rubbish, it were.' He rooted idly in his beard and Corrie was certain she saw something hop out. 'They was comical folk. Never fit in, proper.'

'In what way were they "comical"?' Corrie guessed this Somerset adjective didn't mean 'funny' in the amusing sense.

'Always rowing, for one thing. Terrible arguments I've 'eard comin' from Gibbet Cottage. Screamin' and shoutin' like someone was bein' murdered.'

'And little wonder after the way *he* carried on.' The harsh Irish censure came from Bridget O'Dowd, who was over by the medicine counter, buying haemorrhoid cream for Father John. 'I saw them with my own eyes, so I did. Committing a mortal sin on the beach in his flashy car.'

Corrie turned, surprised. 'What? Simon and Saskia?'

'No, not Saskia. The other one! That silly blonde piece from next door. There she was, in broad daylight, the shameless hussy; feet up on the dashboard and nothing on but the radio! Sure, she'd lie down in nettles for it, that one!' She picked up her bag and stalked out.

Well, well. Simon and Millie. Corrie smiled to herself. And Lullington was such a respectable village full of old-fashioned virtues – if you believed the residents.

On the perimeter of the wilderness that was Dick and Rosemary's 'mature' garden, there stood an octagonal structure built of rubble with a segmented stone roof. It had a studded plank door and one very narrow barred window. The cottage deeds defined it as a 'lock-up' used to hold prisoners prior to them being hanged from the gibbet which stood on Gallows Green Hill. It dated back to the eighteenth century and as such, was a listed building and couldn't be knocked down. In the absence of a garden shed, Dick stored his tools in it.

As Corrie strolled back down the lane that ran behind Gallows Green, she glimpsed someone lurking behind the lock-up. The hooded figure tried, unsuccessfully, to shoulder open the door then slunk around to peer through the barred window. Instead of walking up the path, Corrie inched her way through the undergrowth like Stanley looking for Livingstone. She crept close until she was standing right behind the figure, then:

'Hallo, can I help you?'

The figure must have leapt at least a foot in the air and her hood fell off. It was Edwina.

'Dear me, Corrie, you gave me such a fright.' Her usual confident manner fell apart and she gabbled. 'I was trying to . . . er . . . rescue a cat that I saw jump in the lock-up, but it's all right, it must have climbed out on its own. Lovely day, isn't it? Must dash, I'm Tweeting about a campaign against social networking.' She hurried off.

Corrie was just thinking what a lame excuse it was when she remembered Edwina was allergic to cats and wouldn't go anywhere near one, let alone rescue it. So what was she after in the lock-up? She'd get Jack to take a look.

CHAPTER FIVE

It was about this time that Rosemary noticed the smell in the outhouse that she used as a utility room. It was faint at first but in the summer heatwave, it rapidly became a stench. It reminded her of the time her older brother, Basil, kept a rotting sheep's head under his bed to breed maggots to sell to anglers. When she mentioned it to Dick, she got a typical response.

'We're in the country now, Rosie, you have to expect earthy smells. It's probably coming from that stagnant pond in the garden; something could have fallen in there and died.'

But Rosemary was seriously spooked by now and even her healing crystals hadn't helped. She dragged Dick into the outhouse and made him take a deep sniff. 'The pong's coming from under there.' She pointed to the big chest freezer in the corner. Dick still reckoned it was the drains and said he'd look into it when he had more time.

Corrie was more sympathetic. She agreed she could definitely smell something and it did, indeed, remind her of Basil's rotting ewe. Later, when Rosie had gone for a lie down with a lavender sachet on her forehead, Corrie told Jack what the paperboy had said about the terrible rows he'd overheard coming from Gibbet Cottage.

'What if Simon and Saskia had one violent argument too many? One of them kills the other in the heat of the moment, panics and buries the body under the concrete floor. Then he or she legs it fast, having disposed of the house. It would at least explain their rapid exit, wouldn't it? After all, nobody saw either of them leave.'

Jack, being a pragmatic, unimaginative detective who relied on old-fashioned stuff like facts and evidence, dismissed all this as pure soap opera but he couldn't help noticing that the concrete under the freezer looked fairly new compared to the rest of the floor. He was starting to worry that his joke about 'skeletons under the flagstones' might not be a joke after all.

Dick Brown was oblivious to gossip and assumed his complete lack of interest in the private lives of his neighbours would naturally be reciprocated. Consistent with this philosophy was the salvo of well-meaning advice that he and Rosemary had received from their city friends before they left Bristol:

Once you've moved, keep quiet for at least five years. Never go poking your nose in, organizing, offering advice, changing things, making suggestions or interfering. Don't join any committees, organizations, councils (local or parish) at least for the said five years, unless it's in a very junior role doing menial tasks that the locals wouldn't be seen dead doing. As an outsider, you must bide your time, serve your apprenticeship and hold your tongue until you're accepted.

Privately, most of Dick's business colleagues thought he was insane even to consider moving to the countryside, miles from any decent theatres and restaurants. And it couldn't do his career much good, being off the beaten track like that. There'd be no rich, influential dinner party clients out there in the sticks, among the carrot-crunchers. But the Lullington villagers had high hopes for Dick Brown. It was quickly discovered that he was a professional man with fiscal expertise and as such, he could take his place in the community straight away. Rosemary on the other hand, with her chakras, potions and mystic therapies, was considered a write-off from the start as far as making any practical contribution to village life.

Soon, Dick was approached by Doctor Brimble, local GP and Chair of Lullington Parish Council. The members, he said, would welcome Dick as their new treasurer with open arms, if not open books. Dick was flattered. His rather arrogant, overweening view of himself had convinced him it was only a matter of time before the village recognized and made use of his superior intellect.

'A parish council is a cul-de-sac down which good ideas are lured and then quietly strangled, but don't let that put you off.' Edgar Brimble was a Falstaffian figure and a paradigm for all that was unhealthy. He was overweight, drank too much whiskey and had the kind of complexion associated with a heart attack looking for somewhere to happen. 'We're relying on you newcomers to breathe some life into this village before it dies in its sleep. Do say you'll join us.'

'I'd be delighted. But won't I need to do a handover from your current treasurer?'

Doctor Brimble hesitated slightly. 'There isn't one at present; I've just been keeping a watching brief. The last real incumbent was Donald Draycott, the maths teacher at our local school. Lovely chap; left us a couple of years ago to take a headship somewhere up north. At least, that's what most people believe.'

Here comes the tittle-tattle, thought Dick, expecting rumours of pilfering and misappropriation of village funds. 'And what do *you* believe happened to him, Doctor?'

'He disappeared rather suddenly, about the same time as Thomas Tincknell's first wife, Patsy, amid a good deal of salacious speculation, as you can imagine. But eventually, the village gave up trying to decide exactly what had happened. Of course, there was gossip, but Draycott was an educated man with a first-class degree and Patsy Tincknell had been a farm labourer all her life; first for her father and then for Tincknell. It was impossible to imagine any sort of personal relationship between the two so the village simply decided they'd gone their separate ways.' Doctor Brimble slapped Dick on the back. 'Anyway, we'll see you in the parish hall on Thursday evening, shall we? Half past seven. Mrs O'Dowd provides tea and sandwiches, then afterwards, we all repair to Hangman's Inn for a few jars.'

'Rosie, are there any more eggs?' Corrie was planning to cook a cheese soufflé for lunch and there was only one egg. Dick, it seemed, had not yet embarked upon his organic chicken enterprise.

'Oh dear!' Rosemary was still distracted by the rotting smell that was getting even stronger. 'I'll run down to the village and buy some.'

'No, don't worry. I didn't much care for the eggs in the shop; they looked a bit small and elderly, which doesn't make for a nice, fluffy soufflé. I'll walk out to Tincknell's farm and see if I can buy some fresh, free-range ones.'

On the outskirts of Lullington Barrow sat the untidy sprawl of Black Oak Farm. It had been in the Tincknell family for five generations and was currently worked by Thomas, the dirty, unpleasant old man Corrie had met at the barbecue. Following the sudden disappearance of his first wife, Patsy, he had obtained a quick divorce and married Dimpsy, a young woman more than thirty years his junior. He treated her not as a wife and partner, but as an unpaid farm labourer and provider of any kind of sexual services that he might fancy. Any 'incomer' who was unfamiliar with the ways of the old Somerset farming families, might have questioned why a man like Tincknell bothered with the legal formalities of marriage. But to him, and many like him, marriage to a woman made her your property and from then on, she was yours to do with as you wished; a naive misconception that any modern, educated young woman would have quickly dispelled and with some vigour.

Dimpsy, however, was the eldest of fourteen children, born on a neighbouring farm to Ned and Martha Puddy, a slow-witted couple of a type still found in the more remote parts of the West Country. Unkind locals referred to the family as 'inbreds' since they were almost certainly the result of a series of incestuous relationships which went unreported and unacknowledged. After a few generations, it became impossible to know for sure exactly who was related to whom and, unaware of the importance of genetic diversity, no one really cared.

Thomas Tincknell 'acquired' Dimpsy from the Puddys who were anxious to get her off their hands. Thomas's elderly mother, Ethel, lived with them and between them, she and her son contrived to make Dimpsy's life as hellish as possible. Even her name was demeaning; Dimpsy being Somerset dialect for 'not very bright' and used to describe the failing light on murky evenings. Nobody in the village could recall her real name. But she was young and strong and the only one who could handle Titus, the massive Holstein bull that weighed in at well over a tonne. Systematically ill-treated by Tincknell, the brute was powerful, deceptively fast and bore a dangerous grudge. For safety reasons, since the beast was liable to attack without warning, Titus was kept tethered in a bull pen except for the occasions when he was needed to service the herd. It was always Dimpsy who led him to the field, crooning softly to calm him. The beast went with her, as gentle as a lamb, unless it spotted Tincknell, when it would snort and bellow and pound the ground.

Corrie couldn't raise anyone in the run-down, ramshackle farmhouse with its rotting window frames and slates missing from the roof. She knocked several times and peered through the grimy windows but could see very little in the gloomy interior. Clearly, building maintenance was not one of Farmer Tincknell's priorities because all the sheds and outhouses were in a similar condition. Corrie walked round to the back yard, passing a few scrawny hens in a pen cobbled together from rusty chicken wire. Seeing their poor condition, she doubted there would be any eggs worth buying and had turned to leave when she heard a man's voice shouting threats and vile obscenities. Corrie Dawes had many virtues but minding her own business was not one of them. The verbal abuse was coming from the cowshed. Peering through a broken slat in the dilapidated wooden doors, Corrie could see Tincknell, the man who 'never touched nothin' continental' and two women; one very young and slim, the other very old and fat.

Tincknell had restrained Titus in a pen with side-locking crush gates, pulled so tight that the beast couldn't move. The old man stood in the front cage, safely out of range, viciously beating the animal with a heavy spade. The bull roared and bellowed with anger and pain and was desperately trying to struggle free. Corrie was sickened. Was this how farming folk behaved in this simple, gentle countryside? The young, slim woman was screaming and tugging ineffectually at Tincknell's arm, trying to make him stop. Furious, he turned on her. In between the filthy language and unintelligible dialect, Corrie heard threats and abuse.

'You'm fuckin' bloody useless! I don't know why I married 'ee.'

Corrie remembered something Dani, the Polish barmaid, had said about Tincknell: *He never bring wife to pub. Leave her on farm to do work and look after horrid mother-in-law. Rude man and bully.* So this unfortunate young woman must be Dimpsy, Tincknell's wife, and the fat woman would be his mother.

'Well, you'm for it now, my girl! I'll show 'ee what talkin' back gets 'ee. A bloody good hidin', thass what!' He bore down on Dimpsy, gnarled fists raised, and she backed away, clearly terrified. The fat elderly woman sitting on a hay bale was cackling encouragement.

'Gurn, Tommy, give it 'er, son! 'Er's just half a yard o' pump-water!'

Before Corrie could intervene, Tincknell punched Dimpsy hard in the stomach, then several times in the face, finally knocking her backwards into the deep, neglected slurry pit. Outraged, Corrie burst in through the rotting wooden doors.

'Stop that at once! Leave her alone!' Corrie ran to Dimpsy and helped her climb out of the filth. 'I'm going to call the police! And the RSPCA!' She whipped out her mobile phone and began to punch in Jack's number.

Tincknell bore down on her, threateningly. She could smell the cider on his breath even from a distance. 'I wudden do that if I wur 'ee. 'Tiz none o' your business, you nosey cow!' He turned to Ethel, the old woman who was bouncing up and down with excitement. 'Shall us give 'er some o' the same, Mother? A ducking in the cow shit?'

To her eternal shame, Corrie turned and ran. Trembling and furious, the enduring image, which would haunt her for a long time to come, was of poor Dimpsy, sitting on the edge of the slurry pit, covered in filth. Her lips were split and bleeding and her eye was swelling, almost closed. But by far the worst of it was the pitiful acceptance with which Dimpsy had taken her beating and would no doubt take many more, unless something happened to put an end to her misery.

Corrie was still shaking when she got back to Jack in Hangman's Inn, but now it wasn't from fear, so much as rage and indignation. She smelled foul and her clothes were spattered with manure. While she took a shower, Jack fetched her a large brandy from the bar and a pint of Lullington Gold for himself. Afterwards, she sat on the bed, wrapped in towels, and told him what had happened.

'Jack, it was simply awful. You should have seen the state Dimpsy Tincknell was in. How dare the evil old bastard attack his wife like that! And that fat, smelly old mother of his was just as bad, egging him on. You have to go and arrest him.'

Jack frowned. 'I'd like to, believe me, but will Dimpsy file a complaint against him?'

Corrie chewed her lip, doubtfully. 'I'm not sure she's . . . well . . . all there. She had a kind of vacant, pathetic look. But even so, that doesn't mean she should be beaten up by her husband.'

'I agree whole-heartedly. There can never be any justification for violence of that nature. But if Dimpsy won't complain, the most I can do is issue a warning and caution Tincknell about his threatening behaviour towards you. We'll probably find PC Chedzey has done that umpteen times already.'

Corrie sighed. 'Poor Dimpsy. A tortured life in a seemingly blissful village. What is it about Lullington Barrow, Jack? It's a tiny Somerset hamlet with pretty chocolate-box cottages; it should be a safe, friendly environment. Instead of which, it's full of intrigue, cruelty and dark secrets that no one will talk about.'

Jack took a long pull of his pint and wiped away the foam moustache. 'You're right there. We've only been here a couple of days and already we've witnessed Boobyer sexually harassing Dani, Tincknell beating his wife black and blue and virtual burglars moving Dick and Rosie's furniture around, never mind the funny smell in their utility room.'

'And don't forget Simon and Saskia who argued a lot then disappeared, leaving lots of their stuff behind. And what was Edwina searching for in the lock-up? It certainly wasn't a cat; she's allergic to them.'

Jack shrugged. 'I had a look but there's nothing in there but rats and rusty garden tools. And another thing; according to what Dick heard, the treasurer of the parish council left under something of a cloud, round about the same time Tincknell's first wife disappeared. He went without a word to anyone; not so much as a 'Cheerio, folks, sorry I cooked your books'.'

'And had he cooked the books?'

'Dunno. They've asked Dick to take over as treasurer. If there's one thing he's really good at, it's bean-counting. He'll soon find out if there are any beans missing.'

Corrie lowered her voice in case anyone was passing outside their door. 'Did I mention that Bridget O'Dowd saw Simon and Millie on the beach, having it away in his car? Completely Harry Starkers, she was.'

'What? Mrs O'Dowd? Now, there's an image I'd rather not carry around in my head.'

'No, silly! It was Millie who was naked.'

'Blimey,' murmured Jack. 'What a village!'

'Think I might have traced your two suspects, Guv.' It was Sergeant Malone, ringing from the Metropolitan Police Station.

'Good man, Bugsy. What have you got?'

'After what you said about a possible international connection, I contacted a few of my mates in the 'funny buggers'.'

After some thirty-five years as a copper, Sergeant Malone was still in touch with many of the blokes who joined the police service at the same time but had now moved on to higher things, including the Intelligence and Anti-Terrorist Agencies. The reason Bugsy hadn't moved on with them had nothing to do with his ability; it was simply that he liked being a thief-taker. He had no time for 'shiny-arsed uniform carriers' like Chief Superintendent Garwood, who sat at a desk all day, dodging complaints from the public and totting up overtime claims. A stocky, rotund man, Malone was addicted to fast food and grazed constantly, believing that low blood sugar sapped his powers of detection. Cynical, loyal and unfazed by corpses, however gruesome their condition, he was a valued and valuable member of Jack's murder squad. Added to which, he was a good man to have on your side in a fight.

'The Intelligence Spooks have been on the trail of Simon and Saskia de Kuiper for some time but whenever they get close, the couple slip through the net. There's a bunch of extradition orders from police all over the world. They stick with the same Christian names but their aliases are well exotic. I've got Andropov, Marceaux, Rodriguez, Fischer, Montague-Smythe and something that looks like it should come with a side order of fried rice.'

'Blimey! What are they wanted for?'

'Involvement in illegal arms trafficking with the Middle East, among other things. The clue's in their false identities: Russian, French, American, German, British and Chinese; countries that are the biggest producers and exporters of arms. And their organization isn't fussy who it sells to; dictators and rebels alike, as long as they've got the cash. Estimated turnover of over two hundred million; about the same as Arsenal Football Club. It's a nasty business. Guns can end up in the hands of child soldiers, some as young as twelve.'

Jack was doubtful. 'It can't be the same Simon and Saskia, can it? I mean, what the hell would they be doing living in a West Country village?'

'Why not? Where better to lie low when the heat's on, than a village up the arse-end of Somerset? Last place you'd look. And the company that tops the list of the world's hundred largest arms manufacturers is right here in the UK. You can buy yourself a Eurofighter-Typhoon jet, a Trident nuclear missile submarine, a couple of AK-47 assault rifles . . .'

Jack shuddered. 'Did you get any photos of Simon and Saskia?'

'Only one and it isn't very clear. Funnily enough, they aren't too keen on posing for photos. I'll buzz it to your phone. The organization they work for is based in the States but these two could be anywhere in the world by now. What do you want me to do next, Guv?'

'Nothing right now, thanks. I need to be sure that the couple who lived in Gibbet Cottage really are the Bonnie and Clyde of gun-running. If so, we'll need to go through all the stuff they left behind to see if we can find any leads. I may need you here with me, Bugsy.'

'Just say the word, Guv.'

CHAPTER SIX

That evening, Jack invited Dick and Rosie's Gallows Green neighbours for a drink at Hangman's Inn. Once there, he proposed to show them the photo on his phone to see if they could identify Simon and Saskia. He was still doubtful. Assuming the de Kuipers hadn't broadcast to the village what they did for a living, why had they been treated with such widespread dislike? Granted they were 'incomers', but so were Dick and Rosie and they seemed to get along all right. Apart from when they asked about Simon and Saskia, of course.

The folk from Gallows Green were chatting amiably around one of the pub tables. After Dani had brought everyone drinks, Jack passed his phone to Marcus.

'Is that the couple you knew as Simon and Saskia?'

At the mention of their names, the buzz of conversation ceased abruptly. Marcus took the phone and looked at the photo for some time without reacting, then:

'No, I don't think so, old boy. Wrong colour hair for a start. Saskia had black hair, this woman's blonde.' He passed the phone to Giles who glanced at it and nodded agreement. 'No, definitely not them. What do you think, Peter?'

Peter peered at it. 'No, not Simon and Saskia. Er . . . where did you get this photo?'

'Oh, just a long shot from police archives,' replied Jack, casually. 'Obviously not your hastily departed neighbours so no chance of returning their stuff. Sorry, Dick. Looks like we'll have to dispose of it some other way.'

There was a pregnant pause and a few sideways glances, then they carried on chatting, changing the subject entirely. Jack's copper's nose told him they were lying. But why?

Outside in the pub garden, Jeremy and Aleksy were playing together in the evening sunshine. Exhausted from racing, they both fell on their backs on the grass and stared up at the blue sky.

'I like it here,' announced Jeremy. 'It feels sort of safe; not like Bristol.'

'What was wrong with Bristol?' asked Aleksy, in his precise English.

'There were boys who ganged up on you and stole your stuff. If you didn't hand it over, they bullied you and made you fight. Some of them even carried knives. I hated it.'

Aleksy closed his eyes. 'I hate it here.'

Jeremy sat up and looked at his friend. 'Why? I think Lullington's really cool.'

'That's because you're not a Catholic and you don't have to sing in the choir and be an altar server.' Tears were beginning to force themselves from beneath his closed eyelids.

'So don't do it if you hate it so much. That's just daft. Tell your mum you don't want to.'

'My mother is a very devout Catholic. God would punish her if I didn't do what Father John tells me.'

Jeremy jumped up with all the outrage a ten-year-old boy can summon. 'That's absolute bollocks, Lex! God can't do anything to you, or your mum.'

'I pray to Him to let me go back home.'

'What? To Poland?'

'No, my real home. But my mother says we must stay, no matter how much we hate it, because here she has work; at home we should be very poor. We have no choice.'

Full of pity for his friend, Jeremy asked: 'Do you want to come home with me and play games on my computer?'

Aleksy leaped up. 'No thanks. I'm going to find my mother.' He ran back into the Inn leaving Jeremy kicking angrily at a plant trough and wondering what he could do to help his friend. It was just as he'd always suspected: religion was stupid and all it did was hurt people and make them miserable.

Back inside Hangman's Inn, Corrie had drunk enough Sauvignon Blanc to release her inhibitions and make her inclined to say exactly what she thought about people. In this instance, it was Thomas Tincknell. In a loud voice that could be heard all over the pub, she asked, 'D'you know what I saw today? I saw that horrible old Tincknell man beating his young wife. He punched her till she fell in a pit full of cow manure. Don't you think that's terrible?' She paused, waiting for some sort of response but nobody spoke. 'WELL?'

It was Ted Boobyer who answered. 'Old Thomas has a bit of a temper and Dimpsy winds him up sometimes. You don't want to take no notice.'

'He don't mean nothin' by it,' said another man. ''Tiz just 'is way.' There were general murmurs of agreement from around the pub.

Corrie turned on Ted. 'Well, you would say that, wouldn't you?' Jack was scared she was about to blurt out how they'd seen him harassing Dani, so he tugged at her sleeve, but she shook him off. 'Dimpsy's a strong young woman but she didn't attempt to defend herself. Why? I'll tell you why; because she's lived her whole life believing male domination is normal and acceptable. First her father and brothers, then her husband. What a miserable bloody existence! Men in this village seem to think women are possessions to be treated however they please.' Corrie was really in her stride now; the wine fuelling her sense of injustice. 'You're still living in the dark ages. It's time you woke up and smelt the . . .' she thrashed about for the right analogy . . . 'smelt the shit that's right under your noses!'

Constable Chedzey collected his tankard of cider off the bar and strolled across to try and placate Corrie. She was an incomer and couldn't be expected to understand country ways.

'You see, m'dear, young Dimpsy's a few apples short of an orchard. She needs a little tap from time to time to keep her in check. Teach her what's right.'

That did it. Corrie pulled herself up to her full five feet and stood toe to toe with Chedzey. Jack knew from experience she was about to blow like a Texas oil gusher and kept his head down.

'A LITTLE TAP?' Corrie yelled into the constable's startled face. 'You call what I witnessed 'a little tap'? Dimpsy Tincknell's lips were split and bleeding. She had a black eye and I shudder to think of her internal injuries. It's ABH, Police Constable Chedzey. Assault occasioning Actual Bodily Harm! What are you going to do about it?'

Bert Chedzey had never been challenged like that in all his thirty years as a country bobby in Lullington Barrow and certainly never by a woman. He didn't quite know how to deal with it. 'Well, I could 'ave a word, I s'pose, but—' He was saved from further punishment when the door opened and Father John came in, his frock wafting around him in the evening breeze like an un-guyed tent.

'Trouble I'm afraid,' he announced in the funereal tones he usually reserved for the Last Rites. 'Dimpsy Tincknell has run off. Thomas is furious, of course, and says he has no intention of doing the lazy so-and-so's work. He's rather the worse for drink and has gone to look for her with his shotgun. He intends to drag her back by the hair.' He trotted calmly to the bar where Ted Boobyer had his glass of wine already poured. He made a great play of swirling it round the glass, breathing in the bouquet and finally taking a big gulp and swilling it around his mouth. Having decided it was drinkable, he nodded to Ted who left him the bottle.

'Well?' said Corrie. 'Isn't anybody going to do anything?' There was silence while everyone paid close attention to their drinks. Corrie cast about her. 'If Dimpsy Tincknell is badly hurt, or worse, you all deserve some of the blame.' She eyeballed the old priest. 'I'm surprised at you, Father. "All that is necessary for the triumph of evil is that good men do nothing".' It went very quiet.

'Have I mentioned the smell in our utility room?' It was Dick Brown's pathetic attempt to puncture the uncomfortable silence. 'It seems to be coming up through the floor underneath the freezer that Simon and Saskia left behind.' Glad of the distraction, everyone became greatly consumed by the Browns' nasty smell.

'Probably your drains, old man,' offered Marcus. 'Have you moved the freezer at all?'

'No,' said Dick, 'it's a monster and it's full of food; too heavy.'

'Could be a dead pheasant or rabbit wedged somewhere,' suggested Giles. 'Game can get very high in hot weather.'

There were other suggestions ranging from ''Ave 'ee emptied yer wheelie bin?' to hints that the stink might be associated with Rosemary's aromatherapy.

'Rosie thinks it might be a dead body.' Dick tittered, self-consciously. 'Utterly ridiculous, of course.'

'Whose body do you think it might be, Rosemary?' asked Peter.

She glared at him. 'Maybe you could tell me! There's something odd going on here, something you're not telling us. Where are Simon and Saskia? Why won't anyone talk about them? Is one of them buried under Gibbet Cottage?' The awkward atmosphere had upset Rosie and her voice had an edge of hysteria. At a nod from the others, Peter reached across and put his hand on hers.

'Now why on earth should you think a thing like that, Rosemary? There's no mystery, my dear, I promise you. It's just that one or two of the legalities were relaxed with regard to the sale of Gibbet Cottage and with Jack, here, being a policemen, it seemed wiser not to mention it in case he felt compromised or obliged to arrest us all.' He took out his pipe and sucked at it, unlit. 'Simon and Saskia had a big business deal to finalize in Amsterdam and they needed to move fast and liquidate some assets. They wanted a quick cash sale on Gibbet Cottage; no estate agents, no surveys, no long-winded tax inquiries or capital gains nonsense. They offered the house to us, their neighbours, at a price we couldn't refuse, so we clubbed together and bought it privately, as a kind of Gallows Green consortium. They signed a sale document and our solicitor sorted out all the red tape after they'd gone. Then we put it on the market and you and Dick turned up and put in an offer the following day. Simon and Saskia made a quick exit, the consortium made a quick profit and you got a bargain. Everyone's a winner.'

Peter and the others clearly considered that an end to any further speculation.

'Thank goodness we finally got to the bottom of that,' said Dick, an hour later. He was pouring coffee for Jack and Corrie at the kitchen table. 'No more nonsense about bodies and intruders moving the furniture, eh, love?' He gave Rosemary's shoulder a squeeze. She looked uneasy.

'It all seemed a little glib to me; like they'd been rehearsing it. Don't you agree, Corrie?'

Corrie nodded. 'There were lots of nods and winks between Marcus, Giles and Peter.'

'And,' said Rosie, 'it still doesn't explain the pong in the outhouse. It's really sickly and disgusting now. We may have to call the Environmental Health people.'

Corrie sipped her coffee, thoughtfully. 'How about this for a scenario? What if the Gallows Green 'consortium' are the killers? They wait until Simon and Saskia have signed over the cottage, then bump them off, sell the cottage to Dick and Rosie and keep all the money.

The de Kuipers could both be buried under the cement in the utility room.'

Rosie gave a muffled whimper and dabbed lavender oil on her temples.

Jack groaned inwardly. That's right, Corrie. Wind her up even more. 'But why would they do that? What's the motive? Certainly not the money because it's obvious none of them needs it.' If Bugsy was right, he knew rather more about the de Kuipers than he had divulged, but even if they were arms smugglers, it still didn't explain why they were hated in Lullington Barrow. 'What was it that made them so unpopular in this village? Witchcraft? Wife-swapping gone wrong? What?'

'Does wife-swapping ever go right?' asked Corrie, curiously.

They were still mulling this over when there was a knock on the kitchen door. Marcus, Giles and Peter stood there armed with pick axes.

'We could see Rosemary was still worried,' explained Peter, 'so we thought we'd help you move the freezer and take a proper look underneath. We'll dig up the concrete if you like.'

Peter, Marcus, Jack and Giles each took a corner of the heavy chest while Dick hopped about, supervising the operation. As the freezer finally came away from the corner, the stench became overpowering and the women backed away, hankies over their noses.

'Tip it up, chaps.' Giles, on his hands and knees, reached into the underside of the freezer. 'I think I've found your bodies, Rosie.' He emerged holding up two enormous decomposing rats by their tails. 'Here are your culprits. Crawled underneath, probably already dying from rat poison, then got trapped in the condenser. This one . . .' he swung it towards them, '. . . was obviously about to give birth.' As he shook the rat, several decaying babies fell from her abdomen. Both corpses, fangs bared in death, were dripping their reeking entrails onto the concrete floor and the stink proved beyond doubt that they'd found the source of the problem. Giles chuckled. 'You said you could smell a rat, Rosie, and you were right.'

The three men sauntered back across Gallows Green to their houses.

'Just a couple of dead rats, then,' said Giles.

'But not *our* rats, of course,' drawled Marcus.

'More's the pity,' sighed Peter.

They strolled in silence for a while, then Peter asked, 'Do you think the Browns believed our story about the sale of the cottage? I tried to make it sound as convincing as possible.'

'It convinced me, Pete,' said Giles. 'Especially the bit about relaxing a few of the legalities. We certainly did that.'

'Well, I, for one, am unrepentant,' declared Marcus. 'Simon and Saskia were a poisonous couple. They made many people's lives a misery, not just ours. Lullington Barrow's better off without them, no matter how many laws we broke in getting rid of them.'

'That detective inspector's no fool. I'm not sure he swallowed it entirely,' said Peter.

'And there are still a lot of loose ends that we need to tie up before we're in the clear,' said Giles.

Peter nodded. 'I'll make a start tomorrow. Let you know how I get on.'

'Be careful, old man.' Marcus was wary. 'A lot depends on this. And we have the ladies to consider. We're all agreed that Millie, Edwina and Jane mustn't know what we've done.'

'Agreed,' said Peter.

'Most emphatically,' declared Giles.

CHAPTER SEVEN

St Mary's Church of the Blessed Virgin dated back to the thirteenth century. Its tower could be seen from several miles out to sea and at one time, it was whitewashed and served as a mariner's beacon. As a church, however, it was undeniably ugly. On each corner was carved a grotesque gargoyle in the shape of a gorgon's head that medieval Somerset folk so enjoyed. The gargoyle on the south-west corner appeared to be devouring a human being, probably some unfortunate saint. Village mothers used this imagery to terrify their unruly children.

The early village of Lullington Barrow had been situated just south of the church and close to the sea, but with the drainage of the Somerset marshes, the village had moved further inland and the original Lullington was now covered by large sand dunes. Laid out amongst these dunes was Lullington Barrow Golf Course. The course was designed in the traditional manner of nine holes out and nine back. The first nine skirted the sand dunes and coastline northwards, then turning inland and southwards, down the coast, past the church and back into Lullington.

One of the consequences of the shifting village was that St Mary's Church now stood bang in the middle of the thirteenth fairway, known to golfers as The Church Hole. It was a difficult par five that extended across the cemetery and out the other side. As with all golf links, the challenging factor was the wind and its unpredictability. This meant that churchgoers had to watch out for wayward golf balls when walking up the path. Stray balls had been known to hit people, sometimes injuring them quite badly and several car windscreens had been smashed. A hefty, florid-cheeked member of Lullington Barrow Riding Club claimed her hunter had been summarily dispatched by a blow to the head while she was still in the saddle. Having had a few near misses herself, Bridget O'Dowd claimed she took her life in her hands whenever she went to clean the church and declared she deserved 'danger money, so she did'.

Another consequence of the shift was that the church now had no realistic protection from the Bristol Channel apart from a boundary wall that had been breached on several occasions by high tides which flooded the church and did a good deal of damage. The bishop continually expressed his disappointment that Father John hadn't raised sufficient money for the repairs, hinting that it was the old priest's holy responsibility to screw as much money as possible from his dwindling parishioners by whatever means he could.

The golf clubhouse, on the other hand, was spacious and comfortable and reflected the affluence of both owners and members. There was a Michelin-starred restaurant that could seat a hundred diners, a health spa, beauty salon and gym. The bar had French windows opening onto a covered terrace overlooking the course. It was here that Jack, Corrie and the Gallows Green neighbours were enjoying a drink while watching the sun set behind the dunes and the last golfers, completing the eighteenth hole.

'Originally,' mused Marcus, noting the predominance of Rupert Bear trousers and diamond-patterned slipovers, 'golf was restricted to wealthy, overweight businessmen. Today it's open to anyone who can afford the hideous clothes.'

Millie, excitable as ever, pointed to an impressive trophy on a glass shelf behind the bar. It was a golf ball mounted on a heavy marble plinth. 'Marcus got a hole-in-one with that ball, didn't you darling?'

Deprecatingly, Marcus described in his deep, mellifluous voice how he achieved his hole-in-one at the thirteenth. 'It's a tricky one, The Church Hole, and it had never been done before, so it seemed appropriate to mark the event by mounting the ball onto a decent trophy.'

Corrie was impressed. 'That lovely green marble sets off the ball perfectly, Marcus. It's as if it's sitting on grass.'

'It's Connemara marble. Mrs O'Dowd loves it. When she cleans here, she takes it home and polishes it till it gleams, bless her.'

A ubiquitous cleaner such as Bridget O'Dowd would probably service most of the larger houses in Lullington, mused Corrie, which would explain how she acquired all the gossip.

'What's your handicap, Marcus?' asked Dick, a keen golfer himself.

'Millie, when she's shopping with my credit card.' His loving smile took the sting out of the remark and Millie laughed and squeezed his thigh.

Marcus and Millie, observed Corrie, had all the appearances of a very happy marriage, so either Marcus knew nothing of Millie's hanky-panky with Simon or he was more forgiving than most husbands. The other possibility was that the mouth-watering Marcus had exacted his revenge by disposing of his wife's lover but that simply didn't bear thinking about.

Lullington Barrow Parish Council was made up of the same nucleus of male parishioners who ran everything else in the village: Doctor Brimble, Ted Boobyer, Constable Chedzey, Marcus and Peter. Giles had been invited to stand but said he spent too much time abroad to maintain a useful continuity so it was Edwina who came along to take the minutes. Other members, such as the postmistress and the nursery school teacher, made up a quorum but said and did very little and agreed with everything that was proposed.

Dick, as the incoming treasurer, had taken the books home with him prior to the meeting and carried out a thorough audit, as Jack knew he would. Edgar Brimble asked Edwina to read the minutes of the last meeting, which were sparse to say the least, then welcomed Dick and thanked him for taking over. When the time came for his report, it made interesting listening.

'I'd say your previous treasurer had been doing an extremely good job, until a few months before he disappeared. Then, quite large sums went missing from the council's funds without any supporting evidence for the expenditure and were concealed by false accounting.' He scanned the faces around the table. 'You say Draycott went up north to take up a headship. Was he under severe stress before he left? In cases like this, the underlying cause of fraud can usually be traced to a specific problem; a gambling habit that got out of control, alcoholism or possibly addiction to drugs. I've even known a case where the reason for the embezzlement was an extravagant young wife.' Dick addressed the Chair. 'Was that likely in this case, Doctor Brimble?'

'Absolutely not. Draycott was a good man and a first-class maths teacher. And he wasn't married. I'm sure I can't think of a single reason why he should suddenly feel it necessary to defraud the parish.' He looked around at the others. 'Does anyone have any ideas?'

Nobody had, or if they did, they weren't telling. Like many bankers, Dick was not the most sensitive to people's feelings and totally oblivious to an atmosphere of any kind. Had he been receptive to auras, like his wife, he would immediately have detected a change in the mood of the meeting which dispersed very soon after his revelation. Having unearthed a potential crime, Dick felt he should report it to Jack.

'There's certainly a case for Draycott being required to answer charges. He could get seven years for false accounting. I'll get my sergeant to do a trace.'

But having tried every database available to the police, Bugsy drew a blank. 'Draycott disappeared off the face of the earth, Guv. The National Insurance and tax people have lost track of him and his bank still holds funds in his name that haven't been accessed since he disappeared. He's either legged it abroad to avoid getting nicked or he's dead.'

Next morning, Dick and Marcus had arranged to play golf and it was promising to be something of a needle match since they had similar handicaps. Jack and Giles, who didn't play, were going along to watch, followed by lunch in the restaurant. Millie had gone shopping and Edwina was mounting a campaign against litter, specifically targeting discarded chewing gum. Her leaflets bore the slogan: 'We'll Tell You Where To Stick It'. Only Peter and Jane were at home on Gallows Green. Corrie and Rosie strolled on the beach before the sun got too hot.

'Rosie, you are glad you moved to the country, aren't you?' It seemed to Corrie that far from a gentler, simpler life, living in Lullington, particularly Gibbet Cottage, was causing her younger sister more anxiety than peace.

Rosemary sighed. 'Yes, of course. I know it mightn't seem like it sometimes, but take no notice of me, it's my over-developed sensitivity. I feel things more acutely. Dick loves it here and so does Jeremy, so that's good enough for me.'

As they passed the church, they stopped to listen to the choir practising. The young voices rang out pure and true across Gallows Green. At the end of the anthem, the church door burst open and a dozen or so small boys came tumbling out, laughing and shouting, glad to be in the sunshine after the gloomy church. Aleksy was among them but he was walking sedately, a sad look on his face.

'I worry about that child,' said Rosie. 'He's much too solemn for a ten-year-old. Too much religion and too little joy. He's Jeremy's best friend, but even Jerry says he's miserable most of the time and wants to go back home.'

'Where's home?' asked Corrie. The accent still evaded her.

'Poland, I think. Dani, his mother, is a single parent and came here to work. She was very lucky to get a job and accommodation with the Boobyers.'

Secretly, Corrie suspected luck hadn't come into it. Carlene was working on that one and Corrie suspected she knew what the outcome would be. As they caught up with Aleksy, she called to him. 'Hello, Lex. How are you today?'

'I'm fine, thank you, Mrs Dawes.' The boy stopped and politely shook Corrie's hand, which she thought was charming, if a little quaint.

'The singing was lovely,' said Rosie. 'Do you like being in the choir?' To her horror, the boy's eyes filled with tears. He tried hard to force them back but ended up knuckling his eyes and sobbing.

'No, I don't! I hate it. And I hate God for making me a Catholic.'

He ran off, leaving both Corrie and Rosie feeling helpless and upset. They walked in silence across Gallows Green and towards Gibbet Cottage, each lost in her own thoughts, until Corrie asked, 'Did you light the fire before we left?'

Rosie frowned. 'No, course I didn't. We're having the hottest summer for decades. What made you think I'd lit the fire?'

'Because,' replied Corrie, breaking into a sprint, 'there's smoke coming from the roof of your house!'

When they reached the front door, it was wide open and smoke was billowing down the stairs. 'Quick!' shrieked Rosemary. 'Call the fire brigade.' Corrie was punching 999 into her mobile as she ran. Then a figure emerged, covered in soot and carrying a fire extinguisher that was still half-heartedly dribbling foam.

'It's all right,' croaked Peter. 'I think I've put it out.' He paused, overcome by another paroxysm of coughing from the smoke. 'I'm afraid your attic's a mess, Rosemary.'

They went up to look and Peter was right; everything was blackened and charred. 'Looks like the fire started in those tea chests,' he choked, wiping his smarting eyes. 'I reckon it was the sun shining through the skylight window onto all that paper.'

'Oh Peter,' gasped Rosemary, 'thank goodness you spotted the smoke in time. If the thatch had caught fire . . .' she didn't dare articulate the consequences.

'How did you manage to get in?' asked Corrie.

'Oh . . . er . . . the door was open,' answered Peter, coughing hard. 'I'd better get back, Jane will be worried.' He hurried back to his house across Gallows Green with Rosemary still shouting her thanks after him.

The men came back from the golf club straight away after Corrie phoned Jack and told him what had happened. They all trooped up to the attic to assess the damage.

'Bloody hell, Dickie, that was a near thing,' said Giles, 'the whole house could have gone up and spread to the others on Gallows Green.'

'Whatever was in those tea chests, it won't be any good now. It's completely destroyed,' said Marcus, poking about amongst the charred paper.

'Lucky you left the door unlocked, Rosie,' said Dick.

'But I didn't. I distinctly remember locking it when I left to meet Corrie.'

'You must have left it open, sweetheart. How else could Peter have got in?' Dick gave Rosie a pitying look that implied she was being absent-minded again.

'Maybe he picked the lock,' offered Corrie.

Jack dismissed this. 'Don't be daft; it'd take forever to pick an old iron lock like that. By the time he'd finished, there'd have been no door left attached to it. The whole house would have burned down.'

'There's no mystery about how Peter got in,' explained Marcus. 'Tell 'em, Giles.'

'Spare key under the plant pot in the porch. And before you read us the riot act about security, Jack, everybody in the village does it. Simon and Saskia must have left theirs behind.'

'Well, anyway, it's a valuable lesson about how dangerous the sun's rays can be, magnified through glass,' said Dick.

'It couldn't have been the sun.' Rosemary was adamant. 'The house would have to be facing south-west, and it doesn't. It was one of the things I checked before we bought it. I couldn't live anywhere that faced south-west, it's the Devil's Back Door,' and she gave Dick a glare that defied him to contradict her.

Late that evening, in the bar of Hangman's Inn, Jack and Corrie were deep in thought, each struggling with questions that needed answers. Jack was wondering how long he could justifiably delay telling Sergeant Malone's 'funny buggers' that he had traced two wanted arms couriers to an address in Somerset but that any useful leads they might have left behind had gone up in flames. Chief Superintendent Garwood was going to love that. Then there was the revelation that everyone left their spare door keys under plant pots, so anyone might have gone into Gibbet Cottage while Simon and Saskia were out, and similarly, Simon and Saskia could have raided any of their neighbours' homes. Jack wasn't sure what that proved, but the possibilities for smugglers on the run were infinite.

Corrie was pondering on more humanitarian issues; specifically, the increasing stress and anxiety of her sister, the abject misery of a little boy, Ted Boobyer's behaviour with barmaids and what would happen to Dimpsy Tincknell when her brute of a husband caught up with her. She broke the silence.

'Jack, why do you suppose Marcus, Giles and Peter volunteered to help dig up Dick and Rosie's floor?'

'Just being neighbourly, I guess.'

'I don't think it was that. They were suspicious. Did you notice their faces when the smell turned out to be just rats? It was almost as if they were disappointed. As if they were hoping it would be something else.'

'You're letting this village get to you, Corrie. Mind you, I admit it isn't all garden gnomes and honeysuckle round the door. If everyone leaves their keys under pots, someone might easily have broken into Gibbet Cottage and rearranged Rosie's furniture while she was out. But why? That's the bit I don't understand.'

'And the fire's still a mystery. You heard what Rosie's Feng Shui made of Peter's Olympic flame theory; she doesn't believe the sun's rays ignited it. Do you suppose someone set light to those documents on purpose? I keep getting a creepy feeling that Simon and Saskia are back and they're hiding somewhere in Lullington, waiting to collect what they left behind.'

Jack was wondering whether it was safe to tell Corrie what he'd found out about the de Kuipers or if she'd start hopping about like Miss Marple on speed, desperate to get involved. He was saved from making a decision by Bridget O'Dowd, who burst in, out of breath and hairnet all awry, looking for Constable Chedzey. She found him playing darts.

'Bert, you're here, so ye are! Old Mother Tincknell has raised the alarm. The woman's a Catholic when it suits her and Father John has been summoned to her bedside. She's seen neither hide nor hair of Thomas or Dimpsy for two days and she's whining that there's no food in the house. Sure, the old besom could starve for a month and she'd still be fat as a pig. Father John wants me to cook her meals and he's arranged for farm helpers to see to the stock. He says you're to organize a search party.'

Next morning, the whole village, men, women and children, turned out to join in the search. Corrie had come to know the Lullington villagers rather well over the last few days and guessed that their enthusiasm was more to do with morbid curiosity than community spirit. They treated it almost like a day out, taking cider and sandwiches and speculating cheerfully about what Thomas might have done to Dimpsy and the horrors they might find.

PC Chedzey, basically a lazy man, asked Jack, as the senior police officer, to take charge of the operation. Officially, Jack was on Avon and Somerset's territory and professional etiquette demanded that he should step back, but he'd been requested to take over and frankly, he doubted if PC Chedzey could find his bum with both hands, let alone two missing persons. More importantly, intuition told him action was needed right away if they were to avoid injury, possibly even death. Observing all the protocols would take time.

Having established that Dimpsy had not fled back to the Puddys, her family home, and that no one had seen Thomas since he stormed off drunk and armed with a shotgun, the obvious place to start was Black Oak Farm. Jack directed the main body of villagers to fan out across the fields, led by Dick and PC Chedzey. Corrie persuaded a tense Rosemary to stay home, promising to keep her informed of any developments. Meanwhile, Jack searched the farm buildings with Doctor Brimble and the rest of the Gallows Green crowd. Father John declared he would dearly love to join them but his 'rheumatics' prevented him. He and Bridget O'Dowd stayed with Ethel Tincknell, giving her comfort and the occasional nip of brandy. The old girl alternated between snivelling with self-pity and outbursts of venom against Dimpsy, who, she said, had ruined the farm and her son's life and deserved whatever had befallen her. She didn't care if they never found Dimpsy; she just wanted her Tommy back, safe and sound.

They searched the farmhouse and outbuildings, poked about in feed bins and silos, tore down abandoned sheds and took the ancient dairy apart, piece by piece. They found nothing.

A sudden thought occurred to Doctor Brimble while they were searching the cowshed. The bull pen was empty. 'Where's the bull? Where's Titus?'

'God help us if he's escaped,' said Peter. 'Dimpsy's the only one who can handle him. Should we get a vet, Jack, in case he needs putting down?'

'Let's find the beast, first,' said Marcus, who given the choice, would rather have had Thomas put down than poor old Titus. 'He could be in the next county by now.'

Jack had almost run out of ideas. He doubted very much if Thomas and Dimpsy were elsewhere in the village – somebody would have reported seeing them. And given that Thomas had never been out of Somerset in his life, it was highly unlikely he'd venture 'abroad' now, and neither would Dimpsy. But where *would* they go? Jack racked his brains.

'Corrie, you've been in this cowshed before. What's that?' He pointed to a big concrete pit, sunk into the ground and full of manure. It had been there so long that grass was beginning to grow on the surface except for one end where the contents had been disturbed.

'It's a slurry pit,' answered Edwina. 'Black Oak Farm is obviously run organically. They gather animal waste and unusable hay and slowly convert it into a natural fertilizer which is then spread on the fields. Much more environmentally friendly than artificial fertilizers full of chemicals that get into rivers, kill the fish and destroy the ecosystem.' She leaned over the edge and peered in. 'This pit hasn't been emptied for years, though. Pooh!'

Corrie shuddered. 'It's very deep. When Tincknell punched Dimpsy, she fell backwards into it, nearly up to her neck. I had to pull her out.'

Everyone had the same thought at the same time. Only Millie articulated it. Her hand flew to her mouth. 'Oh Christ! She's not in there, is she? He hasn't thrown her into that pit?'

One by one, the men rolled up their sleeves. Giles squatted down on the edge, his gum boots squelching in the sludge. 'Do you want us to climb in, Jack?'

Jack stopped him. 'I don't think so, mate, thanks all the same. It's too dangerous. I'll call the fire brigade and get them to pump it out. If there's nothing in there, there's no harm done.'

When the firemen started to pump out the tank, the gases were so choking that the chief fire officer made everyone go outside and his men put on respirators. Even out in the fresh air, eyes were smarting from the ammonia.

Jane, the thoughtful one of the group, was shocked. 'Poor Dimpsy. If she wasn't dead when he threw her in, she must be by now. How could he do such a thing? Why didn't we stop it? We knew she was being ill-treated and we just turned a blind eye rather than make a fuss.'

'Hold on, love,' cautioned Peter. 'We don't actually know if she's dead yet, do we?'

But when the chief fire officer emerged, pulling off his mask, his expression said it all. He spoke quietly to Jack. 'I think you'd better come and look at this, Inspector.'

Careful not to disturb what could well turn out to be a crime scene, the firemen had hauled up a bundle from the bottom of the pit. It was dripping with cows' excrement and urine and wrapped loosely in feed sacks, tied up with bailer twine. They placed it on the cowshed floor and stood back. Jack went in with Doctor Brimble, telling the others to stay outside. But Corrie had to see for herself. She felt just as guilty as Jane. After Tincknell attacked Dimpsy, Corrie had turned and run. Why hadn't she made Dimpsy go with her?

As they cut away the blood-soaked sacking, Corrie braced herself. Tincknell, incensed by Dimpsy running away, had kicked and punched his wife once too often. He had beaten her to death and dumped her body in the slurry pit, probably hoping it would rot before it was discovered. And in this toxic village, thought Corrie, he might well have got away with it; but not with Inspector Dawes on his case. She wondered where Tincknell was now. Wherever he'd gone, Jack would track him down. The bundle, clearly a corpse, was unwrapped in silence. As Jack gently uncovered the face, Corrie gasped. It wasn't Dimpsy; it was Thomas.

CHAPTER EIGHT

Doctor Brimble's professional opinion was that Thomas Tincknell had been thrashed to death by person or persons unknown. He had a fractured skull, probably inflicted with a blunt force instrument, and numerous broken bones. Before dying, he had bled profusely from a number of deep puncture wounds in his chest and abdomen made by some kind of pointed device around four centimetres in diameter. He estimated that death had occurred in the last twenty-four hours.

'Hard to be more precise, Inspector, due to the effects on the body of the slurry contents. It's designed to break down organic material. But I'm only a country GP; the post mortem should give you more. One thing I can be sure about, though, Tincknell didn't die of natural causes. Even if it turns out to be one of those messy farm machinery accidents, someone wrapped him in sacks afterwards and dumped him in the pit in an attempt to conceal the body.'

'Will you be heading up the investigation, Inspector Dawes?' Constable Chedzey was anxious to shift responsibility. He wasn't used to dealing with a crime of this gravity. It was well above his pay grade, and he was retiring in six months. His pension beckoned and a nice quiet life playing bowls. He'd reported Tincknell's death to the Avon and Somerset HQ at Portishead double quick; their response had been pragmatic and budget conscious. If there was a Detective Inspector from the Metropolitan Police Murder Investigation Team right there on the spot, who better to deal with the case?

Jack scowled. 'Strictly speaking, PC Chedzey, I'm on holiday and I have no jurisdiction here, but I'll do what I can until someone else comes to take over. And don't forget, we still haven't found Dimpsy. She could be wandering about out there, confused and terrified.'

'So could that ruddy great bull,' muttered Chedzey.

*

Jack's mobile rang half an hour later and he winced when the name of his boss flashed up. That's all he was short of; a flea in his ear from Detective Chief Superintendent Garwood.

'Is that you, Dawes? What the hell's going on there?'

'I'm very well, sir, thank you for asking. And yes, I'm having a very pleasant holiday.' Not for the first time, Jack decided Garwood had been playing truant the day they taught interpersonal skills at Hendon. That's if they ever did.

'I've just been speaking to the deputy assistant commissioner who's had a call from the deputy chief constable of Avon and Somerset. Seems you can't stay out of trouble even when you're supposed to be on leave.'

Here we go, thought Jack. Garwood's had complaints about me treading on the toes of the local police and operating outside my jurisdiction. He could imagine top brass working themselves up into a right old tarnish. 'Well, sir, there's been a suspicious death here and I was just caretaking the investigation, making sure the crime scene wasn't contaminated, until another SIO arrives. Obviously I shall return to the Met now that—'

'No you won't,' barked Garwood. 'The DAC and the DCC want you to stay until the case is concluded and I've extended your absence indefinitely. Just get on with it, man, and try not to rack up too much overtime. Keep me informed. That's all.' And he rang off leaving Jack staring at a silent phone.

Now he was officially in charge, Jack knew he needed backup from someone he could rely on; someone with more brains and enthusiasm than PC Chedzey who, under pressure, was about as animated as one of the scarecrows dotted about the fields. He phoned Sergeant Malone who answered straight away, despite having a mouthful of fruitcake.

'Hello, Guv. I was just going to phone you. I've got some more guff on the de Kuipers. Looks like they've diversified into something even more dangerous than gun-running.'

'I didn't think there was anything more dangerous than gun-running. But first off, has anything lively occurred in MIT since we last spoke?'

'No, boss. It's about as exciting as a nun's knickers.'

'Right. You can bring me up to date on the de Kuipers in person when you get here. Don't try to drive; the motorway's hell. There's a train from Paddington in half an hour; can you be on it?'

Malone gulped the last of his cake. 'You bet. Are things hotting up in the sticks, then?'

'You could say that. I've got a suspicious death on my hands and Garwood's made me the SIO.'

'Blimey, Jack, you get all the luck! Murder seems to follow you around. Who is it? Simon or Saskia?'

'Neither. Someone's topped one of the yokels. He was a violent, malicious old bully who liked using his fists on women but we still have to find out what happened to him.'

'Right, Guv. I'm on my way. See you later.'

'Your mate in the Licensed wossnames dug up some choice dirt on Ted Boobyer, Mrs D.' It was Carlene ringing Corrie from London. 'Dunno what you was expectin' but this geezer's been largin' it, big time. He's one creepy guy. It's all on your laptop; shall I read it to you?'

'No, thanks, Carlene, I think I'll understand it better if I see it for myself. What's the 'Cuisine's' order book like for the next day or two?'

'Nuffink till Fursday week, Mrs D. It's the heat. No one wants Cordon Bleu grub; they're scoffin' salad and ice cream from M&S.'

'Good. Use the business account to buy a train ticket to Lower-bridge. It's the nearest station to Lullington Barrow. There's a train from Paddington in half an hour. Don't forget to change at Bristol or you'll end up in Cornwall. You can bring me up to date on Ted Boobyer when you get here; bring my laptop with you.'

The train from Paddington was packed with refugees from the swel-tering city, escaping to the West Country while the weather held. DS Malone struggled on board with his overnight bag, sweat dripping off his chin. He spotted one vacant seat next to a young woman with tormented magenta hair and a stud through her eyebrow. Cautiously, so as not to encroach on her personal space, he shoe-horned his bulk into it. She smiled and plucked out her earphones.

'Got enough room, mate? I can squash up a bit if you like?'

'Thanks, love.' Malone smiled back and breathed out.

'Wot about this wevver, then? I'm dry as a camel's scrotum.' She reached into the backpack between her feet and pulled out a plastic container and a bottle of water. She drank most of the water then flipped open the box.

Malone recognized the contents. 'That's Bakewell Tart, isn't it?'

'S'right. D'you wanna slice?'

'Not half, it's one of my favourites. My guv'nor's wife makes a cracking Bakewell Tart.'

Carlene chiselled off a slice with her nail file and passed it to Bugsy. 'Bet it isn't as good as this. My boss is a proper professional chef. She runs her own catering business with a posh name: "Coriander's Cuisine". But she's not at all up 'erself; she's dead cool.'

When they realized they were each talking about the same Jack and Corrie Dawes, they chatted non-stop.

'What a coincidence, two strangers sitting next to each other on a train but heading for the same place to meet the same people,' said Bugsy.

'When I was little, my mum used to say that there ain't no such fing as strangers; only friends you 'aven't met yet.'

'That's a nice idea. Where does your mum live, Carlene?'

'She's in a maximum-security booze clinic in Hackney.'

By the time they reached Lullington, Bugsy had learned all about Carlene's early upbringing in a children's home and her juvenile brushes with the law – *Tracy Beaker wiv attitude, that was me, but I'm goin' straight now, ain't I?* – and she knew that he was a long-serving detective sergeant in the Met called Michael Malone but that everyone called him Bugsy because of the film. The real surprise came when the two turned up together at Hangman's Inn where Jack and Corrie were waiting.

'Hello, Carlene, what are you doing here?' asked Jack.

'I'm doin' some detective work for Mrs D,' she said, proudly; then she remembered. 'Only I'm not supposed to say nuffink.'

'Nice to see you, Bugsy,' said Corrie, ignoring Jack's raised eyebrows. 'Have you come to help Jack with the suspicious death?'

'Yeah, and I've got some more gen on the de Kuipers and the arms racket they're running. Starting to look really serious. We may have to take Gibbet Cottage apart.'

Corrie turned to Jack and raised her eyebrows back.

*

The search for Dimpsy continued without success. Some folk thought she'd killed her husband in a mad frenzy, 'what with 'er bein' a bit soft in the 'ead, like', and then run off in terror. But the smart money was on them both having been murdered by someone else for the cash that Tincknell had stashed away and Dimpsy's body would eventually be discovered lying in a ditch somewhere. Meanwhile, Titus, a tonne of ferocious Holstein bull, was still on the loose. And because Tincknell had been too mean to pay for the animal to be disbudded as a calf, it had grown an awesome set of horns. Both Inspector Dawes and the vet warned villagers not to approach the brute as it was now running wild, probably freaked and very likely to attack.

In the bar of the Hangman's Inn, Dawes and Malone were each downing a pint of Lullington Gold while Bugsy brought Jack up to date.

'My mate in the 'funny buggers' says the de Kuipers have got hold of a list of dissidents planning to overthrow the repressive regime in another of the big Arab states. As well as selling arms to both sides, they're offering information about an insurgent network hidden within the government's own security system. The list of names goes to the highest bidder.'

Jack whistled. 'Blimey, Bugsy, that's tantamount to suicide if the de Kuipers get caught.'

'And according to my mate, you don't even want to know about the interrogation techniques if they're captured. They don't muck about, the Arabs.'

Jack went quiet while he thought. Bugsy strolled across to the bar to chat up Dani and buy cheese rolls, scotch eggs and pork pies. He returned, munching. 'Pity about the fire in your brother-in-law's attic. There might have been some useful clues in that stuff.'

'Suppose it was started deliberately?' suggested Jack. 'What if someone wanted to destroy any trace of the de Kuipers?' He told Bugsy about Rosemary's conviction that someone had been in Gibbet Cottage and moved the furniture. At the time, Jack had dismissed it as one of Rosie's bizarre fancies but now he wasn't so sure. It could have been a search that went wrong. 'The fact that the de Kuipers disappeared at a moment's notice suggests someone was on to them but no one in the village will talk about it. I showed the neighbours the photo but they all denied categorically that it was Simon and Saskia.'

'But you think they were lying?'

'I'm certain they were. If I can't tell when someone recognizes a face by now, I'm in the wrong job.'

'That kind of suggests that the villagers don't want the de Kuipers traced.'

'Right. And they sure as hell don't want them to come back. On the other hand, maybe they know that they can't come back, because they're already dead.'

'So what next, Jack? Do we tell Intelligence that we've located the de Kuipers' last known address? They'll be down here mob-handed and take Gibbet Cottage apart, beam by beam, looking for leads as to their whereabouts.'

Jack scratched his chin. Rosemary would have hysterics. 'Let's give it another couple of days, Bugsy. They might turn up elsewhere. I don't want to destroy Dick and Rosemary's home unless it's absolutely necessary.' He didn't mention Corrie's creepy intuition that Simon and Saskia might still be close by, or his own, very real suspicion that they had left behind their list of rebels, waiting for a chance to retrieve it, safely. The information was, no doubt, extremely profitable if you could stay alive long enough to spend the money. He half-hoped it had gone up in flames because while it existed, it endangered everyone on Gallows Green.

Bugsy and Carlene had been given rooms in Hangman's Inn and it was in her chintzy bedroom that Carlene showed Corrie the information on her laptop. Corrie read it in silence.

'He's done time, this geezer,' observed Carlene, laconically. 'Two years in the Scrubs and a ten grand fine.'

'Yes, but not for sexual offences, which is what I expected. This is even worse and could have dreadful repercussions for some people here in Lullington.' Corrie chewed her lip. 'And it explains quite a lot of things, including why his wife's name is over the door as licensee of Hangman's Inn instead of his.'

'It prob'ly explains why he's holed up in a dump like this. Keeping 'is 'ead down . . . but not 'is nose clean. Still up to 'is old tricks, by the look of it, just a different pub. What we gonna do, Mrs D?'

'Nothing for the moment. I need time to think and, if I can, do some damage limitation. Don't say a word to anyone, Carlene, especially not to Mr Jack.'

'Schtum!' Carlene made a zipping motion across her purple-lipsticked mouth.

'So what kind of dirty work have you got poor little Carlene doing?' Jack cornered Corrie as soon as he was able. 'I thought you were teaching her to cook, like you, not interfere in police matters that are dangerous and liable to get her into trouble, also like you.'

Corrie snorted. 'Don't be so stuffy. It's just that business with Ted Boobyer and Danika. I couldn't stop thinking about the look on her face when she was running away from him. Sort of hunted. I guessed he might have done something similar before so Carlene was checking him out with the Licensed Victuallers for me.'

'I thought so!' Jack pounced immediately. 'I knew you wouldn't be able to mind your own business and stay out of it. So what did Carlene uncover?'

Corrie crossed her fingers behind her back. 'Nothing yet, we're still working on it.' She didn't want to tell Jack the whole truth because he'd have Border Control officials steaming in with their sirens and handcuffs before she'd had a chance to work out the best way to handle the situation. She turned the tables on him. 'And anyway, what's all this about the de Kuipers running an arms racket? And why might you have to take Dick and Rosemary's home apart?'

Jack looked sheepish. 'I was suspicious, like you, so I got Bugsy to call in a few favours from his mates in the Intelligence Agency. It looks serious, Corrie. The Arab Spring generated a lot of private profiteering, especially in the black market arms trade. From what we've discovered, Simon and Saskia de Kuiper – and that's only one of their aliases – are right in the thick of it, selling to the highest bidder.'

'Bloody hell!' breathed Corrie, who rarely swore. 'And have you reported their last known whereabouts to Bugsy's "spooks"?'

'Not yet but I think I'll have to soon. If your legendary intuition proves correct and the de Kuipers did leave something valuable behind . . .'

'. . . they'll be coming back to collect it. They may already have tried.'

Jack was thoughtful. 'Mm. It isn't that that's worrying me. It's who else might come here looking for the same thing.'

Corrie gasped. 'What . . . Arabs? In Somerset?'

'Who knows? It's a risk I don't want to take. I think Bugsy and I ought to take a good look around Gibbet Cottage, see if we can find anything.'

'Well, don't disturb Rosie's Feng Shui whatever you do; she'll get one of her headaches and we'll never hear the last of it.'

Always a restless, fidgety sleeper, Rosemary tossed and turned. She had just decided to get up and make some camomile tea when all hell broke loose. The new security lights and alarms that Dick had installed all went off at once. She leapt out of bed and ran to the window, just in time to see a shadowy figure in the overgrown garden making off across the shrubbery, and towards the wall that separated Gibbet Cottage from Marcus and Millie's garden.

Dick wore earplugs and a sleep mask at night, and was still snoring, blissfully unaware of the bedlam going on outside. Rosemary shook him, crossly. 'Dick, wake up! There's someone in our garden. What's the use of burglar alarms if you're not going to wake up when they go off? We could be murdered in our beds. Quick! Get out there and catch him!'

'Catch who?' mumbled Dick.

'The burglar, of course. I saw someone running across the garden and trying to escape into Marcus and Millie's.' She grabbed her phone and dialled Corrie who swiftly woke Jack.

'Quick, there's someone in Rosie's garden. They've triggered the alarms.'

Jack yawned. 'It's not Titus, is it? I draw the line at bullfighting during the night.'

'No, Rosie says she saw an intruder running away. It could be Dimpsy.' She lowered her voice. 'Or it might be those Arabs you were so worried about.'

'Okay, I'll wake Bugsy and we'll get over there.'

Dick pulled on trousers then switched off the lights and alarms. Grabbing an old billhook from the outhouse, he hacked his way through the overgrown wilderness, more to satisfy Rosie than with any real expectation of catching an intruder. He found nothing and was beginning to think an animal had set off the alarms when he saw something move over by the stagnant pond. There it was again. A rustling in the coppice. Too big to be fox or a badger, it began to move swiftly away and Dick gave chase, thorns and brambles tearing at his clothes. Just as he got close, something solid flew up out of the darkness and hit him once, very hard in the face. Pain and the spurt of blood were instantaneous; then everything went black.

CHAPTER NINE

'How's the nose, Dick?' Despite the severity of the situation, Jack had to fight back helpless laughter.

'Like looking down at a big strawberry,' moaned Dick in a nasal voice. 'It bloody hurts.'

They were sitting round the kitchen table. Rosie had made peppermint tea and was burning incense to calm everybody's nerves.

'Some bastard hit me,' said Dick. 'No chance of you catching him, I suppose?'

'Sergeant Malone is searching the surrounding area with your friend, Constable Chedzey. They'll speak to your neighbours in case they saw something. You say the intruder could have escaped over next door's wall, Rosie?'

She wrinkled her nose. 'Maybe. But they could just as easily have jumped the fence into the lane that runs along the back of Gallows Green. It was impossible to tell. It all happened so fast. Could it have been Dimpsy, do you think? She must be out there somewhere. She's a strong girl and could easily vault a wall.'

Jack glanced at Corrie and knew exactly what she was thinking; that it was either Simon or Saskia, back to collect something they desperately needed. Corrie had no way of knowing how dangerous that 'something' was – but Jack had.

Word travelled fast round the village that Dick Brown from Gibbet Cottage had been attacked in his own garden. Neighbours came to visit, less to offer any kind of sympathy than to poke their prying noses in. Speculation was rife, ranging from 'that zilly vool, Dimpsy, 'er's gone proper mental now' to ''tiz my belief his missus knocked 'im out with one of 'er potions'.

When Constable Chedzey produced a garden rake with blood on it, the village considered the business at an end. Who needed "they murder detectives from up London"? Trust old Bert Chedzey to get to the bottom of it.

'Seems to me, Mr Brown, you was running fast through that tangle you calls a garden, when you trod on the business end o' this 'ole rake.' Bert held it up, triumphantly pointing to the bloodstains. 'The other end flew up and smacked you on the neb. Mystery solved.'

Coupled with the fact that Sergeant Malone's house-to-house inquiries revealed nothing out of the ordinary, it seemed as though there was nowhere else to go. But Jack and Bugsy weren't convinced and neither was Dick.

'I know the difference between a garden implement striking me by accident and someone whacking me with it.' His nose still had a glowing, bibulous quality and his voice had worsened to a neigh. 'And someone set off the house alarms. I was attacked, I tell you!'

Jack put a reassuring hand on his shoulder. 'I believe you, old man, but we have to find out who did it and what they were doing in your garden. And without any co-operation from your neighbours, that could take a while.'

While all this was going on, Corrie and Carlene had been discussing how best to handle the dilemma they now faced concerning the illegal and unpleasant activities of Ted Boobyer. Carlene was all for 'gettin' down wiv the sleazy geezer and, like, givin' 'im some grief'. Attractive though the prospect was, Corrie decided it could do more harm than good to the victims of this mess; namely Danika and Aleksy. It was Danika she approached first.

'Dani, could I have a word?' The friendly barmaid, blonde hair in a ponytail, was in the lounge bar, clearing away glasses and wiping the tables. She smiled when she saw Corrie.

'Of course, Mrs Dawes. What can I do for you?'

Corrie dropped her voice. 'Well, it's more what I can do for you. Jack and I saw you and Mr Boobyer together the other night, and you looked very unhappy about the way he was treating you. I'd like to help.'

Dani's face filled with anxiety and she lowered her eyes. 'Please, do not speak about it. I can manage.' She started to move briskly away. 'I must go now; get on with work.'

'No, I'm sorry, dear. I'm afraid I need some answers. What country do you and Aleksy really come from?'

'Poland. We are Polish.' There was real fear in her voice.

'That's not true, is it? I think you're in this country illegally and that Mr Boobyer made money out of smuggling you in and employing you. Now he's taking advantage of you sexually because he knows you dare not report him. That's right, isn't it, Dani?'

Danika sank onto a chair and buried her face in her hands. 'We are from Albania, Leksy and me. I have elderly parents there who need the money I send. There is little work in Albania.' Corrie offered her a tissue and she blew her nose. 'Mr Boobyer paid men to bring us to UK. How do you find out?'

'Because Ted Boobyer has imported and employed illegals before and been sent to prison for it. We can't let him get away with it again, Dani.'

She looked up at Corrie, sadness in her eyes. 'Will they send us back?'

'I won't lie to you, I think they might.'

Danika sighed. 'Aleksy won't mind. He hates it here. He wants to go home to his grandparents. And me, I am homesick, too. This village is not the life I had hoped for us. Mr Boobyer make me have sex with other men here and he charge them money. I am always afraid; scared someone will find out and report me.'

It was even worse than Corrie suspected. Boobyer was actually pimping the poor girl. She put an arm around her. 'It's no way to live, Dani, forever looking over your shoulder. But don't do anything just yet. I want to see if there's any way we can make things easier for you. But eventually, you will have to tell the authorities everything, so they can put a stop to Boobyer and the people he trades with.'

When Corrie told Carlene of Dani's plight, she was full of compassion and her cheery round face darkened. 'Poor fing. That's real manky; 'avin' to do it wiv some ugly, smelly old sod 'coz he's bigger'n you and you're scared to say no. We gotta put a stop to 'im, Mrs D.'

Corrie looked hard at Carlene, barely seventeen but already streetwise and cynical. She knew something of the girl's background; she'd had a bad start but it had clearly been worse than she wanted to discuss. The girl seemed to have grown up with the whole rotten world on her shoulders. Corrie gave her a squeeze. 'Trust me, Carlene, we will.'

Following Dick's unsettling incident with the garden rake, Rosemary became obsessed with clearing the garden of the wilderness that had reclaimed it. Feng Shui, she said, applied to the outside of a house as well as indoors, and events had shown that theirs was beset by bad, unhappy energy. Dick finally agreed to make a start at shifting the worst of it. Jack, having an interest in anything that might be found hidden on Gallows Green estate, offered to help. He and Bugsy had already turned over Gibbet Cottage pretty thoroughly and found nothing out of the ordinary. They had even taken up some loose floor-boards, knocked on the walls and excavated behind the huge inglenook in search of a secret hiding place. If the de Kuipers had left anything valuable behind, it was certainly well hidden. Rosemary had followed them around, twittering anxiously and putting things back where they belonged. Now she was worried about what they might find outside in the woodland.

'You will be careful, won't you, Dick?' she called. 'Don't forget that huge bull is still on the rampage.'

Dick laughed. 'Don't be daft, Rosie. Wherever the brute has gone, I doubt very much if he's hiding in our woodland.' But he was. As Dick hacked into the undergrowth and Jack and Bugsy dragged the branches free, there was a snort followed by a bellow and the enraged bull crashed out of the coppice, his massive head lowered to charge. Dick was rooted to the spot, mesmerized by the huge horns which were stained with dark red, dried blood. Until this moment, he had never faced any animal more dangerous than a goat. He raised his billhook in a desperate attempt to defend himself and Jack and Bugsy both shouted and waved their arms, hoping to divert the beast's atten-tion. It was just yards from Dick, nostrils steaming and eyes rolling, when a soft voice called out, 'Titus. Stand, boy, it's all right. Come here to me.' The bull stopped in its tracks, hesitated, then slowly turned around. Dimpsy emerged, filthy and bleeding, from her hiding place in the medieval lock-up. She looked shattered and starving and had obviously been living rough for some days. Titus ambled over to her, calm and biddable. She gently rubbed his head, also stained with blood, then grasped his nose ring and tied the trailing rope to the lock-up bars.

'My God,' whispered Dick, scarcely daring to breathe. 'That was a close one.' Sweat dripped unchecked from his brow and he badly needed a drink.

While Bugsy phoned PC Chedzey to call off the search and find the vet, Rosemary wrapped Dimpsy in a blanket, took her indoors and gave her tea laced with brandy, which she'd never had before. The young woman seemed vague and confused, staring around Rosie's opulent kitchen with awe. Given her previous life, it must indeed have seemed like a palace.

Dimpsy had a wash and was comfortable now. Rosie treated her cuts and Corrie made her a sandwich, which she wolfed down. Rosemary wouldn't allow anyone to question the girl until she had been checked over by Doctor Brimble. He reported many scars and old, badly-healed fractures but nothing life-threatening. She was, however, two months pregnant. Corrie despaired. Yet another young woman in this village, who, in Carlene's deathless prose, had been forced to 'do it wiv some ugly, smelly old sod 'coz he's bigger'n you and you're scared to say no'. Corrie remembered the vicious punch in the stomach that Tincknell had inflicted on Dimpsy only days earlier and wondered if he had known she was pregnant. He had been perfectly capable of trying to make her miscarry. A pregnant wife would be unable to cope with heavy farm work.

Inspector Dawes and Sergeant Malone, now back in their comfort zone of murder investigation detectives, sat opposite Dimpsy across the kitchen table. In the absence of a solicitor or social worker, Corrie, Carlene and Rosemary sat alongside her, a formidable female presence, sitting in as appropriate adults. Dick, still shaking, had gone in search of more brandy.

Dimpsy had been humming quietly to herself; happy for the first time in years. Then suddenly she spoke. 'They won't hurt Titus, will they? It weren't his fault. '

'What weren't . . . I mean, what wasn't Titus's fault?' asked Jack.

'Tell us what happened to Thomas,' demanded Bugsy. 'Who killed him?'

'Was it you who put him in the slurry pit, Dimpsy?'

'What did you hit him with, love? You can tell us.'

Both men had instinctively reverted to their successful interrogation double act.

'Oi, oi! Leave it out!' Carlene protested over the barrage of questions. 'Give the poor cow a chance to fink.'

Dimpsy smiled, grateful for female support which, until now, was totally foreign to her. 'I don't mind tellin' what 'appened. It were Titus. He killed Thomas, but he never meant to.'

Jack's voice became gentler. 'Just tell us how it happened, Dimpsy.'

'Titus hated Thomas 'coz he was cruel to 'im. He'd tie 'im up in the bull pen and hit 'im with a spade till he bellowed with pain. If I tried to stop 'im, he'd hit me, too. He enjoyed it. It made 'im feel brave and strong, hurtin' a big animal like Titus. Bringin' him to his knees.'

'What a horrible man,' said Rosemary.

'Hands up anyone who ain't sorry the bull got 'im,' muttered Carlene.

'In the end,' continued Dimpsy, 'Thomas wouldn't go near Titus 'less he were penned up and the gate were padlocked from outside. On the day Thomas died, he was beating Titus and I tried to stop him. He turned on me and said he was going to give me another hiding. I ran away because . . .' she lowered her eyes, '. . . I was feared for my baby.' Her hands instinctively went to protect her belly. 'Thomas came after me with his shotgun and I thought he were going to kill me so I went back to the farm with him and got on with my work. Thomas climbed up to mend a bit of leaky roof in the cowshed. He was drunk and must have lost 'is grip on the ladder and fallen in the bull pen. Titus would have attacked him straight off.'

'And in a confined space, Thomas wouldn't have been able to escape,' concluded Corrie, shamelessly leading the witness. 'The bull must have trampled and gored him to death.'

'That would certainly agree with the doc's assessment, Guv,' said Bugsy. 'Fractured skull, broken bones and puncture wounds from the horns.'

'Did you see it happen, Dimpsy?' asked Jack. 'Did you witness Titus killing Thomas?'

She shook her head, then looked Jack squarely in the eye. 'No, Inspector Dawes. I were on my way to the house to see if Ethel were all right. I'd been gone a while and she used to pee 'er pants, if I didn't take 'er to the lav. When I heard Titus bellowing and Thomas screaming, I ran straight back but Thomas were all crushed and covered in blood. I unlocked the pen and Titus pushed past me and out the gate into the lane that leads to Gallows Green.'

'Dimpsy, why didn't you call someone? Get an ambulance?' asked Corrie.

Dimpsy became vague and confused again. 'Don't know. I were scared. I thought they'd shoot Titus if they found out. I didn't know what to do.'

'So what *did* you do?' asked Jack.

'I got some sacks, wrapped Thomas up and put him in the slurry pit. I thought he'd be safe there. Safe from foxes eatin' 'im and crows peckin' 'is eyes out. Then I ran off and hid.'

'You didn't go into the house and tell Ethel her son was dead?' asked Corrie.

Dimpsy's expression hardened. 'No, I never. 'Coz she'd 'ave blamed me.' She began humming to herself again. 'Can I 'ave another sandwich?'

After a while, Dimpsy asked if she could walk Titus back to Black Oak Farm and feed him, but by now the vet and his team had taken the animal away. Rather than upset her further, Jack suggested they drive her back in PC Chedzey's police car and she liked that idea. When they went inside the farmhouse, Corrie was stunned by the filthy condition. The flagstones were black with grime, the wood round the windows was rotten and several buckets dotted about the room suggested that the roof leaked. Acrid smoke belched from the old solid-fuel cooker that hadn't been swept since it was put in forty years ago. Everything was coated in coal dust. Corrie thought that if she stood there much longer, she would be too.

Carlene wrinkled her nose. 'It's mingin' in 'ere.' She pointed to the cooker. 'That bleedin' range would take days to heat anyfing up. Be quicker to eat it cold then lie with a hot water bottle on your belly.'

There was worse to come. In the parlour, which reeked of cabbage water and incontinence, the district nurse was sitting with Ethel, who was still grizzling with self-pity. She wore a filthy cardigan with stale food down the front, a long black skirt, torn and shabby and her swollen, dropsied ankles spilled out over the tops of grimy carpet slippers. As soon as the old woman saw Dimpsy, she struggled up from her chair; a tremendous effort for someone over twenty stones and geriatric.

'It were you, you little bitch!' She jabbed a blackened fingernail at

Dimpsy who cowered. 'You locked 'im in there, didn't you? I knows it. You trapped my Tommy in the pen with that gurt big brute. You knew that bull hated 'im.'

The nurse tried to calm her. 'Sit down, Mrs Tincknell, Your blood pressure's sky high. You mustn't get excited.' But it was a waste of time. The old woman was almost foaming at the mouth and struggling to get at Dimpsy. It took both Dawes and Malone to restrain her.

'Let me at the wicked little cow! I'll give it 'er! She killed my Tommy of a purpose. I want 'er dead.' Then she suddenly clutched at her chest, gasped, and collapsed in a substantial heap on the filthy rug, taking Jack and Bugsy down with her.

The two detectives were back in Hangman's Inn, about to try a pint of the local cider as recommended by the landlady. A copy of the *Lullington Herald* was on the bar. The article on the front page contained a report of Tincknell's sudden death with comments from the locals: *Landlord of the nearby Hangman's Inn pub, Ted Boobyer, said: 'Mr Tincknell was a well-known and respected member of the Lullington Barrow community and will be sadly missed'*. Malone could never understand why people who had been miserable pieces of shit during their lifetime suddenly acquired virtuous qualities after death. He held up his glass and regarded the contents with suspicion.

'Well, Guv, what did you make of all that? Do we believe Dimpsy's story that Tincknell fell off a ladder into Titus's bull pen?'

'We'll have a hard job proving otherwise. If, as I suspect, the post mortem confirms the forensic report and Tincknell died from being crushed and gored by a bull, who's to say it didn't happen exactly like she said?'

'And Old Mother Tincknell's in hospital under sedation, so no point asking if she'd heard anything when the rumpus started. She'd most probably lie, anyway. All we could charge Dimpsy with is failing to report a death and illegally disposing of the body. And with her being a few beers short of a six-pack, she'd be deemed unfit to plead and walk. Speaking of beer, let's see what this famous Somerset apple juice is all about. It's allegedly made by locals in that clapped-out old cider mill we passed on the way here. Cheers!' The cider tiptoed down Malone's throat as smooth as silk, tasting of nothing more sinister than fruit. Then, suddenly, the pin shot from the hand grenade and something exploded inside him, punching him in the stomach, making him gasp for breath. 'Gawd help us!' he spluttered as soon as the fit of coughing stopped.

'What's it like?' asked Jack, who hadn't plucked up the courage to try his yet.

'Delicious,' croaked Bugsy, his throat raw and stinging as if he'd swallowed a glass of hot creosote.

'So no suspicious death and we're back to finding the de Kuipers and their "swindlers" list – that's if they're still alive.'

CHAPTER TEN

With Eucharist over, Father John retired to his sacristy through the priests' gospel entrance to change out of his vestments and pour himself a very large glass of wine. This one was a particularly fine St Emilion from his private cellar; nothing at all like the insipid filth he had dished out half an hour earlier during the Sacrament. Never mind the blood of Christ, chip vinegar tasted better, but the stupid bumpkins of Lullington Barrow gulped it down zealously and went away believing they were full of grace. Fat chance. He smiled contemptuously to himself. He knew exactly what these peasants were full of and it wasn't grace! Over time, he had discovered all their dark secrets and there wasn't one of them without some nasty skeleton in a cupboard somewhere. What sins he didn't learn in the confessional, he winkled out of Mrs O'Dowd, the village busybody, who gossiped about everyone. Like many priests, such knowledge gave him a very powerful and privileged position in the village and in Father John's case, it also fed his prurient curiosity.

This evening, Father John kept the door slightly ajar, so he would spot Aleksy tiptoeing past after his duties as altar boy. The child would escape if he could and that was not to be permitted; the priest had been looking forward to this all day and now that those damnable de Kuipers were no longer around, he could indulge himself without threat of discovery. Soon he glimpsed Aleksy's blond head and, with impressive agility for a man of sixty who claimed to be rheumatic, he sprang to the door and pounced on the boy.

'Come in, my child. I've been waiting for you.'

Aleksy wriggled as hard as he could but Father John pulled him inside and quickly locked the door. It wouldn't do to be interrupted by some tiresome member of the congregation wanting confession or advice about their pathetic pastoral problems. His enjoyment of this beautiful young boy was much more urgent.

'Please, Father, let me go. My mother is outside, waiting for me,' Aleksy begged with tears in his eyes.

'Now, now, Aleksy, that's a lie isn't it? And God doesn't like liars. I know your mother isn't waiting for you; I just saw her go past on her bike. She's doing some shopping, isn't she?'

With Aleksy held forcibly on his knee, he made him drink some of the wine. The boy spluttered, hating the taste and retching. Father John poured more and forced it into Aleksy's mouth.

'No more, please, Father, it makes me ill.'

The old priest showed no mercy and made him drink until the glass was empty, leaving Aleksy sick and light-headed. If his mother, a devout, practising Catholic, had ever noticed the child's condition when he returned home, the priest knew she would not dare comment or complain. And she was certainly in no position to report him to the authorities.

'Now, then, Aleksy, you know what we do next. Take off your trousers.'

The boy was full of dread, knowing what was to come. Tears poured down his cheeks.

'Please Father, I don't want to. Please let me go. I don't like it.'

In the face of resistance which made it uncomfortable, no pleasure at all, Father John threatened his victim with the most powerful weapon in a priest's armoury: eternal damnation.

'You know you must do as you're told, Aleksy, because Jesus demands it. If you persist in this wicked disobedience, you and your mother will be condemned to hellfire and suffer everlasting separation from God. Is that what you want? Because I can make that happen.'

The church was deserted now but outside the gospel entrance, a woman had spotted Aleksy being dragged into the sacristy and heard the key turning in the lock. Now she was eavesdropping, her ear pressed to the door. She had been suspicious for some time but now she clearly overheard the priest's vile demands and the boy's pitiful sobs. Enough! No more! He had to be stopped. She crept around to the epistle door, through which priests were supposed to exit from the sacristy. Gently, she tried the handle. As she suspected, in his mounting excitement, the old priest had forgotten to lock it. Very quietly, she eased it open just a chink and stood behind it without revealing herself. But Father John heard and was furious.

'Who's there? How dare you? Go away! You've no business in here while I'm hearing this child's catechism.'

Sensing opportunity, Aleksy wriggled off the old priest's lap and made for the door. Slipping through the narrow gap, he sprinted down the nave and out into the fresh air as fast as he could. He fell several times, dizzy from the wine he'd swallowed, and was sick twice in the hedge, but he didn't care; he was so relieved to have escaped the torment. And so grateful to whomever had been behind the door.

The priest was scarlet with rage and frustration. He yelled at the woman who had now come right in. 'What do you think you're doing? You'll pay for this! I'll—'

But the woman didn't wait to hear what Father John would do. She took a heavy object from her shopping bag, walked purposefully towards him and brought it down hard, just once, on top of his bald head. He slumped to the floor with a deep wound in his skull from which blood began to seep. For some moments, she waited, but he didn't move. Tentatively, she checked that he was dead, then bowed her head and crossed herself.

Briskly, she took a pair of rubber gloves from her bag and pulled them on. The priest's disgusting penis was still hanging out of his pants. Quickly she poked it back in and zipped up his trousers. Then she opened the cupboard where the vestments and other paraphernalia were stored and stuffed his body inside, first placing a bin liner over his head to prevent the blood from spreading. Such blood as there was, she was able to wash away with neat bleach. Conscious that modern forensics were very thorough, she rinsed the water down the sacrarium instead of the drain. When she was satisfied that as far as feasible, she had removed all traces, she locked the door and went home. Later, under cover of darkness, she returned to the sacristy and, still wearing rubber gloves, she dragged Father John's body outside. She arranged him on the path leading to the church, face down and with his arms outstretched in the form of a cross. Before she left, she took a golf ball from her pocket, smeared it with the priest's blood and tossed it into the long grass.

Late that night, a freak tide breached the crumbling and pitifully inadequate wall around St Mary's. The raging sea water surged through the church, sweeping hymn books off pews, washing away hassocks and flooding all the other trappings of Christian worship including the altar furniture. In the morning, a shocked deacon was hurrying from the church to the parochial house to inform Father John of the disaster when he almost fell over the priest's body. It lay face down, arms spread as if in supplication, on the path that crossed both the cemetery and the thirteenth fairway of the golf course. There was some dried blood and a gash on his head.

The deacon covered Father John's body with his cloak and immediately ran to fetch Constable Chedzey, who equally rapidly summoned Inspector Dawes and Doctor Brimble. The four men knelt round the corpse while the torrent of the Bristol Channel continued to flow, unconstrained, through the church, cleansing the sacristy where the old priest had met his death and effectively washing away any evidence that might have remained.

The doctor examined the body briefly before offering his opinion. 'My view, and I have every confidence that it will be confirmed by autopsy, is that Father John suffered a single blunt force trauma to the top of his head, consistent with a blow from something small, hard and spherical, most probably a golf ball, given where he is lying. He was an elderly man with a brittle skull; the blow would have been sufficient to kill him instantly.'

Sergeant Malone was already carrying out a preliminary search of the surrounding area and returned with a blood-encrusted golf ball in a plastic forensic envelope, a supply of which he always carried about his person. He passed it to Inspector Dawes.

'It was in the long grass. What d'you reckon, Jack? Is this the culprit or have we got another suspicious death on our hands?'

The deacon protested. 'Oh surely not! Father John wasn't simply a shepherd of the faithful; he worked tirelessly for the glory of God through his selfless service to all his parishioners. He was both friend and confidante; loved by everyone in the village. You can't think that his death was anything but a tragic accident.'

'Or an act of God,' observed Malone, wryly. 'What with that and the sea destroying your church; that's two acts of God in the one night. Bit excessive, I'd say.'

For once, the affronted churchwarden was speechless and bustled away to inform the bishop that Lullington Barrow had lost its beloved priest.

Forensics examined the golf ball and whilst they were able to confirm that the blood on it was indeed Father John's, it was impossible to state beyond any doubt that it was the blunt force instrument that had killed him. On the other hand, they couldn't prove it wasn't, because the indentation causing a fractured skull and death was definitely made by a small and extremely hard round object. Despite extensive searches, no weapon fitting that description was found, leaving Dawes and Malone with the convenient golf-ball solution. The toxicology report found a large amount of red wine in Father John's system but not enough to affect his ability to look out for himself.

The villagers told each other it was an accident waiting to happen; there had been several golfers playing the course the previous evening. Hadn't they always said that anyone who uses that path regularly runs the risk of getting smashed on the head, sooner or later? It was nobody's fault. And in the light of the forensic evidence and the autopsy report, they were confident the coroner would subsequently reach a verdict of death by misadventure.

Malone had been brought up a Catholic but the crimes he'd witnessed whilst in the police service and the knowledge that more than seventy-six per cent of violent prisoners claimed to be Christians had finally persuaded him he had been duped. As a lapsed Catholic, therefore, he had no qualms about investigating the dead priest's background, just in case someone had a reason for wanting him dead. If he dug up anything solid, he'd tell Jack and the boss could decide if it was worth pursuing.

When told of the demise of Father John, the bishop made a rare visit to Lullington Barrow. A tall, cadaverous man with a permanent expression of lugubrious disapproval, he examined the devastation that had once been St Mary's Church of the Blessed Virgin, but which was now St Mary's Church of the Sand, Seaweed and Lumps of Driftwood. The church was constructed largely of permeable, carboniferous limestone from the nearby Mendip Hills. Seawater had seeped through the faults in the north wall of the nave and dislodged the statue of the Virgin Mary from the niche in which she had stood since the fifteenth century. In what was left of the porch, a dead jellyfish floated in the holy water stoup. But most worrying was the tower, which had been built in the

Perpendicular style but didn't look like remaining perpendicular for much longer.

On balance, the bishop decided that the hazards of deadly golf balls, coupled with the ever-present threat to the church from the heavy seas at high tide was sufficient to justify deconsecrating what remained of the building. He could then have the ruins pulled down and sell the land to the owners of the golf club. It had never, after all, been much of an earner. Congregations and contributions had been small if Father John's perpetual excuses were to be believed. A profitable sale would go much further to appease the ever-hungry coffers of the Catholic Church. Added to which, there had been some rather unfortunate allegations about Father John in his last three parishes and it had become increasingly difficult to hush it up, which was why the man had finally been exiled to St Mary's. The bishop knew that if he got up to his old tricks with the choirboys in a place like Lullington Barrow, it would be much easier to brush under the carpet. But fortunately that was no longer his problem. He was free of a tiresome priest and a financially under-performing church in one fell swoop. God did, indeed, move in mysterious ways. All in all, the bishop was well satisfied with the outcome.

'Not bein' funny or nuffink, but I reckon we're makin' a right bog-brush o' this job,' announced Carlene at breakfast.

'How do you mean, love?' asked Malone, amused at the 'we'. It seemed that Carlene now considered herself an honorary member of the team. He'd smothered his full English breakfast with ketchup until it looked, according to Carlene, like a 'monkey's abortion' which he assumed must be a culinary term.

She gestured eloquently with her fork. 'Well, you've only gotta look at our clear-up rate. Dead people two; police nil.'

'Thomas Tincknell's death was an unfortunate accident,' said Jack.

'Ya think?' Carlene speared a sausage with her fork, dipped it in Malone's ketchup and bit off the end.

'Why? Don't you?' asked Corrie. She was increasingly impressed with Carlene's powers of deduction and it did no harm to listen to her, even if her sense of justice was slightly less merciful than Judge Jeffreys'.

'Don't get me wrong, Mrs D, the old geezer was a shit and got what was comin' to 'im. But ask yerself: what was 'e doin' up a ladder mendin' a leak in the cowshed roof? After all, 'e never mended nuffink else, did 'e? The place sucked; doors 'angin' off and rain comin' frough the ceiling. Dunnit seem a bit random to you?'

'And do you have similar theories about the death of Father John?' asked Jack, intrigued.

'Yeah, well, it sticks out a bleedin' mile what 'e was up to, the dirty old bugger.'

Jack, Corrie and even Bugsy put down their knives and forks, completely riveted.

'Yes, go on, Sherlock,' urged Malone. 'What was he up to?'

'He was fiddlin' wiv the choirboys, wasn't 'e? Poor little sods were too scared to say nuffink. I've seen it before. Not wiv vicars, like, but blokes put in charge o' kids. Ought to have their bollocks cut off; a smack on the 'ead's too good for 'em, innit?' The case for the prosecution concluded, Carlene picked up a piece of toast and dipped it in her fried egg.

For once, Corrie was speechless; mostly with revulsion at the mere idea of a trusted priest abusing helpless children. Surely it couldn't be true, could it? But Jack was gripped by Carlene's shocking indictments and pushed her further.

'Do you have any particular choirboys in mind?'

Carlene swallowed her toast and washed it down with tea. 'That little foreign kid, for a start. I can always spot the misery and shame on an abused kid's face. And of course, 'e wouldn't dare tell 'coz of 'is mum.' She caught Corrie's warning look and remembered she wasn't supposed to say anything about Danika and Aleksy being in the UK illegally. 'I mean, she's dead religious, goes to Mass and everyfink. Wouldn't want the old priest pullin' the plug on 'er direct line wiv God, would she?'

Just at that moment, Aleksy burst into the dining room, chased by his mother, who was trying to grab him before he reached the guests' table.

'Is it true, Inspector Dawes? Is Father John really dead?' His face was ecstatic.

'Yes, I'm afraid it's true, Aleksy,' replied Jack. 'I'm very sorry.'

'I'm not!' The boy skipped round the room chanting, 'Thank you, God. Oh, thank you, God. Oh, thank you, God.'

Danika seized him. 'Stop it, Leksy, that's a wicked thing to say.' She steered him away, apologizing profusely.

Carlene glanced casually at the others. 'See? Told ya.' She helped herself to more toast and smeared marmalade on it. 'Golf ball, my arse ... 'scuse my French. It wouldn't surprise me if someone lamped the old perv.'

'Well, what do you make of that?' asked Corrie, dumbfounded. Carlene had gone to her room to tweak her hair into its customary state of magenta anguish, leaving the two coppers and Corrie to mull over her razor-sharp but worryingly matter-of-fact observations.

'Sometimes,' said Jack, still reeling from the shock, 'I think we detectives should think critically, like Carlene. I mean, I never spotted anything wrong with Aleksy. Did you, Corrie?'

'Actually, yes I did, and I wish now that I'd done something about it. Rosemary and I thought Leksy was much too solemn and joyless for a little boy of ten. But it never occurred to either of us that he was being sexually abused and even when we spoke to him, he never gave us the smallest clue. I only met Father John a few times but I find it hard to believe he was a monster. He seemed so kind to the choirboys.'

'That's how the bastards get away with it,' said Malone, bitterly. 'All smarmy and pious in public but cunning and manipulative behind locked doors. I did some snooping of my own, Guv. A complete background check. I found plenty of allegations against Father John but nothing was ever proved. The bishop just kept moving him around when things got awkward. You can see why. Allegations can lead to criminal prosecutions of not just the abuser but civil lawsuits against the church's diocese where the abuse was alleged to have occurred. That would reflect badly on the bishop and the Catholic Church, so the hierarchy keep that kind of thing locked up real tight.'

'What do you think, Jack? asked Corrie. 'Do you reckon someone "lamped the old perv"?'

'I don't know, but in the interests of a complete and thorough investigation into a suspicious death, I think Bugsy and I should have a few words with the bishop before he scuttles back to the safety of his fortified palace.'

CHAPTER ELEVEN

They found the bishop in Father John's parochial house enjoying a leisurely lunch cooked for him by Mrs O'Dowd. He had discovered Father John's well-stocked wine cellar and was planning to relocate a few cases of the most excellent 2006 Châteauneuf-du-Pape into the boot of his car before he left. He had also carried out a precautionary search of the priest's bedroom and removed some extremely irksome magazines and photographs from under the mattress. He would burn them in the palace incinerator when he returned. Having congratulated himself on having seen the last of a troublesome priest and a second-rate church, he was less than pleased when two Metropolitan policemen arrived, wanting to question him. He suspected he knew what they were after but he had successfully stone-walled such delicate issues many times before, particularly with regard to Father John, so he appeared calm and unfazed when Mrs O'Dowd showed them in.

'Gentlemen, how can I help?' The bishop dabbed his mouth delicately with his napkin.

Dawes and Malone produced their badges, which the bishop examined at some length before handing them back. Big guns this time. It was usually some local police constable going through the required procedures, having received complaints from a hysterical mother. It had been a simple matter to obfuscate sufficiently to convince the officer that it was all gossip and hearsay and that the child was a liar. Then the bishop would assure the police that he would conduct a full investigation into the allegations and they could safely leave it in his episcopal hands. And this they thankfully did, because it was a subject that most people found distasteful and would rather leave to someone else. However, looking at these two detectives, especially the fat, scruffy one, he doubted they would be fobbed off quite so easily and he was glad he'd had the foresight to remove the child porn magazines. That village idiot, Constable Chedzey would never have searched

Father John's rooms but he was quite sure these Met officers would.

DI Dawes began the questioning. 'We're investigating the death of Father John. I'm sorry for your loss.'

The bishop looked suitably solemn. 'Thank you, Inspector; I fear he will be greatly missed in Lullington Barrow.'

Not by one little lad, he won't, thought Malone, grimly.

'But I don't quite understand,' continued the bishop. 'What exactly is there to investigate? I understood it was a tragic death by misadventure. Father John's skull was smashed by a wayward golf ball.'

'That may well prove to be the case, Bishop, but a background check on Father John's past has thrown up some rather unsavoury allegations,' said Malone, eyeballing him. He'd had some dealings with Catholic bishops as a lad and he knew they saw themselves as unimpeachable: protected by the Pope and outside the law. Well, not on his watch.

The bishop sat back in his chair and steepled his fingers, warily. 'That's all they were, Sergeant – allegations. You need to understand that Catholic priests are men of deep and regular prayer, steeped in sacred scripture and educators in the faith. They work tirelessly for the glory of God through service to His people. In order to fulfil all those roles, Father John had to become very familiar with the lives of those to whom he ministered and this can sometimes be misinterpreted by mischief-makers.'

Bollocks, thought Malone.

As if sensing his cynicism, the bishop treated Bugsy to a cold, hard stare. 'I must warn you that if you attempt to besmirch Father John's admirable reputation when the poor man is dead and unable to defend himself, the Catholic hierarchy will take the matter very seriously. There will be robust complaints to both your Metropolitan commander and the chief constable of the Avon and Somerset Constabulary, with whom I frequently have dinner.'

DI Dawes looked him firmly in the eye. 'Is that a threat to try to prevent a thorough investigation of this suspicious death, Bishop? Because if so, I must warn *you* that in my book, nobody, including your Catholic hierarchy, is exempt from charges of obstruction and perverting the course of justice. Added to which, I'm surprised that given your high regard of Father John, you don't seem anxious to be certain of exactly how he died.'

The bishop was seething with rage inside, but maintained his calm, pious demeanour. 'What evidence do you have that Father John's death was suspicious?'

'Well, for a start,' said Malone, 'not everyone in Lullington Barrow is sorry he's dead. I could introduce you to a little lad in the choir who's overjoyed about it.'

The bishop made a mental note to obtain the name of the wretched child from Mrs O'Dowd then lean on his mother, before the gutter press got to her.

'Would you mind explaining,' continued Dawes, 'why Father John had been assigned to four different parishes in the last five years?'

'Because, as I have already stated, he was an admirable and very effective priest. He was able to take an ailing, backsliding parish and transform it into a caring, God-fearing community. Because of his success, I confess I used him shamelessly to restore such parishes, time and again.'

'Right,' said Malone. 'So the reason you had to keep moving him had nothing to do with the allegations of child abuse made against him?'

'Absolutely not! Members of the church hierarchy have continually argued that unwholesome media coverage of what are actually very rare cases has been excessive. This has resulted in the public making all sorts of allegations against innocent priests without proof or evidence, simply to cause the maximum trouble and embarrassment to the Church.'

Dawes plugged away, relentlessly. 'In addition to cases of actual abuse, much of the press scandal focused around members of the Catholic hierarchy who did not report abuse allegations to the civil authorities and who, in many cases, reassigned the offenders to other locations where the alleged predators continued to have contact with minors and had opportunities to continue to sexually abuse children. In defending their actions, some bishops contended that the prevailing psychology suggests men could be cured of such behaviour through counselling.'

'Is that what you believe, sir?' asked Malone, who reckoned men were only cured of such behaviour through the application of a couple of bricks.

'I couldn't possibly comment, Sergeant. I have never had to deal with such men in any of my dioceses.'

'So you don't believe someone might have found out about Father John's proclivities and decided to put a stop to him?'

'Certainly not! He was killed by a golf ball.' The bishop stood up, indicating that as far as he was concerned, the audience was at an end. 'Now, if you don't mind, I need to arrange Father John's funeral and decide the future of St Mary's Church.'

The two detectives strolled back to Hangman's Inn, hands in pockets, deep in thought.

'Who was the last person to see Father John alive, Bugsy?'

Malone consulted his notebook. 'Mrs O'Dowd, his housekeeper. She attended Mass, then went back to the parochial house to cook Father John's dinner. She said she spoke to him to tell him when his meal would be ready just before he disappeared into the sacristy. That was the last time she saw him.'

'Wasn't she worried when he didn't come home for his dinner?'

'I asked her that; she said, no. She used to leave his meal in a warm oven and go home because he often took a long time to de-robe and cleanse the vessels of the sacrament.'

'What does that mean? I don't know much about the rituals of the Catholic Church.'

'There's a special sink in the sacristy called a sacrarium. It bypasses the sewer and discharges straight into the earth. The priest uses it to wash sacred vessels so that no particles of holy substances end up in the sewer but are returned to the earth. When I was a lad, the leftover consecrated wine was poured down the sacrarium, but today, I think it's supposed to be consumed by the celebrant priest and his faithful attendants, not thrown away.'

Jack was impressed. 'I'd forgotten you were brought up a Catholic, Bugsy.'

Bugsy grinned. 'Yeah. Those Jesuit monks have a lot to answer for.'

'I wonder if Father John consumed the sacramental wine that was left over. It would account for the pathology report of a high level of alcohol in his system.'

'Doubt it. His taste in fine wine was much more expensive; you saw what he was like in the pub, sniffing the bouquet and rolling it round his gob. And being the conscientious kind of priest he's turning out *not* to be, he probably just chucked the cheap stuff down the drain.'

Several thoughts were buzzing about in Dawes's brain, vying for attention. 'Is St Mary's still flooded, Bugsy, or might we find something useful?'

'Shouldn't think so, Guv. Once the tide turned, it swept everything back out to sea, like a mini-tsunami.'

'Might be worth a look, though. And tomorrow, we'll have another word with the housekeeper, Mrs O'Dowd. She may have seen something suspicious but considered it either unimportant or disrespectful in some way to Father John. She seemed very fond of him.'

Two deaths in rapid succession had jolted the inhabitants of Lullington Barrow out of their comfortable, unchanging routine. They were disturbed by the sudden loss of two of the village's most familiar figures and despite Constable Chedzey's reassurance that both deaths were the results of unfortunate accidents – caused by bull and ball respectively – gossip was still rife. Lurid speculation was, after all, the villagers' favourite hobby and they were very good at it.

Old Ethel Tincknell had taken a turn for the worse and was considered unfit to return to Black Oak Farm. Social Services had found her a bed in a nursing home but medical opinion was that she was unlikely to last much longer because of her age, weight and high blood pressure, which was exacerbated by frequent outbursts of hysterical grief for her son.

'If my Tommy were alive, you'd never dare dump me in this bloody prison. And that wicked little bitch what killed 'im is still walkin' free; livin' in my Tommy's lovely house!'

Ethel had never fully grasped the fact that murderers were no longer publicly hanged and was willing herself to stay alive long enough to see Dimpsy convicted and with any luck, swinging from the gibbet that stood on Gallows Green Hill. No amount of reasoning would shift her as her feeble mind became increasingly demented. She rambled constantly about 'her Tommy's nest egg' that she insisted was hidden on the farm. When asked where, she refused to say.

'I don't want that murderin' little cow to get 'er thievin' hands on my Tommy's savings.'

Dimpsy had indeed returned to the farm and, according to Dr Brimble, she was managing very happily on her own. He had persuaded her, without much resistance, to undergo proper antenatal care and to avoid any heavy lifting. She was clearly looking forward to the birth of her baby and had even agreed to a scan. Dawes and Malone were still undecided as to whether she would have to answer charges with regard to her failure to report a death and unlawful disposal of her husband's body, but in view of her obvious learning difficulties, her pregnancy and the lack of any real evidence that she had contributed in any way to Tincknell's death, Jack thought it very unlikely that the CPS would even look at it. Dimpsy, of course, seemed blithely unaware of any concerns about her legal position and now that Thomas and Ethel were no longer there to torment her, the only blot on her landscape was that they wouldn't let her have Titus back.

The bishop's visit had been widely discussed. When Mrs O'Dowd announced in the village shop that she had overheard His Excellency speaking on the phone about pulling down what remained of St Mary's Church and selling the land to the golf club, it caused widespread alarm and despondency. Although only a handful of worshippers ever bothered to attend church, the village was nevertheless set against change of any kind in Lullington Barrow. The next nearest church was at least ten miles away; a traumatic journey for folk who rarely ventured further than the village green. Many blamed Father John for drawing attention to himself by getting killed – or more pertinently, for drawing attention to Lullington. The village demographic rarely changed and that's how they wanted it to stay. Others blamed Dick and Rosemary. When the de Kuipers disappeared suddenly, everyone had breathed a sigh of relief and slept easily in their beds again. Then those Browns from the city had taken over Gibbet Cottage with their minimalistic, arty-farty, tight-arsed, bare-board notions that deemed it vulgar even to put a rug on the floor. After that, everything had started to go wrong again, hadn't it? It was always the same. 'Incomers' brought trouble. And now there were two London coppers tramping all over Gallows Green, poking their noses in where they weren't wanted and asking damn-fool questions. Where would it all end? they asked each other.

In Gibbet Cottage, the realization that something as big and dangerous as a Holstein bull could lurk, undetected, in their private patch of woodland had determined the Browns that they must clear away the worst of the undergrowth – and sooner rather than later. Although Dick had made a tentative start when they found Titus, he realized it was too big a job to manage on his own. Since none of the Lullington folk did anything for anybody without being paid, Dick hired a couple of farm labourers to help with the heavy work. Neither man was particularly bright but they made up for it with muscle and after a few hours, they had hacked a reasonable clearing through the brambles and overgrown thicket. This revealed a large expanse of surprisingly green grass and fully exposed the stagnant pond in the middle of the coppice. It was deep, smelly and congested with tangled weeds. At five o'clock, the men took their day's money and made for Hangman's Inn to spend it, promising – but never intending – to return next day. It was too much work for too little pay; even on top of their dole money. Dick wondered vaguely about the country myth that 'brawny-chested sons of the soil toiled from dawn to dusk'. They hadn't started until eleven and then stopped at one o'clock for their bread, cheese and cider. At least that part was authentic.

When she saw the men leave, Rosemary came out to join Dick, bringing with her a couple of preprandial gins and tonic. Now the pond was properly exposed, she began planning a tranquil water feature with a small fountain and water lilies. It would look lovely with all that greenery around it and as long as she ensured the water flowed *towards* the house, it would be perfect Feng Shui, creating harmony and allowing chi to enter their home. Of course, the water would need to be completely purified first and approved as free from any dangerous bugs by Environmental Health. Then she could call in that excellent landscape gardening company she'd found in her *Homes and Gardens* magazine. She walked around the perimeter, poking into the sludge with a stick to see how deep it was.

'Poo! What a pong! Hand me that spade the labourers threw down, Dick. I want to see if I can touch the bottom with it. '

Dick sighed. He'd barely sipped his gin and tonic and was hungry for his dinner but he obediently passed her the spade. She plunged it deep into the pond. There was a clang as it hit something metal and glanced off, causing her to lose her balance and teeter precariously on the edge; one elegantly-shod foot in the muck.

'Careful, darling,' admonished Dick, 'you nearly fell in and it's probably teeming with bacteria and deadly viruses.'

'Actually, old fruit,' said a deep, cultured voice behind them, 'that bog Rosie's stirring up is the overflow from your septic tank.' It was

Marcus from next door, carrying a very expensive-looking leather travel bag. 'You're suffering from soakaway failure, Dickie. If I were you, I'd see to it before it gets any worse.'

'Thanks,' said Dick, thinking how everyone in the city took main drainage for granted. 'I'll have it treated professionally.'

Marcus dropped his bag on the newly discovered lawn, took Rosemary's gin and tonic and downed it in one. 'Wonderful. Just what I needed.' He took her hand and kissed it. 'I've come to beg a favour, my delicious, exotic Rosebud, and I know you can't refuse me anything.'

Rosemary giggled. 'You really are a terrible phoney, Marcus. What do you want?'

'Phoney? Moi? I'm mortified! Utterly cut to the quick!' He feigned hurt for a couple of seconds, then: 'The fact is, I have to go to Dubai for a few days. It's a big business deal.'

'Wow, Dubai. How very glamorous,' breathed Rosemary.

Dick scowled at her. 'Only if you can afford their luxurious hotels. Even Dubai has its slums.'

Marcus waved a languid hand. 'You know how it is, Dickie, old man. Some of us drink champagne in the fast lane and some of us sip tea from a thermos in a layby off the B380. We all make our own special contribution in life.' He turned to Rosemary. 'What I came to ask is whether you'd keep an eye on Millie for me. She hates being left on her own and gets mildly depressed when I'm away.'

'Yes, of course I'll look after Millie,' said Rosemary. 'How long will you be gone?'

Marcus hesitated and the dazzling, almost constant smile faded slightly. 'I'm not sure at the moment. I'll be in touch. Thank you, my delectable Rosie, I love you madly.' He kissed her cheek then picked up his bag and strode away.

'Why us?' asked Dick, tetchily. 'Why not one of the other neighbours on Gallows Green? We've only been here five minutes – we hardly know Millie.'

'Because the other neighbours are never home. And anyway, would you want Environmental Edwina keeping an eye on you?'

'Good point,' conceded Dick. 'Besides, I doubt we'll see much of Millie anyway; she'll be off shopping as soon as Marcus has gone.'

But Millie wasn't off shopping. When Rosemary popped next door with some tea tree oil and a healing crystal, Millie was sitting cross-legged on the floor with a nearly empty bottle of vodka in her hand. Her blonde hair was lank and tousled and tears had ravaged her mascara. The exquisite, heart-shaped face was red and puffy with weeping. This wasn't mild depression; it was something much more distressing.

'Millie, whatever's the matter?'

'Marcus has left me.'

Rosemary was shocked. Whatever she'd been expecting, it certainly wasn't this. But Marcus was impossibly handsome and a terrible flirt, so it wasn't entirely unbelievable. She pulled out her mobile. Robust, female reinforcements were needed to deal with this situation. She phoned Corrie. Her sister was much better in emotional situations and would know exactly what to say. Five minutes later, Corrie arrived with Carlene and immediately took control. Carlene went to the kitchen to make 'bucketloads o' coffee 'coz Millie's well 'ammered'.

'Millie, I'm sure Marcus hasn't left you,' said Corrie briskly. 'He absolutely adores you, anyone can see that.'

'But he's always away from home,' snivelled Millie, working her way through a box of Kleenex, 'and he keeps going on about money and how extravagant I am. I don't mean to be, truly I don't. But I get so lonely when he's away, so I buy things to cheer myself up. Expensive things. And then I get into debt. All wives do it, don't they? You understand, don't you, Corrie?'

Corrie didn't but it wasn't a good time to say so. To her, it was a simple case of cause and effect. Millie was decorative but dim and seemingly unable to square the obvious circle.

'Did he actually *say* he was leaving you?' asked Rosemary. 'Only he told Dick and me that he was off on a business trip to Dubai.'

'He didn't say it in so many words,' sniffed Millie. 'He just said he had to go away to sort things out and he wasn't sure when he'd be back. I think he must have found out.' She was looking down at her hands, twirling her wedding ring round and round. 'You see, I did a very silly thing. I had an affair. Well, it was only a one-off actually. It meant nothing – nothing at all. I just felt so miserable and neglected and I'd had too much to drink.'

'Don't worry, love,' said Carlene, emerging from the kitchen with mugs of coffee. 'We've all been there and it's dead shitty but you just 'ave to chillax and move on.'

Corrie hadn't 'been there' and she'd have been amazed if Rosie had, but Carlene meant well. 'This one-night stand, was it with Simon?' Corrie asked, remembering Mrs O'Dowd's lurid account of seeing them 'committing a mortal sin' in Simon's posh car.

Millie looked up, her eyes wide. 'Yes, how did you know? Have you found them?'

'Found what?' asked Rosemary, puzzled.

'My letters. The ones I wrote to Simon. Saskia got hold of them. She was so beastly to me. She said if I didn't pay up, she'd give them to Marcus and he'd divorce me and then I'd be penniless because I was too stupid to keep myself. She was really nasty. When I told Simon to make her stop, he just laughed. Then they both disappeared and I thought it was all over and I was so relieved. But now Marcus has gone . . .' She burst into fresh sobs and looked accusingly at Rosemary. 'Did you give my letters to Marcus?'

Rosie was affronted. 'No, of course not. I wouldn't do a thing like that and anyway, I don't know what letters you're talking about. If they were in those tea chests in the loft, they went up in smoke, along with everything else.'

'Never put nuffink in writin', that's my advice,' said Carlene, sagely.

'Do you know if Marcus took his passport with him?' asked Corrie.

Millie stumbled off to look and returned, shaking her head. 'No, it's still in his desk.'

So he hadn't gone to Dubai, then. Corrie reckoned that if the de Kuipers had been into blackmail, it probably hadn't been confined to poor, witless Millie. There were plenty of other potential victims in Lullington Barrow with secrets that they'd prefer remained that way; Ted Boobyer and the late Father John to name just two. Everything that was murky and unexplained still seemed to lead directly back to Simon and Saskia and it was becoming clearer why they were so comprehensively disliked by the village. Corrie's intuition told her that many more transgressions would crawl out of the woodwork before this couple was stopped; that's if someone hadn't stopped them already. What she couldn't understand was why a pair of international arms traffickers involved in multi-million deals would waste their time blackmailing the yokels in a grotty little place like Lullington Barrow. She needed to talk to Jack.

CHAPTER TWELVE

In the ruins of St Mary's Church, Dawes and Malone stepped carefully over displaced masonry and the piles of detritus that the sea had washed up. As well as clumps of green algae and dead marine creatures that had been marooned when the tide receded, there were plastic bottles, tin cans and even an odd sock festooning the beak of the eagle-shaped lectern. The building had now been deemed unsafe and the deacon, ludicrous in his hard hat and surplice, hopped around them, anxiously.

'I really don't know what it is you hope to find, officers. I've already salvaged anything of value as instructed by His Excellency and sadly, nothing is left of the spiritual essence of this lovely old church.'

Dawes put a hand on the deacon's shoulder. 'All human life is here but the Holy Ghost seems to be somewhere else.'

The deacon bristled. 'I really don't think that's an appropriate remark for a member of the police service, Inspector.'

'Not I, Deacon – Anthony Burgess. He was talking about Catholicism and I think I'm beginning to understand what he meant. Tell me, did Father John have a laptop?'

'Yes. He said it was important for the church to use new media to reach out to young people. He was very computer literate and—'

'Is his laptop still in the parochial house?' Jack knew that if it had been there when the bishop visited, he would undoubtedly have taken it away with him along with anything else incriminating.'

'No, it isn't. Soon after Father John's tragic death, I borrowed it, intending to email other members of the Catholic clergy concerning our terrible loss, but I'm afraid I haven't quite got the hang of how to use it, yet. I was thinking I might ask one of the choirboys to show me; they're so comfortable with all the new technology and—'

'Would you please fetch it straight away? Don't switch it on or fiddle with it; just bring it to me.'

The deacon was horrified. 'I'll do no such thing. The laptop wasn't church property; it was Father John's private possession. He may be dead, but I've no intention of breaching his confidential—'

'We can get a warrant.' Sergeant Malone spoke gruffly from behind, making him jump. 'And by rights, I could do you for obstruction and perverting the course of justice.'

The poor deacon blustered. 'What? Why? I don't understand.'

Malone eyeballed him. 'Obstructing a police officer in the course of his duty includes any intentional interference by physical means, giving misleading information or refusing to cooperate. You've already disturbed what might turn out to be a crime scene by removing certain items from the church without permission. Fabricating or disposing of evidence is perverting the course of justice and carries a maximum sentence of life imprisonment so I'd do as Inspector Dawes says and fetch that laptop, if I were you.'

The deacon gulped. 'Yes, Sergeant. Right away.' He scuttled off.

'I've a pretty good idea what we'll find on it,' said Malone, grimly. 'Still, it doesn't prove someone topped him, does it?'

'Maybe not,' agreed Dawes, 'but the circumstantial evidence is piling up.'

'We could always question that little foreign lad, the barmaid's kid. You saw how he carried on when you told him Father John was dead.'

Jack frowned. 'I don't want to do that unless it's absolutely necessary. If Carlene's right and Aleksy *has* been systematically abused, the last thing he'll want to do is talk about it. We'll keep that as a last resort. After all, we've no evidence that the old priest wasn't killed by that golf ball you found. Forensics went along with it.'

'Yeah, boss. Just because he was an evil bastard and deserved to be exterminated like the vermin he undoubtedly was, doesn't mean someone actually went ahead and did it.'

Dawes surveyed the devastation. 'I don't think there's much for us here, Bugsy. But before we go, show me the sacristy and the sacrarium you were talking about.'

The sacrarium basin was still there but the elderly plumbing had been in need of urgent repair, even before the sea overwhelmed the site defences. The pipe connecting the sacrarium directly to the ground had fractured and been swept away, leaving the earth, into which centuries of consecrated sacramental hosts had drained, completely exposed to the elements. Malone knelt down, his back to the inspector.

Remembering his sergeant was once a practising Catholic, Jack asked, 'Would you like me to go outside and leave you for few minutes, Bugsy?'

'No thanks, Guv, but you can hold this for me.' Malone produced one of his omnipresent plastic evidence envelopes and passed it to Jack. Then he took out his penknife and began scraping up earth samples from beneath the sacrarium. 'Doubt if we'll find anything after the seawater has been all over it but forensics like a challenge.'

After the ten o'clock news had finished on TV and the girls had still not come back from Marcus and Millie's house, Dick decided to use what was left of the light to excavate the pond, seeing as Rosie was so keen to make it into a water feature. He dug out most of the weed and some rather nasty eels, but then his spade hit metal again. The old cistern, or whatever it was, was firmly wedged in the sludge at the bottom. It was no use; it would have to come out before any company would even consider tackling the septic tank and soakaway problem.

Sometime later, after a great deal of puffing and groaning, he finally managed to get a rope around it and heave it, dripping, to the surface. It wasn't an old water cistern after all, it was a sealed deposit box; surprisingly modern, like the ones they used on submarines. Dick had seen one before at the bank. Judging by the weight, it was full up with something, but by this time, Dick was dripping himself so he hosed away the raw sewage then dragged the box into the garage and went off to shower. Tomorrow, he'd get some tools, prise it open and see what was inside. If, as he suspected, it was simply full of junk, he'd take it to the rubbish tip and dump it. On the other hand, it was a strange thing to find in a pond full of effluent. He'd get Jack to come and help in the morning. He needed a witness in case there was something suspicious about it. He couldn't afford to get mixed up in anything dodgy – he had his bonus to consider.

Dawes and Malone caught up with Bridget O'Dowd early next morning, at her first cleaning job in the golf club. She was polishing the trophies that stood along the glass shelf, behind the bar. Already, the room reeked of metal polish, furniture wax and bleach.

'Mrs O'Dowd, I wonder if we might have a word.'

'What about?' She sniffed and continued polishing, furiously.

'Can you tell us about the last time you saw Father John?' asked Dawes, politely.

'I've already told *him*.' She jabbed a thumb at Malone. 'Don't you lot keep notes?'

'Yes, I realize you've already made a statement, but it now seems you were the last person to see Father John alive and we were wondering whether there was anything more you can tell us. Something that might have occurred to you since.'

'Like what?'

Malone consulted his notebook. 'On the evening of Father John's death, you attended Mass, then went back to the parochial house to cook his dinner. You told him what time his meal would be ready just before he disappeared into the sacristy. That was the last time you saw or spoke to him.'

'That's right, so it is. I left his dinner – chicken vindaloo, pilau rice and naan bread – in a warm oven, as usual, then I went home. That was the last I saw of him.'

'Did you see anyone loitering in the church after you left? Maybe someone from the village or even a stranger?'

Mrs O'Dowd put down her duster. 'And why would there be? I'm always the last to leave; me and the deacon, that is. We left after tidying up.'

'Didn't the deacon ever go into the sacristy with the priest after Mass?' asked Malone. 'To help cleanse the sacramental vessels and dispose of any leftover wafers and wine?'

Mrs O'Dowd looked Malone firmly in the eye. 'Sometimes he did. But on this occasion Father John said he didn't need him and he could go home. The deacon left just before I did.' She glared at Dawes. 'Why are you asking all these questions? Father John was conked on the head by a golf ball and it killed him, so it did. It was the Lord's will and that's that.'

'Why would the Lord want Father John dead?' asked Dawes.

'Sure, it's not for me or you to question the Lord's purpose. He moves in mysterious ways and if He chose a golf ball as his instrument of mercy, it's not for the likes of us to cast doubt upon it.'

'You worked as Father John's housekeeper for a number of years, all over the diocese. You must have got to know him very well. Were you fond of him?'

Bridget O'Dowd's mouth snapped open and shut like a rat trap. 'Father John was a priest. It wasn't my place to be fond of him.'

Malone decided they'd tiptoed around the real issue for long enough. 'Did he ever show an unnatural interest in the altar boys, Mrs O'Dowd?'

She looked wary but not shocked. 'And if I believed that, wouldn't it have been my holy duty to do something about it? Now, if you're finished, I've another cleaning job to go to.' She gathered up her voluminous shopping bag and her cleaning materials and stumped out.

Malone scratched his head. 'Well, Guv, that's as good a piece of stonewalling as we're ever likely to encounter from a witness. Was she withholding evidence, d'you reckon?'

Dawes was doubtful. 'Blowed if I can tell, Bugsy. And to be frank, I'm not sure I care any more. I'm pretty certain the technical boffins will find evidence of child porn on Father John's laptop and it'll be their job to do some electronic tracking to find out if he was part of a ring. After that, it'll be up to the vice squad to decide what civil lawsuits they can bring against the bishop and his diocese. There's every chance that young Aleksy was one of his victims, but since the priest is dead, there seems little point in putting the child through more misery by interrogating him. We've done enough to satisfy the requirements of a thorough investigation.'

'I agree, Jack. We've found nothing to suggest someone "lamped the old perv", like Carlene thought, so I say we go with the golf ball theory.'

With two suspicious deaths cleared up to the satisfaction of both the Met's deputy assistant commissioner and the deputy chief constable of Avon and Somerset, all that remained was the de Kuiper dilemma. In Jack's book, it was far more important than the timely demise of a wife-beater and a child-abuser. So far, he had backed off from reporting what he knew to Intelligence but he couldn't stall for much longer and then the Spooks would be all over Gibbet Cottage like a rash. Dick, Rosie and Jeremy would almost certainly have to move out and the Lullington Barrow villagers would have apoplexy. He wanted to discuss how to handle the Browns with Corrie before he *cried havoc and let slip the dogs of war.*

*

That same morning, Corrie and Rosemary had plans to play a round of golf followed by lunch in the clubhouse, so Jack and Bugsy wandered down to the bar of Hangman's Inn for a swift half and a ploughman's.

'Any news on the capture of the de Kuipers from your mate in the "funny buggers"?'

''Fraid not, Jack. They seem to have dropped off the radar and the Intelligence lads are shitting themselves trying to get details of the insurgent network inside the president's own security force before an auction for the names sparks off a full-scale Arab war.'

'Have you told Intelligence we've traced the de Kuipers' last known whereabouts to Lullington Barrow?'

'Not yet, Guv. I was waiting for you to give me the nod.' He took a long slug from his glass of Lullington Gold and wiped his top lip with his sleeve. 'You don't seriously think Arab rebels will turn up in Lullington, looking for 'em, do you?'

'I bloody well hope not. On the other hand, they must be desperate to get their hands on that document before the president does, or it'll be a blood bath of executions and a serious setback for their revolution. How good is their intelligence, d'you reckon? Are they likely to have traced the de Kuipers to Lullington Barrow?'

'Doubt it, Guv. I mean, if our Spooks, with all their contacts, haven't been able to find out where they went, I doubt if the Arabs have, either. Unless, of course, someone on the inside has tipped them off.'

Lullington Barrow Golf Links were within easy walking distance of Gibbet Cottage if you took the shortcut down the lane that ran along the back of Gallows Green. Corrie and Rosie engaged in rare, sisterly gossip as they trundled their golf trolleys down the leafy track in the morning sun, not yet at its blistering zenith. Corrie had borrowed Dick's clubs and having been told they were very expensive, she was a little nervous about using them. There were few people around this early in the morning. The villagers weren't early risers and there was no sign of life in any of the neighbouring cottages.

'I expect Millie's still sleeping off her hangover,' remarked Rosie. 'Do you think Marcus really has left her for another woman?'

'Doubt it,' said Corrie, guiding Dick's golf trolley carefully around a flattened hedgehog. 'Where would he find another witless, Marilyn Monroe lookalike who lets him come and go as he pleases?'

'So where has he gone, then? And why did he say he was going to Dubai on business?'

Corrie sighed. 'Rosie, you can never be sure what's going on in a man's brain but it's nearly always closely connected to whatever's going on in his trousers or his wallet. And men rarely leave their wives until they have a replacement lined up. For them, marrying their mistress simply creates a vacancy. But I think Marcus is totally besotted with Millie so it has to be something to do with all the money she spends.'

'And he's always away from home, trying to earn more.' She was silent for a while, mulling it over, then: 'Giles is abroad again, in Amsterdam. Edwina says he's producing a documentary about the history of wooden clogs and their effect on the Dutch economy.'

'Can't wait to see it,' observed Corrie, without enthusiasm.

'While he's away, Edwina's mounting another of her environmental clean-up campaigns. Last time I saw her, she was painting "Wipe Out Graffiti" on placards.'

Corrie giggled. 'That's odd. After all that stuff about Milan and Rigoletto; I thought she liked Italians.'

'What?' Rosie looked puzzled.

Corrie smiled. Rosie was too thin and intense to have a sense of humour. 'Ignore me; I'm being facetious. I haven't seen much of Peter and Jane recently. They shout "hello" over their fence, then they nip back indoors.'

'Hmm.' Rosie chewed her lip. 'I know what you mean. Almost furtive, although I can't think why. Peter's an absolute hero as far as I'm concerned. He single-handedly saved our house from burning down.'

The morning was idyllic. Blue skies, fluffy white clouds and ducks swimming contentedly round the pond. Corrie was almost beginning to think that the countryside wasn't so bad after all. Jack had investigated the two suspicious deaths to his satisfaction and in both cases, the coroner had swiftly brought in verdicts of 'death resulting from an accident following an unusual event that was unanticipated by everyone involved'. It just remained for Danika and Aleksy's future to be sorted out and they could all go back to London, leaving Dick and Rosie to settle into their new home. It seemed doubtful now that the de Kuipers would ever return to Lullington; they were probably miles away in Syria or Yemen, flogging arms to anyone with enough cash to pay for them. The concept of Arabs coming all the way to Somerset to snatch something valuable that Simon and Saskia had left behind now seemed melodramatic and highly unlikely. Corrie stopped to drag her trolley out of a pothole in which the wheels had become wedged. Rosemary sauntered dreamily on ahead.

Suddenly, the serene tranquillity of the morning was shattered by the throaty roar of a powerful vehicle with someone's foot hard down on the throttle. Behind them, a huge black limo, some seventeen feet long, accelerated up the lane and slewed to a halt beside Rosie, the driver still wildly revving the engine. A fat, swarthy man with a bushy black beard jumped out of the back and grabbed Rosie. Terrified, she struggled and screamed out, 'Corrie help me!' The man hit her once, very hard, and yelled something in a foreign, guttural language. Then he bundled her and her golf bag into the limo.

For a split second, Corrie froze, like a rabbit in headlights, unable to believe what was happening. Then she was furious. Muggers after Rosie's golf clubs! What a bloody nerve and in broad daylight! How dare they manhandle her little sister like that! She let go of Dick's precious golf trolley and ran, just managing to grab the edge of the car door before it could slam shut. She clung on, grimly, as the car started to pull away, yelling as loudly as she could. 'Help! Help!' Even as she shouted, she knew it was useless. If anyone had seen the attack, they most certainly wouldn't get involved – this was Lullington Barrow. Just as her fingertips lost their grip on the door, strong arms reached out and seized her, dragging her into the back. Next thing she knew, Corrie was lying face down on the floor of the sedan as it roared away. Her arms were twisted painfully up her back and someone fat and hairy was kneeling on her.

CHAPTER THIRTEEN

With everyone away 'doin' stuff', Carlene found herself at something of a loose end. Lullington Barrow had little in the way of amusement for young people as most of the villagers were either little kids or 'dead old'. She decided that all the teenagers must push off somewhere lively once they were old enough, and who could blame them? Apart from farming, the only 'industry' was cider making. She'd had a look round the old cider mill at the far end of the village and it was like a museum; full of screws and wheels for grinding up apples. At the time she'd visited, it had been deserted and she didn't reckon anyone had made cider there for yonks, judging by the dust and rats. She was more interested in the history of Lullington Barrow and was fascinated by the macabre gibbet up on Gallows Green Hill. She'd read in one of the tourist brochures on the desk at Hangman's Inn that less than 180 years ago, criminals actually swung in the breeze for all the village to see. On impulse, she decided to climb up the hill and take a look at the replica gallows which now adorned the summit.

The view from the top was breathtaking, especially to someone who had spent all her short life in the less salubrious parts of Hackney. The brochure had said that on a clear day you could see Glastonbury Tor. Carlene shaded her eyes to look – and there it was, rising from the heat haze that hovered over the Somerset Levels and crowned by the roofless St Michael's Tower: the Isle of Avalon. How awesome was that? She took a deep breath. It brought out the spiritual side of you, up here, and she exulted at how her life had changed since she came to work for Mrs D. She loved her job and took it very seriously, keeping copious notes on everything she learned and trying as hard as she could to do everything well. Mrs D was ace, a real smart lady, and Carlene liked and respected Mr Jack. Together, they made her feel she was an asset to the business, unlike her care workers and probation officers who had treated her like rubbish. No good for anything except signing on and nicking things, they said, so she'd done precisely what was expected of her. Well, all that was behind her now. She would work hard, save hard and eventually, she hoped to be able to move out of the halfway-house hostel and rent a tiny flat of her own. She could do it; she knew she could, now that she had a good job and real support behind her. And it was great that Mrs D trusted her to help with her sleuthing. Even Sergeant Bugsy was a good laugh; he'd started calling her Sherlock. They were a cool team and, unbelievably, she felt part of it.

Carlene reached up to the noose that hung from the gallows and gave it a tug. The rope was frayed and perished. Couldn't hang anyone from that, she decided. It'd never take the weight. Looking down over Lullington Barrow, she was amazed at how much of the village she could see from Gallows Hill. There was Hangman's Inn with that slimeball, Ted Boobyer, sweeping the yard; next to the inn was St Mary's Church, all battered and ruined by the sea. And a bit further south, she could see Gallows Green and Gibbet Cottage quite clearly, even the recently exposed patch of green lawn and the darker area of woodland. She could even see Jeremy and Aleksy playing on their bikes. What a change there'd been in that poor little kid's life since the old priest had carked it. These days, he never stopped smiling. She hoped the sick old perv was roasting in hell.

She sat down on the grassy knoll, her back against the wooden strut of the gallows and turned her face to the morning sun. For the first time in her life, she was really happy because for the first time in her life, she had a real future to look forward to. Through half-closed lids, a sudden movement down on the ground caught her eye. A speeding saloon was tearing up the lane that ran along the back of Gallows Green. It was a big black job with tinted windows, unusual for this naff village where everyone had ancient Fords and Skodas with tatty trailers on the back. Even from this distance, she recognized the make of this monster; it was a Cadillac Escalade. Back home in Hackney, a Jamaican drugs baron drove about in one just like it, chucking petrol bombs through the windows into the clubs and brothels owned by his rivals. Not many brothels in Lullington, though. Carlene watched the car pull up violently alongside two women wheeling golf trolleys. Then a fat, bearded bloke jumped out and strong-armed the first lady into the passenger seat after smacking her hard about the head. The second woman dropped her trolley and ran to help the first one, clinging on to the car door by her fingertips as it raced away. Then hairy hands reached out and she was dragged inside, too. What the hell was occurring? It looked like a kidnap but it couldn't be, could it? Not in a dead and alive hole like Lullington.

Then Carlene's blood ran cold. She recognized the second woman's scarf; an unusual design of vivid pink and orange splodges. It was silk, real mega gear; the one she'd given Mrs D for her birthday. She'd saved up for weeks to buy it. And the other lady must be Mrs Brown, her sister. They were in deep shit; that was obvious. Carlene could see they hadn't got into the car voluntarily. She scrabbled in her pocket for her mobile, ready to dial 999. Bugger! She'd left it on the bedside table in her room.

Now she was running, helter-skelter down the hill, sometimes falling and rolling over and over in her haste. Mrs D and Mrs Brown needed her help. Neither of them was savvy enough to get out of this on their own. They weren't used to being jumped on by fat hairy blokes; they wouldn't have a clue how to take care of themselves. You had to have lived rough for a while to be streetwise. Carlene didn't allow herself to dwell on why they'd been snatched or what might happen to them. She just knew she must reach the road in time to see what direction they took, maybe get the registration of the Cadillac, although it stood out like a tiara on a tart in Lullington Barrow. As soon as she got down, she'd raise the alarm and Mr Jack and Sergeant Bugsy would come to the rescue.

Corrie gasped. The weight of the fat, oily assassin kneeling on her back was forcing all the breath from her lungs. Her arms, twisted up her back, were hurting badly. She mustered what little bravado she could.

'Who are you? Where are you taking us?' she wheezed. 'You won't get away with this, you know!' She knew, even as she spoke, that it was a pathetic thing to say. Neither man took any notice.

Rosie had collapsed on the floor in the front, weeping pitifully. She had an inflamed cheek and incipient black eye from the vicious slap she had received. 'Please let us out. We haven't any money. Take the golf clubs; they're worth quite a lot.'

The driver, a tall, slim man in an immaculate charcoal suit, spoke quietly. The black eyes above the trimmed moustache were without emotion. 'I think you know that it isn't your money we want, Mrs de Kuiper. It's something much more valuable.'

So that's it, thought Corrie. These men think Rosie is Saskia. It was just as Jack had feared; the Arabs really *had* come to find whatever it was that Simon and Saskia had left behind. 'She isn't Mrs de Kuiper,' insisted Corrie. 'Her name's Rosemary Brown and she's my sister. Let her go.'

'You lie!' shouted the fat bearded man, kneeling harder. He twisted Corrie's arms until she screamed out in pain. 'Be silent until we tell you to speak.'

Lying on the floor, the two women couldn't see where they were being taken until the limo pulled up a short while later. Without a word, the two men pulled Corrie and Rosie from the car and shoved them towards an old shed, roughly twenty feet long.

'No talk,' insisted the bearded one. 'Get in there.' To emphasize the order, he pushed Corrie through a set of doors in the centre of the long side and it was then that she got a look at him. His olive-skinned face was marred by a long, deep scar. It started in his beard, crossed his nose and cheek and bisected one eye, twisting the lid into a hideous disfigurement. Corrie could only guess at how it had been caused. Once inside the shed, the big nostrils in the hooked nose flared as he inhaled the pungent smell of sour, rancid apples. His one good eye scanned the road outside in case they'd been spotted and followed.

'It is safe here?' asked the driver. His bearded companion nodded then forced both women down onto their knees on the dusty floor. Rosie whimpered with fear and pain.

Corrie glanced quickly about her. They were in the old cider mill, described in the tourist guide as an important part of Lullington Barrow's cultural heritage and well worth a visit. She hadn't reckoned on visiting it quite like this. The ancient machinery consisted of a crusher and two wooden cylinders, one with teeth and the other with corresponding slots, which meshed together and ground the apples to a pulp. The press was where the crushed apples were squeezed by lowering a formation of screws with levers. It looked to Corrie like a medieval instrument of torture and she realized now why the Arabs had brought them here.

'What are you going to do with us?' she demanded, with more

pluck than she felt. 'I should warn you, my husband's a policeman, he'll—'

The driver, tall, slim and smelling of sandalwood cologne, was far more composed than his colleague but the tone when he spoke was not friendly.

'All we require is that you tell the truth. If you do that, you will not be hurt. Where is your husband, Mrs de Kuiper?' He was complacent, knowing he had the initiative. The demand was quiet, authoritative.

'He's at work in his office in Bristol. His name's Dick Brown. He works for the bank,' Rosie gabbled.

'If you continue to lie, I cannot guarantee your safety. Mohamed, here, has a cruel, violent temper, particularly with uncooperative women.'

Corrie noted the accent, guessed it was Syrian but only because it was similar to that of one of her rich, dinner party customers who hailed from Damascus. She plucked up courage.

'Listen to me! We don't—'

'No. You listen!' countermanded the bearded one, with scarcely a second's pause. 'We are the avenging Sword of Islam, spawned in war-torn Kabul from the seeds of revolution! Our Holy Jihad, nurtured in our beloved country, is to wreak vengeance on the enemies of Allah and a free state. The president-dictator is an evil, many-tentacled monster who is trying to strangle our nation by every means possible. It is the will of Allah that he be hacked down. Vengeance will be swift! Our weapons are kidnap, hostage and assassination.' His good eyeball was rolling fanatically round in its socket.

The slim kidnapper was smart; always professional, always in control. Corrie had to give him that. So far, they had been ruthlessly efficient without resorting to gratuitous violence that might render their captives unable to talk. Inside the shed, the sun was now baking in its intensity. Through squinty eyes, Corrie saw that the bearded man was now standing back, brandishing a gun in case the women tried any kind of resistance. Again the professionalism. No common crooks, these. This was an organized anti-government force. Someone's government. But Corrie had no idea whose.

'Please,' begged Rosemary. 'Won't you tell us what this is all about?' She was terrified and her voice, intended to be firm, came out sounding like Minnie Mouse.

The Arab with the gun pointed it at Rosemary as though he intended to use it. 'You are Saskia de Kuiper! You have yellow hair and we have observed you coming from the de Kuiper house. No more time-wasting. Where is it?'

'Where's what?' stammered Rosemary. 'Please! I'm not Saskia de Kuiper. They moved away and we bought their house, you see, and—'

'Shut up!'

Corrie crawled across to comfort her trembling sister. At the sudden movement, the one-eyed man with the gun instinctively turned his weapon on her and fired wildly. It was a snatched aim. The bullet whined angrily as it struck a metal girder supporting the roof in the ancient shed.

'No more questions,' the leader snapped. 'Just answers; or we kill you both.'

Since they had no idea what it was these terrorists thought they had, Corrie reckoned they were in for a very long interrogation or a very short life expectancy. 'Killing us would be stupid, wouldn't it? If we're dead, we can't tell you anything. And what would you do with our bodies? They'll be found and when you're caught, the forensic evidence will prove you did it.'

The leader smiled grimly. 'We passed a pig farm near here, I think. There is petrol in the car. Burned bodies fed to pigs will never be found. You have exactly one minute to provide me with the exact location of the item you have stolen that belongs to the people's revolution.'

Corrie was seriously miffed at being shot at, never mind the threat of ending up as barbecued pig swill. She struggled to her feet and faced the impassive one who was clearly the more intelligent of the two Arabs. 'Look, we don't know what you're talking about and we don't know anything about your revolution. This is clearly a case of mistaken identity. I suggest you go back to whichever ghastly state you came from before you get into serious trouble. We have laws in this country and you and your gun-happy friend have already broken several of them.' She went to Rosie and helped her up. 'Come on, Rosie, we're going home. This whole thing is a farce and I refuse to take any further part in it.'

The proud Arab was filled suddenly with rage, angry that she had no respect, this middle-class *taghouti* woman. He grabbed the hair at

the back of her head and twisted it fiercely in his grip, forcing her to face him.

'Mrs de Kuiper *will* tell us what we want to know, I promise you.' He spoke rapidly in guttural Arabic to the bearded man who grasped Rosemary and dragged her across to the apple crusher. He grabbed her hands and shoved them hard into the teeth of the press.

The leader's voice was icy calm. 'Where is it? Tell us now or I shall allow Mohamed to break all of your fingers, very slowly.'

The bearded man began to turn the screws that lowered the crusher. It creaked and groaned like a medieval rack but it worked perfectly as the two Arabs had ensured it would.

'No! No! Please don't hurt me!' Rosemary screamed and screamed as the pressure increased and she felt the bones in her fingers slowly starting to crunch. Horrified, Corrie screamed too, and tried to struggle free to help her sister, but her hair was tightly in the Arab's grip and her shoulder felt as if it was being wrenched from its socket.

'Tell us where you and your husband have hidden the list of our brave rebel fighters, Mrs de Kuiper, and we'll stop.'

'Please, don't hurt her!' Corrie begged. 'We haven't got what you want! She isn't Saskia de Kuiper, she's Rosemary Brown. Please let her go!'

Then, as suddenly as it had begun, it ended. The decaying wooden doors burst open and Carlene rushed in, screeching like a banshee. She had spotted the Cadillac Escalade parked outside the cider mill with Mrs Brown's golf bag lying abandoned on the front seat. She could hear agonized screams coming from inside the shed and knew she couldn't wait for the police. Needing some kind of weapon, she grabbed the club with the heaviest head and raced to the rescue. With scarcely a moment's hesitation, she took in the situation and cut down the bearded Arab with a ferocious blow behind his knees. Taken completely by surprise, he yelped, let go of Rosie and fell forward onto his chest. Still screeching, Carlene leaped on his back and straddled him, pummelling the man's face into the stony ground with hard, sharp blows whilst screaming obscenities that would have shocked him deeply, had he understood.

Taking advantage of the unexpected diversion, Corrie wriggled around, brought her knee up hard in the second man's groin and felt his grip ease as he shrieked with pain. It was sufficient for her to

struggle free and deliver another debilitating blow to his solar plexus with a clenched fist. Her last punch, a punishing right hook, made perfect contact with the point of his jaw. It was like a power cut; the Arab's lights went out instantly as he staggered backwards, cracking his head against the wall.

Carlene didn't hesitate; she grabbed the golf club and welted her dazed Arab over the head with the business end as he lay struggling beneath her. Then, gently, she loosened the screws and extricated Rosemary's crushed fingers from the press. Poor Rosie was hysterical with terror and Carlene gave her a little shake.

'Come on now, Mrs Brown, getta grip, love. You're gonna be fine. I don't fink nuffink's broken, just a bit squashed. But we don't wanna hang about here, do we?' She gripped the arms of both traumatized women and raced them out of the mill as fast as she could. In their patriotic zeal, the Arabs had left the keys in the Cadillac. Carlene jumped into the driving seat. 'Ace! I've always wanted to drive one o' these. Come on, quick! Get in before those wally-brains come after us!' Battered and stunned, the two women half-scrambled, half-fell into the back.

'Anyone gotta mobile?' yelled Carlene, over her shoulder. 'We 'ave to tell Mr Jack what's 'appened.'

The two women looked at each other vaguely and shook their heads.

'Never mind. Let's get out of 'ere.' Carlene gunned the engine, rammed it into gear and they sped away, tyres spinning on the melting tarmac. Halfway down the lane that ran behind Gallows Green, there was a bump as if they had run over something. Corrie looked out of the back window and saw the remains of Dick's golf trolley and clubs, lying mangled in the middle of the track where she had dropped them.

In the cider mill, the two Arabs staggered to their feet, dazed and disbelieving. They had been chosen for this mission after undergoing stringent training. The Kidnap and Hostage Operations against Enemies of the Revolution had been run by the best Shi'ite instructors from Lebanon and were considered the optimum in preparation. The training covered moves and countermoves in negotiation for ransom or release of prisoners, kidnap and evasion techniques and the attitudes and modus operandi of all police forces in the western world. Where had they gone wrong? They had been defeated, but worst of all – by

women! The shame was not to be borne. They had failed and in their honourable culture, there was only one punishment for such failure.

The suave, hook-nosed rebel picked up the gun from where his fanatical, one-eyed companion had dropped it. Without a word, he shoved the bearded man to his knees, pushed his head forward and placed the muzzle against the back of his neck. He pulled the trigger then . . . 'Allahu Akbar!' He raised the gun to his own temple.

CHAPTER FOURTEEN

The Cadillac Escalade roared up outside Hangman's Inn and slewed to a halt just inches short of the flower tubs. Inquisitive locals, drinking their lunchtime cider, rose idly from their chairs and drifted over to the window to see what all the commotion was about. When Carlene hopped out of the driver's seat, there was a ripple of astonishment tinged with disapproval. When she ran round to open the doors and help out two very shocked and wobbly ladies, one with a black eye and a scarf wrapped around her hands, everyone crowded to the door to have a better look. *What had they incomers been up to now, the dozy articles?*

Inside the pub, hidden away in a booth in the snug, Dawes and Malone were working their way through platefuls of cheese and pickle and convincing each other that the Arab uprising was nothing to do with them. All they had to do was inform Intelligence of the de Kuipers' last known address and they could go back to the Met without any further involvement. They'd personally searched Gibbet Cottage, from top to bottom; even taken up a few loose floorboards but had found absolutely nothing. Then they'd thrashed their way through the woodland and the coppice with no success. This whole business of arms trafficking, revolution and torture now seemed totally unreal; like something out of an SAS thriller. This was rustic Somerset, not the Middle East.

Liz Boobyer hurried over to their booth. 'Think you'd better come, Jack. Your Corrie and her sister are outside and they're in a bit of a bad way. Looks like they've had an accident.'

'What!' exclaimed Jack, jumping up. 'They're meant to be playing golf. How can two respectable ladies possibly have an accident playing golf?'

'Maybe one of 'em fell in a bunker,' quipped Bugsy. 'That sand gets everywhere.'

Dawes and Malone pushed their way through the throng that had gathered outside and couldn't believe what they saw.

'Corrie, what the hell has happened to you?' Jack's voice was gruff with anxiety.

Corrie opened her mouth to tell him but nothing would come out. She was trembling violently. He tried to take her in his arms but she yelped with pain. 'Sorry, darling . . . shoulder . . . dislocated, I think.' Jack took off his jacket and draped it gently around her. Even on a hot day, delayed shock made you shiver.

Carlene came forward, steering Rosemary, whose cheek was livid and her eye already half-closed. 'Can someone get the doc for Mrs Brown? Better get 'er 'usband, too. She might need to go to 'ospital.' As if to confirm her battered condition, Rosemary sighed feebly and slid slowly to the ground in a dead faint.

Bugsy carried Rosie into the pub and Liz poured her a brandy but she couldn't hold the glass in her swollen, throbbing fingers, so Carlene held it for her while she sipped. Fortunately, Doctor Brimble was there, having his usual ham and egg salad between house calls. He hurried over with his bag and began to tend to Rosie. Corrie stumbled into the inn with Jack supporting her and took several good gulps of her brandy until she could finally speak sensibly again. Her left shoulder was agony and she couldn't move her arm at all.

The villagers, bursting with morbid curiosity, crowded closer, trying to hear what was being said. Bugsy moved them back, firmly.

'Come on now, folks. Give the ladies some space. They've had a nasty shock and the doc needs room to treat them.'

They moved away reluctantly, some of them still loitering as close as they dared, desperate to know what had happened so they could be the first to gossip about it. The initial consensus was that it could have been a road accident but the big, black beast outside was undamaged, so that obviously wasn't it.

Having treated Rosemary and made her comfortable with a pain-killing injection, Doctor Brimble attended to Corrie. She was more concerned for her sister than herself.

'Is Rosie all right, Doctor?'

'She has badly bruised fingers but luckily, no broken bones as far as I can tell. She kept muttering something about having them crushed in a cider press. She's very shocked and she'll have a swollen cheek and a black eye by morning. I've given her a sedative and she's feeling slightly better. I've called Dick and he's coming straight home from the bank.' He was examining Corrie's shoulder as he spoke. 'You, on the other hand, have an anterior dislocation of the left shoulder. The humeral head has been forced out of its socket. If it isn't reset quickly, it could result in severe pain and restrict the range of motion. Have you ever dislocated it before, Mrs Dawes?'

'No, Doctor.'

'Aah. You won't be familiar with the procedure to put it back, then. Keep your arm in a resting position, perpendicular to the ground.' He bent Corrie's elbow to a ninety-degree angle and slowly rotated her arm. Then he pulled on it sharply and the shoulder popped back into its joint.

'Owww!' Corrie squealed. But the relief was immediate and she relaxed. Jack sat beside her, full of concern but anxious to know what had been going on.

'Sweetheart, are you able to tell Bugsy and me exactly what happened?'

'Oh, Jack, it was awful. They crushed poor Rosie's hands in the apple grinder. She screamed and screamed.'

'Who did? Someone at the golf club?' Jack was completely flummoxed.

''Course not, silly! At the cider mill.' With the pain receding, Corrie was recovering her spirits. 'Do try to keep up, darling.'

'What were you doing in the cider mill? You were supposed to be playing golf.'

'We were walking down the lane behind Gallows Green towards the golf links when we were abducted by two horrible men in that bloody great van-thing, parked outside. God only knows what it is; I've never seen one before.'

'It's a Cadillac Escalade, Mr Jack. Gotta be worth fifty grand of anybody's loot. Goes like shit off a shiny shovel. You all right, Mrs D?'

At the sound of Carlene's voice, Corrie turned and grabbed her hand. 'Oh, Jack, Carlene was magnificent. You should have seen her. She beat up Mohamed, rescued us and drove the getaway car like a demon. Without her, we'd probably both be dead by now.'

'You didn't do too bad, yerself, Mrs D. That right hook was a blinder, never mind the knee in the goolies. I was dead proud of yer.'

Jack shuddered. He was used to Corrie getting into skirmishes but this sounded like a full-scale brawl. He looked at Carlene properly for the first time since the car pulled up outside. She was covered in dust and earth as if she'd been rolling about in the dirt, her tunic was ripped and there were several holes in her tights. Her knuckles were raw and bleeding and her knees were badly grazed. Only her tormented magenta hair looked the same as ever.

'Blimey, Sherlock!' Bugsy was beside Carlene. 'You look like you've been in a fight.'

She grinned. 'You should've seen the other bloke.'

Jack was trying to get his head around what Corrie had told him. One word stood out in a way that he had been dreading. 'Did you say that one of the men was called Mohamed?'

'Yes, I just told you,' snapped Corrie impatiently. 'We were kidnapped by Arabs. They kept saying they were the avenging Sword of Islam and they were going to hack off the president's tentacles.'

Malone winced. 'But why did they kidnap you and Mrs Brown?'

Corrie fidgeted with exasperation at their inability to grasp the situation. 'Because they saw Rosie coming out of Gibbet Cottage and thought she was Saskia de Kuiper. It was her yellow hair that persuaded them. They obviously don't see many blondes in Kabul.'

'So why did they crush her hands in the apple grinder?' Jack was pretty sure he knew the answer but wanted Corrie to repeat exactly what the Arabs had said.

'To make her tell them where she'd hidden something that the de Kuipers stole from the people's revolution. He said something about names at one point, but he didn't say whose names. Of course, Rosie hadn't any idea what they were talking about but they wouldn't believe her. Oh, Jack, she was so frightened. And I was right all along, wasn't I? Simon and Saskia did leave something valuable behind when they disappeared. Do you think they might still come back for it?'

'Possibly; but so might those two Arabs. Will you be all right here if Bugsy and I go after them? I want a few words with the bastard who dislocated your shoulder.' Malone noted Jack's grim expression and decided to turn a blind eye when his boss got hold of the bloke.

The full impact of what could have happened to them finally kicked in and Corrie became tearful. 'He pulled my hair – really hard,' she snivelled. 'I think some of it came out.'

Carlene was furious all over again. How dare the manky foreign gits hurt her beloved Mrs D. 'Let's go and nick 'em, Mr Jack. They can't have got far. We pinched their motor.'

Bugsy pushed her down into a chair. 'You're not going anywhere, Sherlock. You've done enough for one day. Stay here and look after Mrs Dawes and Mrs Brown.'

Carlene's face fell but she did as she was told. She became suddenly aware that she was filthy and starting to stiffen up. She needed a nice, hot bath and reckoned the two coppers could manage without her – just this once.

As soon as Dawes and Malone entered the cider mill, the smell hit them. It wasn't cider apples. It was more familiar than that; the sweet, sickly smell of blood. Years in Scotland Yard's Murder Squad had made the stench of fresh human blood instantly recognizable.

'Reckon we're too late, Jack.' Malone went across to the dead man who was still grasping a gun. The bullet had entered his right temple and there was no exit wound, meaning it was still lodged in his brain. He was lying on his back, his head in a pool of blood that continued to ooze from the wound.

Dawes was already kneeling beside the bearded one who had been shot through the back of the head and had fallen forward onto his face, which was now obscured by blood. He'd probably been kneeling when he was shot; the classic execution position.

'Recognize the weapon, boss?' Malone pointed but touched nothing. 'It's a nine millimetre Caracal semi-automatic. They were developed in Abu Dhabi but nowadays, it's the favoured handgun of most Arab security forces.'

'Revolutionaries as well, it seems. These men were after the names of the insurgents working within the government before the dictator could get hold of them. While the de Kuipers were flogging arms to both sides, the list must somehow have fallen into their hands and they stole it. Worth a lot of money.'

'D'you reckon the de Kuipers are still alive, Guv?'

'These two Arabs obviously thought so. And they were convinced the list of names was hidden here in Lullington Barrow.'

'So what was this? A circular firing squad?'

'More or less. After their female captives escaped and took their armoured car, the leader knew the game was up. He executed his fellow freedom fighter then killed himself. I reckon this is what you can expect for failure in their line of business.'

'Blimey. Good job they don't do that in the police service. There'd be nobody left in Scotland Yard.'

'Oh my dear Lord, whatever's happened here?' It was Constable Chedzey who had been told about some kind of fracas in the cider mill by the eavesdroppers in Hangman's Inn. It was his patch and he'd come storming over in his police car to assert his authority and take control. He'd had enough of these 'comical' London policemen undermining his authority in the village and making him seem like a useless twit. He took one look at all the blood, caught a whiff of the abattoir stench, then rushed back outside. They could hear him losing his lunch in the bushes. Neither Dawes nor Malone took any notice of him.

'Reckon it's time we reported the situation to my mate in the 'funny buggers', don't you, Jack?'

'Yep. When PC Chedzey's finished throwing up, we'll get him to cordon off the mill as a crime scene. How long do you think it'll take for the Spooks to get here?'

'Almost immediately, once we tell 'em the situation.' He scratched his head. 'Where the hell do you think the de Kuipers hid that list? We've looked everywhere in Gibbet Cottage.'

'Could've gone up in smoke when the loft caught fire, but somehow, I don't think so. It was too valuable for the de Kuipers to leave it on show in a tea chest full of papers. Dick and Rosemary might have taken it to the tip. No, I believe it's still somewhere on Gallows Green.'

'But I don't understand! How did Rosemary get so badly hurt? She was perfectly fine this morning and looking forward to playing golf.' Dick Brown had raced home down the M5 at a speed that would surely have cost him his licence and a huge fine had the revenue cameras clocked him. He'd rushed straight to his wife's bedside where she was half asleep, having been given a sedative by Edgar Brimble for the pain and shock. She'd been unable to explain in detail what had happened to her and told him to ask Corrie, which is what he was doing now.

'Corrie, I blame you. You're her older sister; you should have taken better care of her. You've seen her poor face and Christ knows how long it will take for those swollen fingers to heal. All I could get out of her was some nonsense about you both being kidnapped and tortured by Arabs. She's clearly delirious. What the blazes has been going on?'

'Take it easy, Dick,' interrupted Jack.

They were in the kitchen of Gibbet Cottage. Corrie and Bugsy were sitting at the pine table while Carlene kept out of the way, making tea over by the hob. Jack strode about trying not to lose his temper with Dick who behaved like an even bigger twerp under pressure.

'Corrie was injured, too, you know; her shoulder was dislocated. And if it hadn't been for Carlene, I don't care to contemplate what might have happened.'

'It's all to do with the couple who owned this cottage before you,' chipped in Malone. 'We haven't been able to tell you until now but they make their living selling arms to countries like Libya, Egypt, Tunisia and Syria.'

Dick was dumbfounded. 'Do you mean to the governments or the insurgents trying to overthrow them?'

'Both,' said Malone. 'They'll trade with anyone who has the money.'

'But that's terrible. And to think they lived right here in this house; in this village '

'The men who came here this morning and abducted us thought Rosie was Saskia because of her blonde hair,' added Corrie. 'It seems the de Kuipers stole details of rebels trying to overthrow the government from the inside. They intended to sell to the highest bidder. The Arabs tried to make Rosie tell them where the list was hidden but of course, she didn't know.'

'Oh God, poor Rosie. She must have been terrified.' He looked at Jack. 'So that's what you were looking for when you were searching the house and grounds.'

'Right. And very soon officers from the Intelligence Agency will be here to search more thoroughly.' They'll take the place apart, thought Jack, including the thatch.

'You mean . . . the blasted thing's still here somewhere?'

'We believe so. The two Arabs who came this morning are both dead, but more could be on their way. The document they're after is red hot and many lives will be at stake if it gets into the wrong hands.'

Dick swallowed hard. 'So what you're saying is that we could all be murdered in our beds.' He looked at the mug of tea that Carlene had put in front of him. 'Thank you, dear, but I think I need something much stronger.'

Corrie wondered if this was a good time to tell him what had happened to his golf clubs.

The Anti-Terrorist Branch wanted a full report as soon as possible. The bodies of the dead Arabs were invisibly spirited away from the cider mill by Intelligence Agents who were well practised in making troublesome corpses vanish, no questions asked. Teams of operatives went about their business in Lullington Barrow with barely a ripple. Villagers who noticed anything unusual quickly decided it was just some nonsense caused by 'they daft city buggers' and it was safer to stay out of it.

As Jack predicted, agents began searching Gibbet Cottage with a thoroughness and professionalism that was breathtaking to watch. Furniture was taken outside and dismantled, electrical equipment was X-rayed and audio devices were deployed to locate any unusual tremors in places that were inaccessible. Sniffer dogs and their handlers quartered every room and two men climbed up on the thatched roof with long spikes and stabbed their way from one eave to the other. There was talk of removing the thatch altogether. In the two acres of woodland, a thin blue line of policemen poked their way slowly from one perimeter to the other, eyes riveted to the ground. Others climbed trees, hacked through brambles and waded in the stream. A firm specializing in liquid waste management was called in to empty the pond-cum-cesspit. Dick, Rosie and Jeremy had to move out into Hangman's Inn and had been warned to say nothing to a living soul, however trustworthy they believed them to be. Despite being told to stay clear, Dick trailed anxiously around after the agents, constantly reminding them that Gibbet Cottage was a Grade II listed building and as such, was protected both inside and out. All the period features, he told them, must be fully restored after they had finished their search. They ignored him until he got fed up and went away.

Bugsy's mate in the 'funny buggers' issued a chilling warning. 'Replacements for the dead revolutionaries are closer than you might think and they're likely to turn up at any time. You're up against some very dangerous and unpredictable people. Watch your backs.'

*

When Chief Superintendent George Garwood was informed of the situation by the deputy assistant commissioner, he had to sprint to the senior officers' private cloakroom as a matter of urgency. When he returned to his office some time later, he poured himself a very large Glenfiddich. Anything to do with national security filled him with trepidation. It was full of elephant traps of the kind that could wreck his career if things went wrong. Terrorist issues were the responsibility of the Intelligence Agencies and goodness knows there were enough of them. What the blazes did Dawes think he was playing at getting mixed up with Arab revolutionaries? And two of them were dead, by all accounts. Shot in the head. It couldn't get much worse and there was a promotion board looming in the autumn. Until now, he'd stood a good chance of climbing another rung up the ladder; something that was long overdue. And in his jaundiced opinion, the delay was caused mainly by the frequently unorthodox activities of Inspector Dawes. He phoned him, hoping to achieve some damage limitation. As soon as Jack answered his mobile, Garwood launched into a tirade.

'Inspector Dawes, you were assigned to investigate a couple of suspicious deaths in an insignificant Somerset village. They both turned out to be unfortunate accidents. But instead of returning to your duties here, I discover that you're knee deep in dead Arabs. What the hell's going on, man?'

'It's a long story, sir. Basically, my wife and her sister were kidnapped and tortured by revolutionaries who wanted to recover a list of pro-democracy sympathizers plotting to kill the dictator of a repressive regime before he got hold of it and had them all executed.'

'And did your wife and her sister hand over the names?' Garwood was beginning to think this was a particularly unpleasant nightmare and soon, Cynthia would wake him with a cup of tea.

'Well, no, sir. They never had it in the first place. You see, the list was originally stolen by a couple of arms traffickers who used to live in my sister-in-law's cottage. They were planning to sell it to the highest bidder. So far, we've been unable to locate it.'

Garwood's voice rose several octaves. 'You mean it's still there? And more Arabs could come looking for it?'

'That's what the Anti-Terrorist Branch believes. Unless, of course, the gunrunners come and snatch it back first.'

Garwood gulped. What had he done to deserve this? He liked nice, uncomplicated murders that got him good clear-up figures and positive press coverage. Prostitutes, gang leaders and drug dealers; the sort of people that the public didn't mind seeing bumped off.

'Dawes, you and Malone are to hand over all responsibility to the Intelligence Service and return here, immediately. Do you understand?'

'Well, I would, sir. Like a shot. But I've been told I have to remain here until the Foreign Secretary is satisfied that the threat of an international arms dispute between the UK, NATO and the Middle East is averted. He wants a full report on everything that's taken place. I believe the head of the Secret Intelligence Service – that's MI6 – is going to speak to the commissioner, then he'll brief the DAC who will speak to you. Hello, sir? Are you still there?'

The line had gone dead. DCS Garwood was hurrying back to the senior officers' private cloakroom.

CHAPTER FIFTEEN

Balancing precariously on the draining board with one foot in the sink, Edwina had her binoculars trained on Gibbet Cottage.

'Giles, there are two men on the roof next door, poking spikes into the thatch and I can see at least six more through their living room window and a whole host of them in the garden. They're wearing those white cover-all suits with hoods. What do you suppose they're up to?'

Giles was packing his rucksack with food, ready for yet another trip abroad. 'According to Peter who heard it from Dick in the pub, they're pest control operatives. It seems Dick and Rosie are infested with rats and cockroaches and various other unpleasant creatures, including bats. They've had to move into Hangman's Inn while the place is being fumigated.'

'Well, I hope they're not fumigating the bats. They're a protected species. I may have to start a protest campaign.'

'I wish you'd get down off there. Someone will see you.'

Edwina climbed down reluctantly. 'I'm a concerned member of the public. I'm entitled to know what's going on. What if the pests spread to our house?' She stood watching him pack, passing him things from the kitchen table. 'I wonder where Marcus has gone. Millie says he's left her. You and Peter are very thick with him; do you think he has?'

'No, course not. He's away on business, that's all. Millie's a bit emotional, even on a good day. She imagines all sorts of daft things. Marcus is a good bloke; he wouldn't just push off and leave her.'

Edwina was thoughtful for quite a long time. 'Giles, you wouldn't leave me, would you? Not without telling me why.'

Giles stopped packing and looked closely at her. 'Of course I wouldn't leave you, Weena. What's brought all this on?'

She looked guilty. 'I was emptying the pockets of your jacket before taking it to the cleaners. I wasn't spying on you, honestly. Anyway, I found your driving licence and as I was pulling it out, it fell open.

Giles, it said you've been licensed to drive an LGV for over a year. That's a lorry, isn't it? You must have taken a test but you never told me. Why would you want to drive a truck? You're a film producer.'

Giles answered almost at once but the slight hesitation, just for a heartbeat, told her he was lying. 'It's all the heavy film equipment, Weena. It needs to be transported abroad and we couldn't always get a qualified driver so I thought it would be more cost effective if I could drive it myself. I didn't tell you because you're not usually interested in that kind of thing.'

'So there's nothing wrong, then?'

'Nothing for you to worry about.' He kissed her. 'Now, I must dash or I'll miss the ferry. I'll be home in a couple of days.'

After he'd gone, Edwina stood looking out of the window at the men sifting minutely through Dick and Rosemary's lawn with rakes. They must be infested with moles as well. She wasn't a particularly sensitive woman, just the opposite, but she knew something in Lullington Barrow was very wrong. First Thomas Tincknell dies suddenly, then Father John. She had a feeling that something was about to happen which could eventually destroy the whole fabric of Gallows Green and she was scared.

On the opposite side of the green, Peter and Jane were sipping coffee and he was trying to peer out of the window without seeming to do so. They were further away from Gibbet Cottage than Giles and Edwina but it was impossible to ignore the activity.

'Pests,' said Peter, shortly.

Jane looked up from her magazine. 'Pardon?'

'Dick told me they were infested with pests and they've had to get Rentokil people in.'

Jane took off her spectacles. 'I may not be the sharpest knife in the drawer, Peter, but I know the difference between rat exterminators and forensic officers. I think they call it "turning the place over" in those police dramas.'

'I wonder what they're looking for,' he remarked ingenuously.

'Obviously not the same thing that you were looking for when you set fire to the Browns' loft with that smelly old pipe of yours. They'll be after something much more important.'

He looked shocked. 'How did you know that was me?'

'Of course I knew. Haven't I been telling you for ages that if you didn't knock your pipe out properly, you'd set fire to something? It was inevitable. I expect you put it down on one of those tea chests full of paper while you searched.'

'Yes, I did. Stupid of me. But I was desperate to find . . . well, you know what I was after.'

'I know, my dear, and I love you for it.'

'Aren't you worried that those security men might find it?' he asked anxiously.

'No, I've convinced myself that it went up in smoke in the Browns' loft and that's an end of it. And now Simon and Saskia have vanished, that's an incredible bonus and we've nothing more to worry about. I still wonder what it was that made them suddenly sell their house and take off like that but I'm very glad they did. They were evil through and through.'

'Do you think the police will want to question us, when they've finished "turning the place over"?'

'I don't know, Depends whether they think we might have had something to do with whatever it is they're looking for, doesn't it?'

Jane went back to her crossword and Peter went quiet, deep in thought. He was pretty certain he knew what they were after but he'd agreed with Giles and Marcus not to tell the women. Far safer if Jane knew nothing about it.

It didn't take long for Carmichael, the officer in charge of the operation, to get around to questioning the Gallows Green inhabitants. He stopped Giles just as he was leaving with his rucksack.

'I'm sorry, sir, but I shall have to ask you not leave the village; at least until the operation is concluded.'

'All right,' said Giles, shortly. 'But might I ask what all this is about?' Giles was sure he knew but it didn't hurt to have it confirmed.

'You may ask, sir, but I'm afraid I'm not at liberty to tell you. Not yet. Might I have a brief word with you and your wife?'

Giles and Edwina were adamant that they knew little about Simon and Saskia or what business they were in. The de Kuipers had spent much of their time travelling abroad and returned to Gibbet Cottage only briefly, seeming to treat it as a kind of country *pied à terre*. Because of this, people hadn't got to know them at all. They confirmed the story about the Gallows Green consortium buying the cottage cheaply and selling it on very rapidly to the Browns. They understood that the de Kuipers needed to move fast to close an important business deal and no, they had no idea what that deal was about. They hadn't asked. It was none of their business.

It was exactly the same with Peter and Jane. Their statement matched Giles and Edwina's virtually word for word. They assured him they would stay put until they received permission to move. When Carmichael and his team questioned Millie, however, she panicked and called Corrie.

'They keep asking me where Marcus has gone and I don't know! I told them he said he was going to Dubai but then he didn't. I don't think they believed me. I heard one of them say, 'She can't possibly be that dim. She's hiding something.' But I am dim, Corrie. You know I am. And I really can't tell them anything about Simon and Saskia or where Marcus has gone. I didn't dare tell them about the love letters and Saskia blackmailing me; they might have suspected me of doing away with her. Oh Corrie, please help me.'

'Millie, why don't you pack a few things and come and stay with us in Hangman's Inn?'

'But they said I wasn't to go anywhere without permission.'

'No, but I don't expect they'll mind as long as you stay in the village. I'll get Jack to speak to the officers and explain.'

'Oh yes, please. I'll come straight over.'

'Any luck, sir?' Dawes asked Carmichael. Gibbet Cottage had been virtually stripped down to how it must have looked nearly two centuries ago, when it was being constructed from lath, plaster and oak beams. Even the old cob walls had been exposed. Now they were in the double garage, digging up the concrete floor and dismantling shelves of car accessories and tools.

Carmichael looked exhausted. In the absence of anything more comfortable, he sank down onto an old metal box that his men had shoved out of the way while they dug up the garage floor. 'We haven't found a single clue as to where the de Kuipers have gone or where they hid the documents we're looking for. They seem to have vanished into thin air again and covered their tracks extremely well. It's something they're particularly good at. They've had plenty of practice.'

'They could have just taken the list with them when they legged it,' suggested Malone.

'Highly unlikely, in my experience,' said Carmichael. 'The de Kuipers are seasoned arms traffickers. They're well aware of the risks involved in trading with both sides during a revolution. In their business, if you want to stay alive, it isn't good practice to carry the merchandize around with you. If the Arabs catch you, they just take it and you're dead. No, they will be relying on keeping it hidden away to bargain with. That way, they survive; at least for a while.'

'Is there anywhere we haven't searched?' asked Dawes.

'I know what you're thinking,' said Carmichael. 'I'm missing something really obvious but believe me; we've taken this place apart down to the last nail and coat of paint. A mouse couldn't have escaped without being searched.' He fidgeted on the hard box. 'The answer's staring me in the face but I can't see it. Are you sure the Browns don't know anything?'

'Well, Rosemary Brown certainly doesn't. If she had, she'd have told the two Arabs who crushed her fingers. She was terrified. She'd have told them anything they wanted to know.'

Carmichael grimaced. 'She's certainly very voluble when she wants to be. As well as giving us a lurid account of her kidnap together with Mrs Dawes, she prattled on about her house being broken into and her furniture moved, utterly destroying her Feng Shui. Then she claimed her husband was attacked with a garden rake in the middle of the night and described the spontaneous combustion of her loft. It took one of my men an hour and a half to write it all down. She believes it was the work of marauding Arabs and demanded to know what the Secret Intelligence Service intends to do about it.'

Dawes smiled wryly. He could just imagine it. When she was really wound up, Rosie didn't allow anyone a word in edgeways. 'My wife's sister is a little highly strung and she's on a lot of medication at the moment but you can see her point. What happened to her was horrific and she's worried for her family. She has a young son. What if the Arabs had kidnapped and tortured him to make her talk?'

Carmichael scowled. 'I know, Inspector, it doesn't bear thinking about.' He scratched his head, desperate for some clues. 'What about that dapper little bloke – the husband? He's a merchant banker, isn't he? It could be a useful cover; access to global funding, off-shore accounts, all that kind of thing. He could be their cash-flow manager, providing the financial link between the Middle East and the UK. He wouldn't be the first international criminal whose wife didn't know what he was up to.'

Dawes glanced at Malone, who remained silent and deadpan. 'With the greatest respect, sir, Dick Brown's my brother-in-law and he's a good husband and father, but as a master criminal, he wouldn't know where to start.'

'I've met him and I agree, sir,' added Malone. 'I can smell a villain through a brick wall and Mr Brown's harmless. Pompous, toffee-nosed and tight-fisted, but harmless.'

'What about the rest of the neighbours? I questioned them about the de Kuipers and I got a kind of shifty feeling. Their statements were identical as if they'd rehearsed them beforehand; it came across as a communal secret that they'd made a pact not to reveal. Is it possible they know more than they're telling?'

'It's more than possible, sir, I'd put money on it. When I showed them the photo of the de Kuipers, they all flatly denied it was them; said something about Saskia de Kuiper having black hair although she's blonde, like Rosemary. Hence the Arabs' mistake with her identity.'

'What about the two suspicious deaths that happened here recently?' asked Carmichael, clutching at straws. 'Any connection there?'

Dawes shook his head. 'No, sir. One was a farmer gored to death by his bull and the other, a priest hit by a golf ball on his way home. Both accidental and accepted as such by the coroner.' Jack didn't feel it necessary to elaborate about the wife-beating and child abuse. No point muddying the waters; they were murky enough already.

'I'll like to interview that bloke who does a lot of business in the Arab States. The one who's married to the dim-witted blonde with the great legs.'

'That'll be Marcus,' said Malone. 'Unfortunately, we don't know where he is at present.'

'Of course you do, Sergeant. I'm right here.' It was Marcus's deep, cultured voice, edged with his usual debonair flippancy. Casual but immaculate in a leather jacket and designer jeans, he appeared in the doorway of the garage with Dick. 'I've been away on business but now I'm back and I can't find my wife. You haven't locked her up, have you? She's really quite innocent, you know.'

'She's staying at the Hangman's Inn with the Browns and Corrie,' said Jack. 'She needed some support – she was worried about you.'

'Seemed to think you'd left her to face the music, sir,' added Malone.

Marcus, smooth as ever, brushed it off. 'Silly girl. What man in his right mind would abandon someone as gorgeous as Millie? I'll go and reassure her and then I'm at your disposal,' he said to Carmichael. As he was leaving, he noticed the metal box. 'I see you managed to dredge up that old tank from the bottom of your soakaway, Dickie old man. I bet it was quite a struggle.'

Carmichael leaped up as if the metal had suddenly become red hot. He peered down at the deposit box on which he'd been sitting for the last half hour then swallowed hard. 'Where did this come from exactly, Mr Brown?'

Dick became defensive as he always did when he felt he was being criticized. 'It was buried in a stagnant pond in the middle of the coppice, Mr Carmichael. It's just an old deposit box. I managed to drag it out a couple of nights ago when I was clearing the jungle from my garden. That pond was full of the overflow from my cesspit. Clearly, I needed to get a waste disposal company to pump out the effluent but then your men came and did it anyway.' He gave the box a kick. 'This old tank could have sabotaged my entire drainage system. I expect the de Kuipers dumped it there. Appalling behaviour, I call it. Why couldn't they dispose of it responsibly? But what can you expect from mercenary people who make their living selling arms to filthy foreign countries? I think they should all be—'

'Why didn't you mention this before, Mr Brown?' asked Carmichael, cutting him off.

Dick took umbrage and resorted to sarcasm. 'Funnily enough, I'd forgotten all about it in the trauma of my wife being kidnapped and tortured and my home dismantled. The tank seems to be sealed up so I was going to rip it open with my angle-grinder in case there was anything important inside, then take it down to the local tip, but—' He saw the look on Carmichael's face and gulped. 'Oh my God. You don't think what you've been searching for is in there, do you?'

Carmichael was already on the phone to his team ordering oxy-acetylene equipment and balling them out for having missed something as simple as a metal box in the corner of the garage.

CHAPTER SIXTEEN

Carmichael sent everyone away except Dawes and Malone and a small team of his own. They all stood back as an engineer in protective clothing and goggles applied the oxy-acetylene torch to the edges of the strongbox. The flame cut through the metal like a hot knife through ice cream and in minutes, the box was in two halves. Several packages wrapped in a protective covering fell out, each one neatly labelled. Carmichael reached for the largest one that bore the name of a well-known terrorist organization. He pulled out a formidable knife from inside his jacket and ripped the package open. There were many hard-backed files inside containing Dutch and American bonds, probably forged, some elaborate plans, maps and photographs of the munitions compounds of Middle Eastern countries with DVDs and details of arms deals done with known Al Qaeda sympathizers in exchange for heroin. It was the kind of data that could never be securely trusted to the memory of a computer. One parcel revealed a considerable amount of hard cash in 500 euro notes. Skittering around in the bottom of the container were two serious handguns of the kind carried by the two Arabs and which they had subsequently used for their execution. It was quite a haul. Carmichael sifted carefully through the contents while the others waited in silence. Finally, he held up a single page of typescript and whooped triumphantly.

'This is it, guys!' In his hand he held the names of leading pro-democracy dissidents within the security forces of a repressed regime; in the government's hands, this document was tantamount to a death warrant. 'The dictator and his sons would have paid the de Kuipers megabucks for this.'

Dawes and Malone examined some of the stuff. 'This looks like an arms dealer's survival kit,' said Dawes. 'Money and guns for immediate subsistence and enough insurance to generate a steady income after they had established themselves elsewhere.'

'Probably the US or Netherlands, if these bonds are anything to go by. They could have carried on trading from there with hardly a break and accessed all their other funds held elsewhere,' observed Carmichael.

'Why didn't they come back for this stuff?' asked Malone. 'It's worth a fortune.'

'Maybe they tried,' said Jack.

'Maybe they're still trying,' added Carmichael, grimly. What if your sister-in-law was right and Mr Brown really was attacked that night in his garden? It could have been Simon de Kuiper back to recover this deposit box from the pond where he'd dumped it for safety. Then all the burglar alarms went off and he found he was being chased by someone. He clouted his pursuer with the nearest weapon, a garden rake, and legged it, hoping to come back later when the heat had died down.'

'So what's our next move, sir?' asked Dawes.

'As far as you're concerned, there isn't one, Inspector,' said Carmichael. 'We're grateful for your help and the excellent leads you've given us but now our objective is to find and detain the de Kuipers. They don't know we've got their stash so my guess is that one or both of them will make another attempt to retrieve it and very soon. I propose to stake out Gibbet Cottage and wait for them to return. Obviously, this has to be a strictly covert operation and the fewer people who know about it, the better; for everyone's safety. It's a toss-up who'll get here first; the de Kuipers or more Arab revolutionaries. Either way, we'll be ready for them. '

Malone was an old-school copper; he nicked the villains who broke the law and he was no stranger to violent death in all its sickening forms. But all this talk of Arab uprisings, torture and executions left him seriously out of his comfort zone and he could feel his blood sugar dropping. He was more than happy to leave it to the 'funny buggers'. He pulled a jumbo Mars bar from his trouser pocket, peeled back the wrapper and bit off the first third. 'Guess that's you and me finished here, then, Jack,' he mumbled through a mouthful of sticky caramel.

'Not quite.' Dawes was poking around in the bottom of the deposit box. When the guns and ammunition had been carefully extracted and placed in secure bags, there was another package, simply labelled 'Gallows Green'. He offered it to Carmichael who did the business with his cutthroat dagger then looked at the miscellaneous junk that fell out; a bundle of letters, photos, CDs, accounts sheets, planning applications and, screwed up at the bottom, a birth certificate. Carmichael glanced at this last item briefly but the names didn't mean anything. He lost interest and tossed the items to Dawes. 'Looks like some local stuff the de Kuipers picked up from their neighbours. Maybe you'd like to sort it out. I'm pretty sure they're nothing to do with our operation but if you find anything significant, let me know.' He strode away to arrange for Gibbet Cottage to be hastily restored so that it appeared normal, at least on the surface, and to set up the surveillance which was to be named 'Operation Blondie' after Saskia de Kuiper.

That evening in Hangman's Inn, Dawes and Malone sat in a booth in the snug bar with the various items from the strongbox spread out on the table.

'What d'you reckon these were doing in that box, Guv?' asked Bugsy. 'Looks like a load of old junk to me.'

'Me too. But it couldn't have been junk to the de Kuipers or why would they have hidden it there next to the really valuable stuff?'

Corrie poked her head around the corner of the booth. She was carrying a tray of drinks. 'May we join you, gentlemen? Rosie's feeling a little better and I think it'd do her good to join in a bit and try to forget her ordeal.' They slid into the bench seat, Rosemary holding her heavily bandaged fingers aloft so as not to catch them on anything. Her black eye was a real shiner, all the colours of the rainbow, and her swollen cheek made her face look lopsided.

'Dick's here too,' she said. 'He's fretting about our cottage and how it will be depreciating in value at about ten grand a minute.'

Corrie glanced sideways at Jack and he pulled a face back.

Dick looked pale. 'Millie's gone back home with Marcus and Jeremy's asleep upstairs so there's just us now.'

'And me.' Carlene wriggled into the tiny space beside Bugsy. While they were sorting out their drinks, she rummaged about among the objects on the table and Bugsy noticed her damaged knuckles. They were obviously painful and even though he couldn't see the state of her grazed knees under her jeans, he suspected they were worse. Most kids would have whinged but Carlene hadn't complained once. She had guts, this one, and he admired that, but privately, he was sad for the tough life she must have experienced to make her that way.

'What's this, then?' Carlene picked up the bundle of letters. 'These look like the love letters Millie was goin' on about.' Before Corrie could stop her, she'd pulled one out of the envelope. 'Blimey! This is 'ot stuff. Listen. 'My darlin' Simon. I'm achin' to feel your hard—'

'Yes, thank you, Carlene,' interrupted Corrie hastily. 'I don't think we should be reading someone else's letters, do you?' She leaned across and muttered in Carlene's ear. 'Not out loud, anyway.'

Carlene grinned. 'You can see why Millie didn't want 'er old man to get 'old of 'em, though. Where d'you find 'em, Mr Jack? Millie finks Mrs Brown 'ad 'em.'

Dick's expression was of sanctimonious outrage. 'I wasn't aware that Camilla had been conducting an extra-marital affair with Simon de Kuiper,' he declared, pompously. He turned to Rosie. 'Did you know about this, Rosemary? Has somebody informed Marcus? I really think he has a right to see these letters because—'

'Dick, shut up!' said Rosie, sharply. 'You don't know what you're talking about.'

He stared at her, shocked; opened his mouth to argue, then closed it again. Since her ordeal, Rosie seemed to have acquired a strength of character that he didn't know she possessed and he found it rather alarming.

Jack decided that since everyone round the table was fully aware of the present situation and most of them had been involved, sometimes painfully, they were entitled to know what had been going on.

'That metal deposit box you dredged up from the bottom of your cesspit, Dick, contained the information the Arabs were after. It must have been dumped there by the de Kuipers when they made their sudden getaway. It was full of money, guns and other valuable documents. It's all in the hands of MI6.'

Dick breathed a sigh of relief. 'Thank goodness for that. I didn't relish being hacked to pieces or wearing my kneecaps on a chain round my neck.'

Rosie shuddered. 'You don't need to be quite so graphic, Dick. Some of us have already suffered at the hands of mad Arabs.'

'Sorry, darling.' He tried to hold her hand but she squealed and glared at him with her good eye.

Corrie picked up one of the photos. It was a fairly new one and showed a man opening the tailgate of an articulated lorry in what looked like a big city. The licence plate was clearly visible as was the load in the back; several crates of guns and ammunition. In the background, there was a road sign in Dutch. The driver looked shocked and was staring straight into the camera as if it had just flashed. Corrie held it up for the others to see. 'Isn't that Giles?'

They all looked. 'Yes, it is,' agreed Rosie. 'But what's he doing driving a lorry full of guns? I thought he was a film producer.'

'Maybe he's making an undercover documentary exposing illegal gun trafficking,' offered Dick, lamely. 'You know . . . like they do on *Panorama*.'

'Yes, and maybe, just maybe, he's up to his neck in the de Kuipers' racket,' said Malone.

'That's impossible,' said Rosie. 'He's one of our friends. Surely we'd have known.'

'All the same, Jack, I think we should hand this over to Carmichael,' said Bugsy.

'This other photograph's much older,' said Corrie. It was another picture of a lorry. The driver standing beside it was wearing overalls and holding the hand of a skinny little girl aged about six or seven. 'There's writing on the back. It says, "To Edna, love Dad," and it's dated 1982.' The sharp, ferret-like features of the girl had changed very little over the last thirty years. Corrie passed the photo to Jack. 'Look, it's Edwina.'

'But that can't be her dad,' said Rosie. 'She told us he was a diplomat. Very important in the government. This man's a lorry driver.'

Carlene was looking at the crumpled birth certificate. It said the baby was called Michael and he was born on 5 August, 1972. His mother's name was Jane. She looked to see who his father was. Her own mum had given Carlene her birth certificate before they took her away to the booze clinic and there'd been a blank space where her dad's name should have been. She reckoned her mum hadn't known who he was, not for sure. Now, she read the name of this baby, Michael's, father, and did a double take: it wasn't Jane's husband, Peter. Although Carlene was only seventeen, where she came from in Hackney, the man who was named on this certificate was a legend. He'd been a notorious criminal, famous in his day for ruling the underworld in the East

End of London with savage violence. Some of the stories she'd been told had given her nightmares as a child. The workers in the children's home used to say he'd come in the night and nail her to the floor her if she didn't behave. When she heard he'd died in prison where he was serving a life sentence, she'd been so relieved. But what was this certificate doing in the de Kuipers' stash? Wordlessly, she passed it to Corrie, who glanced at the names and gulped. Then she squirrelled it secretly away in her handbag under the table. Her expression warned Carlene not to say anything.

'All these objects seem to be local,' said Jack. 'Does anyone recognize anything else?'

Dick, predictably, was looking at the accounts sheets. 'I've seen these before. They're copies of the accounts of the parish council signed off by Donald Draycott who was the treasurer before me. Even a cursory glance confirms my original view that there are some serious discrepancies here. Draycott had been syphoning off funds on a regular basis. But I don't understand why. Everyone says he was an honest man and a brilliant teacher. Why was he so desperate for money that he'd fiddle the books? It must have gone against all his principles.'

'I think I can guess why,' said Corrie. 'Look at this photo.' She held it up. It showed a man and a woman in a loving embrace. They were having a picnic in a field of bluebells and looked very happy. They were clearly unaware that someone was snapping them.

'Who are they, Corrie?' asked Rosie. 'I don't recognize either of them.'

'That's because they'd both left the village before you arrived. Their names have been scribbled on the back; it's Donald Draycott and Patsy Tincknell.'

'So they *were* having an affair, just as Doctor Brimble and the more prurient members of the village suspected,' said Dick. 'And eventually, they ran off together.'

'So would you, if you was married to a vicious old scrote like Thomas Tincknell,' observed Carlene. 'You wouldn't 'ang about until 'e found out and 'ammered you to death.'

'Pretty obvious what the de Kuipers were doing with all this stuff.' Bugsy was munching a sausage roll and sprayed the table liberally with shards of puff pastry. 'A nice sideline in blackmail. What a diamond couple they must be.'

'And when poor old Draycott couldn't keep up the payments, he fiddled the parish accounts to protect Patsy,' said Jack.

'This CD is just labelled "Marcus",' said Rosie, picking it up. 'Hard to imagine anything incriminating on it, he's so charming and debonair.'

'They're the ones you have to watch,' said Bugsy. 'Now why doesn't this one surprise me?' He stabbed at a photo with a stubby forefinger. 'It's a picture of your friend and mine, Police Constable Gilbert Chedzey, taking a wodge of wonga from a motorist he's pulled over into a layby on the A38.'

'Maybe it's perfectly lawful,' protested Dick, pathetically.

'Yeah, and maybe I'm Barack Obama,' countered Bugsy. 'I reckon PC Chedzey was operating his own system of on-the-spot fines and the de Kuipers caught him at it.'

For the next hour, they sifted carefully and surreptitiously through all the material, concealing it quickly when Liz Boobyer came over to ask if they wanted more drinks. More and more startling revelations came to light: a slightly out of focus picture of Ted Boobyer with his hand up Dani's skirt and copies of forged immigration papers maintaining she was Polish although Corrie and Carlene both knew she had entered the UK illegally from Albania with Boobyer's corrupt help.

Undoubtedly the most repulsive picture was of Father John, taken through the window of his study in the parochial house. He was clearly masturbating over scenes of child pornography on his laptop and was too engrossed to notice he was being observed and recorded. Even from the blurred images on the screen, it was easy to recognize the handsome little blond boy and what was being done to him. He was wide-eyed with fear and obviously crying bitterly.

It went very quiet and nobody spoke for a long time. Then Rosie said she felt sick.

'Oh Dick, that poor child. Why didn't any of us realize what he was going through and help him? I feel so guilty; and when I think how that vile priest wanted our Jeremy to join the choir, become an altar server. He was – what do they call it? – grooming him for abuse.'

Corrie shook her head. 'He'd never have succeeded, Rosie. Any inappropriate behaviour and Jeremy would have fought him off like a tiger then run straight home and told you. Think about it. Jeremy couldn't be coerced by threats of eternal damnation and ex-communication because he knows it's all manipulative rubbish.'

'If that priest were still alive, I'd go round there and give him a bloody good hiding,' said Dick, savagely. 'Whoever hit that golf ball off the thirteenth tee did society a favour.'

Seeing his grim expression, Jack believed that for once, Dick really meant what he said.

'I still reckon someone welted the dirty old bugger,' mumbled Carlene.

'Does anyone know anything about planning applications?' asked Corrie, anxious to change the subject before everyone became irredeemably depressed. 'This one seems to be for a housing development on the edge of Lullington Barrow. There's a letter with it confirming that a rather large amount of cash has been paid into the bank account of the Chair of the parish council in return for signing the approval document.'

Dick held his head in his hands. 'Not Edgar Brimble, too. Is there no one in this village with any integrity at all?' It was a rhetorical question. He took Rosie's hand very gently. 'What have we done, Rosie? We've moved from a city of crime and corruption into a village that's even worse. It's just less obvious, that's all.'

What do you suppose we'll find on these DVDs, Bugsy?' asked Jack, picking up a handful.

'At a guess, films of people doing things they wouldn't want anyone else to know about.' Bugsy took a long pull at his pint. 'What are we going to do with all this stuff, Guv?'

Jack thought for a bit. 'Most of it's personal and as such, it's of no concern to the police and we'd be within our authority to dispose of it. Where a crime may have been committed, we have to follow it up. Father John has already been taken care of and by now, his bishop will have some serious questions to answer. Draycott's long gone and the police computer has been unable to trace his whereabouts. Doctor Brimble may have to answer bribery charges but that's for the council to deal with and out of our jurisdiction. I'll leave you, Bugsy, to interrogate PC Chedzey about his unorthodox interpretation of the Road Traffic Act. That just leaves Boobyer's sexual harassment, Marcus's CD, Millie's letters and some strange photos of Giles and Edwina.'

And, thought Corrie, the birth certificate in her handbag that clearly had serious repercussions for Peter and Jane and more to the point, for their son, Michael.

'Why don't we just post the personal items through the relevant letterboxes?' suggested Dick. 'Then they don't need to know we've seen them.'

'That's a terrible idea!' squealed Rosie.

Dick was puzzled. 'I don't see why.'

'No, you wouldn't,' she said scathingly. 'What if Marcus picks up the letters instead of Millie? What if Edwina doesn't want Giles to see the photo of her with her lorry-driver dad? What if Liz Boobyer doesn't know Ted is trying it on with Dani? Have you any idea how many relationships we could destroy simply by chucking confidential things through letterboxes, just any old how? I can't believe you even suggested it, Dick.'

Dick bridled. 'All right, so what *do* we do with it, then? We've no clear idea what the implications are for most of it. I mean, what about Marcus's CD? That could have all sorts of irregularities on it. And what have Dani's immigration papers got to do with anything? I think, as Jack is a police detective, he should sort it all out.'

'May I make a suggestion?' Corrie desperately needed to circumvent this. She still hadn't worked out how she was going to handle Dani's forged papers and now the birth certificate was an added complication. Once Jack got control, any ability she had to negotiate some damage limitation would be lost. Jack would say she was interfering again, but she sensed some really life-changing events were happening here. 'What if we invite the Gallows Green crowd to a meal, here in Hangman's Inn? Gibbet Cottage is out of bounds while MI6 are staking out Operation Blondie so we can't have it there. While everyone is round the supper table, Rosie and I could give back the items surreptitiously, with the least harm done.'

'Why not just stop 'em in the street when they're on their own and hand it to 'em?' asked Bugsy. Ever the pragmatic copper, he couldn't see a reason for all the subterfuge. In his book, if you'd been up to naughties, you admitted it and took your punishment, which could explain why he'd never had a lasting relationship.

'Because, Bugsy, they never *are* on their own in the street, are they? It could take months and it'd be very messy.'

'Corrie's right. I think we should do the supper. How about

Saturday?' said Rosie. 'I'll ask Liz Boobyer if we can book the private dining room.'

'I could 'elp wiv the grub, if she wants,' offered Carlene.

'What do you think, Jack?' asked Corrie.

Jack knew better than to take on the female Mafia. 'Seems as good a suggestion as any.'

CHAPTER SEVENTEEN

'Okay, what did you do with it?' Jack and Corrie had gone to their room at half past one, worn out mentally but unable to sleep.

'Sorry, I don't know what you mean,' said Corrie, all wide-eyed and innocent. 'What did I do with what?'

'The birth certificate. It fell out of the Gallows Green package when Carmichael slit it open and it was on the table in the pub. I saw Carlene pick it up and look at it, then she slipped it to you. After that, it vanished. I'm not a detective for nothing, you know.'

'Oh Jack, you aren't going to be difficult, are you? I have to give it back to Jane at the private supper on Saturday. It's really important.' She pulled the cork from a rather decent bottle of Bordeaux that she'd picked up at the bar. 'Would you like a nightcap, darling?'

Jack took the glass she offered him but he knew Corrie too well to be bamboozled by booze. 'So whose birth certificate is it?'

'I think it's Jane's son, Michael. Peter told me at the barbecue that he was a rising star in the government, tipped to become the next Home Secretary.'

'Good for him,' said Jack, tasting his wine.

'No, it won't be. Not if this certificate gets into the wrong hands – such as the tabloid press or the Opposition.'

'Why? Did he lie about his age and he's actually ten years younger than the prime minister thinks? I don't see it makes any difference. Most rising star politicians look about sixteen these days. Hardly important enough for the de Kuipers to blackmail Peter and Jane. '

'It's much worse than that. And there's something you don't know about Dani, too, but I don't want to tell you, yet.'

'Okay. As long as she didn't get fed up with Ted groping her and put his dick in the lemon slicer, I don't need to know. And even if she had, it'd take me a very long time to get around to charging her. I'm sure you and your mate in the Licensed Victuallers can stitch up Ted

Boobyer and his gaping flies.'

Corrie was silently thinking that it would be the Border Control Agency not the Licensed Victuallers who would be dealing with Ted Boobyer when the time came. 'Jack, why do you think Simon and Saskia collected all that dreadful information about their neighbours? They're multimillion-pound arms traffickers working for a massive organization of racketeers in the States. They don't need a few quid from blackmail, surely?'

Jack helped himself to a top-up. 'I wondered about that, too. Bugsy reckoned it was spite. When they first came to Lullington Barrow, they were treated like pariahs because they were 'incomers'. They took exception to that so they thought they'd get their own back by finding out the villagers' dirty little secrets and putting the screws on them; watching them squirm. Because they're intrinsically evil, it would have been more for amusement than profit although they must have made a fair whack when you consider how many people were paying them; and that's just the ones we know about.'

'And it would explain why the whole village disliked them so much and were glad when they moved away.'

'Exactly.' Jack swirled his wine, thoughtfully. 'Of course, we still can't be sure they did move away. They may still be hiding out somewhere nearby, waiting to retrieve their very valuable stash, or—'

'. . . they might be dead. Done away with by one or more of their "blackmailees". Maybe they formed a Gallows Green Murder Consortium. Although the Arabs obviously believe the de Kuipers are still alive.'

'Hmm. But then, they wouldn't necessarily know any different, would they?'

Sergeant Malone had been speaking on his mobile for some time. His face was grim as he finally switched it off and stood looking at it. This was a decision that he'd really hoped he wouldn't have to make and for once, the way forward wasn't entirely clear; which was the way he usually saw things. He went to find Inspector Dawes who was tying up loose ends prior to the Saturday night supper, after which he hoped they could all go back home to a semblance of civilization. Now that Carmichael and his men had taken control and were lying in wait for the de Kuipers, there was nothing left for MIT to do. Bugsy found

Jack sitting outside Hangman's Inn on an uncomfortable wrought-iron bench, among the flower tubs that Carlene had nearly demolished with the Cadillac. He was examining some of the items from the deposit box more closely, in particular, Dani's immigration papers. Bugsy sat beside him.

'Jack, do you remember when we searched what was left of St Mary's Church after the flood? I took a sample of the soil from beneath the sacrarium and sent it to the lab.'

'Yep. The sample's come back negative, has it? I'm not surprised. Impossible to find anything after the sea had been all over it, even if there'd been something to find. Never mind, Bugsy. It was worth the effort to ensure a thorough investigation.' Jack went on sifting through the papers. When Bugsy didn't say anything, he looked up and read his expression.

'So they did find something? What was it, mate?'

'They found very faint traces of blood; hardly any at all really. I doubt if it would be enough to prove anything.' He stared out across the Green. 'The blood and DNA matched Father John's although the lab boys said the sample had been contaminated with sodium hypochlorite and as such, it wasn't a hundred per cent reliable.'

'Aah.' Jack was silent while he took in the implications. 'So what are you thinking?'

'That young Sherlock was right all along. Someone "lamped the old perv". Caught him in the sacristy with young Aleksy and administered their own version of the wrath of God. Then they used bleach to wash the blood away down the sacrarium, not knowing that a freak tide would surge through the church during the night and cleanse everything for them. Then they dragged his body outside and left it lying across the path so it looked like he'd been hit by a golf ball; the one they'd already smeared with his blood and thrown into the long grass where they knew the police would find it. My problem, Jack, is that I'm not sure I wouldn't have done the same thing myself. What that so-called Shepherd of God had been doing to little kids over the years was despicable. In my book, it was much worse than what was done to him and I admit I can't work up the enthusiasm to try and nick the killer.'

'Hang on a minute, Bugsy. Don't let's jump to conclusions. If what you suspect is true, what was the murder weapon and where is it now? It'd be almost impossible to cause fatal blunt force trauma by just bashing someone over the head with a golf ball in your hand. But Forensics said Father John's skull was fractured by something small, round and hard, consistent with a flying golf ball. And if he was dragged all the way from behind the chancel of the church, down the nave, through the cemetery and across the path, why wasn't there a trail of blood? The only blood they found was right there, on the spot where he died.'

'They could have put a bin liner, or something, over his head.'

'You're saying this was a spur-of-the-moment killing, unplanned and spontaneous? How many people carry bin liners and bleach around with them, never mind a heavy object shaped like a golf ball? You're the only person I know who goes about with a constant supply of plastic bags on his person. Listen, Bugsy, how about this for a different scenario? Suppose Father John was in his sacristy doing what you said he was meant to be doing, cleansing the sacramental *wossnames* under the tap in the sacrarium, and he cuts his thumb on a sharp bit? His blood runs down the sacred drain and soaks into the earth, contaminated by the household bleach that's been used to disinfect the basin.'

'But, Guv, there aren't any sharp bits on the sacred vessels. They're kept polished and immaculate. And Father John's autopsy didn't mention any cuts on his fingers.'

'Bugsy, it could have been a tiny puncture wound; enough to make him bleed but easily missed by a pathologist. Think about it. Don't you reckon that's a plausible explanation?' Jack gave him a friendly shove. 'Stop worrying, mate; in this job, you have to accept that sometimes, fate metes out the justice.'

Malone looked much more cheerful. 'You're right, Jack.' He hauled himself to his feet, pulled a chunk of genuine cheese from Cheddar out of one pocket and a pickled onion from the other and crammed them both into his mouth at once. 'I'm going to find PC Chedzey and give him the good news that if I have my way, he can kiss his pension goodbye.' He trotted off with more than a spring in his step.

Inspector Dawes remained on the bench for a while, deep in thought. He was a first-class detective and even as he'd said it, he'd known very well what kind of person would carry bleach and bin liners around on them – and rubber gloves. And as for fingerprints, he knew that if he was inclined to check, he'd find the prints of the person he had in mind all over most of the larger buildings in Lullington Barrow, including the church and the golf club. But as Corrie would have pointed out, in addition to being a first-class detective, Jack Dawes was also a first-class human being. He stood up, rubbed the life back into his numb backside and went to see how Carmichael was doing.

DS Malone found PC Gilbert Chedzey in the garden of his neat, well-appointed police house, watering his dahlias, which he hoped would take first prize in the Lullington Barrow Flower Show in August. *Dahlias, Pompon, not exceeding 52mm, six blooms* – he'd won the cup for the last ten years. The Flower Show and the Harvest Supper were the two most important events in Chedzey's calendar. As Malone approached, he put down his watering can and bustled officiously to meet him. He didn't like these London police officers muscling in on his village, making him look like an ineffective country bumpkin, and he'd been waiting for an opportunity to get his own back. Now he had his chance and he was going to make the most of it. He'd show 'em he wasn't the village idiot!

'Ah, Sergeant Malone, I'm glad I've caught 'ee. 'Tiz about that young woman o' yourn what come up on the train from London. Carlene, I believe she's called.'

'What about her?' snapped Malone.

'As I understand it, she's barely seventeen. For that reason, I'm assumin' she don't 'ave a valid driving licence and 'asn't passed her test, yet she were seen by a number o' folk driving a gurt big foreign car up to Hangman's Inn with two passengers in it. I'm sure you don't need me to remind 'ee, Sergeant, that drivin' without a licence is a serious offence likely to incur between three and six penalty points and a maximum fine of £1,000.' Chedzey was in his element now, confident he had the moral and legal high ground and looking forward to seeing the look on this fat, scruffy sergeant's face after he'd wiped the floor with him. 'Tiz more'n likely the magistrates'll ban her from obtainin' a licence for a long time and even when 'er do get one, she'll find 'er insurance bloody expensive for at least five years, that's if she can get anyone to insure 'er at all. We takes the Road Traffic Act a mite serious in this village and we clamp down on folk breakin' the law. I 'opes you've taken the proper steps to 'ave this young woman charged with—' Chedzey froze. DS Malone had pulled a photograph from his inside pocket and was holding it up in front of the constable. It was the one that showed him taking a bundle of notes from a motorist at the kerbside. Chedzey had hoped that now the de Kuipers had gone, and he no longer had to pay them hush money, all that nasty business was over; he wouldn't hear any more about it. How the hell had this bloody London copper got hold of it?

'Can you explain what's taking place here, Constable? And before you answer, I should make it clear that this motorist is being traced by automatic number plate recognition and he will be questioned about the money he's handing over and why. Have you anything to add?'

Chedzey's manner changed instantly from bolshy to sycophantically smarmy. 'You know how it is, Sergeant. We're all men o' the world. A constable's pay hardly covers the essentials, these days . . .' never mind blackmail payments, he thought grimly. 'You 'ave to make a bit extra where you can, 'tiz the perks o' the job. I'm sure you'll see your way clear to—'

Malone went for the jugular. 'Were you aware that Father John was sexually abusing the choirboys? A straight answer, yes or no!'

Chedzey swallowed hard. 'Well, I wouldn't say I was aware, exactly. I mean, you 'ave to expect a bit o' hanky-panky with Catholic priests, don't 'ee? They're all a bit . . . you know.' He flapped a limp wrist to illustrate his point. 'Comes of all that celibacy nonsense. It's not natural. Stands to reason, they 'ave to get it somewhere, don't they?'

'So you knew he was making children's lives a living hell in this village, but you didn't do anything about it?'

Chedzey became defensive then and lapsed even further into dialect. 'It weren't my job, were it? It's church business, innum? The bishop's concern. Don't tell I, tell 'ee!'

'Police Constable Chedzey, you're a disgrace to your uniform, which, I'm glad to say, you won't be wearing for much longer.'

Chedzey was horrified. 'But Sergeant, I retires in six months. The wife's looking forward to a little bungalow in Burnham-on-Sea when we lose this police house. We've got grandchildren to see after and a timeshare in Magaluf.'

'Paid for out of the bribes you've been taking, no doubt.' Malone put the photo back in his pocket. 'You'll be hearing from your senior officer in Portishead very soon.' He strode away, leaving Chedzey wondering how everything had gone so badly wrong. He'd been the local bobby in Lullington for over thirty years and it'd been a nice, cushy little number. The villagers looked up to him; he was the symbol of law and order, but he didn't have to do very much. Now shame and disgrace stared him in the face. Bloody incomers! Why couldn't they go back where they came from and leave everybody alone?

Malone fumed as he walked away. Police officers like Chedzey were the lowest form of pond life and earned them all a bad name. He was a lazy, corrupt bugger and he deserved everything he'd undoubtedly get. Soon, he'd be out of the service officially and until then, Malone suspected he'd be told to take sick leave. He wouldn't be around to take any more backhanders or do any harm to young Sherlock.

As he rounded the bend in Gallows Green Lane, Bugsy spotted Aleksy skipping towards his mother and his home at Hangman's Inn. The lad was a different chap since Father John's death. The failed responsibility of adults to protect Aleksy weighed heavily on Bugsy and he felt the police, at least, owed him an apology.

'Hello there, Aleksy. Can we have a chat, son?' Malone was horrified to see the boy recoil and back away; the cheery round face suddenly wary.

'No, it's all right, honestly. I'm a copper, I work with Inspector Dawes, look . . .' he fished in his pocket for his warrant card and held it out. That bastard of a priest had made the child terrified of any man who approached him. 'I know it says my name's Michael Malone but my friends call me Bugsy.'

Aleksy looked, recognized Bugsy from Hangman's Inn and decided it was all right. They sat down on the grassy bank and Bugsy produced some fluff-covered toffees from a sticky bag in his trouser pocket, offered one to Aleksy and popped one in his own mouth. For a few moments, they chewed in companionable silence.

'Leksy, when you've been a policeman for a very long time, like me, you make yourself believe you can deal with anything. That's what we do. That's what we're paid to do, and that's what the public expect of us. You become thick-skinned, cynical, world-weary. Do you know what those words mean, son?'

'I think so.'

'Then something happens to another human being. Something that lives in your worst nightmares. Something that you can't make right.

Something that I don't have the stomach even to describe. What I'm trying to say is that I'm sorry. Sorry that we weren't there when Father John hurt you. Sorry that we didn't stop it happening in the first place. Sorry for the mother who spawned the bastard and the bishop who knew about it but let it go on happening.' Malone glanced sideways at Leksy who was staring down at his sandals. 'I know it's not good enough, son, not by a long way, but I just wanted to say it.'

Aleksy stood up, smiled and offered Bugsy his hand. They shook, solemnly.

'Thank you, Sergeant Bugsy.' The child skipped away.

CHAPTER EIGHTEEN

Inspector Dawes stole unobtrusively through the woodland behind Gibbet Cottage to check how Operation Blondie was progressing. He was expecting a low-key police presence and a semblance of normality so as not to alert the de Kuipers if and when they returned. Instead, there was vigorous activity amongst the lush green grass and around the stagnant pond where the deposit box had been found. There were large areas taped off as crime scenes within which dogs were barking and straining on the leash. Carmichael was striding around the woodland, shouting orders to his men who were assembling on the green area with spades. A number of forensics experts in the customary white coveralls hovered on the perimeter, ready to move in when summoned. It was bedlam and nobody even noticed Jack's arrival. If the de Kuipers turned up now, they'd turn straight around and be long gone before anyone realized they'd come. Dawes approached Carmichael to find out what was going on.

'Has there been a development, sir?'

Carmichael turned. 'Ah, Inspector Dawes. Yes, there has. I believe we may have found the de Kuipers at last.' He gestured towards the excited German Shepherds. 'The cadaver dogs have located human remains under that patch of grass. As you can see, it's unusually green compared to the rest of the ground, nourished, we think, by decomposing corpses. The size of the area indicates there may be more than one body buried there. My men are about to dig but I'm pretty sure we've found our gunrunners. Looks like the Arabs got to them before we did.'

Dawes wasn't so certain. He'd been here in Lullington Barrow longer than Carmichael and he'd found it a disturbing village full of disturbing people. It wasn't at all impossible that someone in the village had killed Simon and Saskia and goodness knows, there were enough motives to suspect a dozen people. 'But why did those two Arabs turn up here and mistake Mrs Brown for Saskia if they knew the de Kuipers were already dead and buried?'

Carmichael shrugged. 'Maybe the other side got to them first; that's the dictator's followers rather than the pro-democracy lot. It wouldn't surprise me if, when we dig them up, we find they were tortured to death because the dictator wouldn't pay them the money they were asking so they refused to hand over the list. And because the dictator didn't immediately start executing all the rebels in his security forces, the insurgents took that to mean he hadn't yet managed to get hold of their names and therefore the de Kuipers were still alive, so they sent Mohamed and his chum to find them, fast. Does that make sense to you, Jack?'

'Quite frankly, sir, nothing that goes on in this village makes sense to me but I'll try and keep up.' Privately, Jack didn't doubt for a moment that Arabs would have killed them without hesitation, but would they have hung about afterwards to bury the bodies? Probably not.

'What's going on, Jack? Why are these men digging up my lawn?' Dick Brown had spotted Jack making his way over to Gibbet Cottage and decided that as he owned the property, he was entitled to see what the authorities were doing to his house and land.

'Mr Brown, I thought I asked you to stay out of the way until this operation was over,' said Carmichael. But then one of his officers called to him urgently. 'We've found them, sir.'

He hurried over with Jack and Dick close behind. They ducked under the tape and reached the exhumation just as the first skeleton was uncovered.

'This one's had the top of his head blown off with a shotgun at point-blank range,' announced the forensics chief. He held up part of a skull with strands of hair still clinging to it.

'Catch him, someone!' called Carmichael. Two men grabbed Dick as he blenched, reeled and went into a free-fall lawn descent. He was frogmarched away without ceremony.

'Wait a minute,' warned Carmichael, as they carefully disinterred the other skeleton, which had been carelessly thrown in beside the first. He approached the forensics expert. 'How much can you tell me about these remains right now, before you take them to the lab?'

The man pursed his lips. 'Not much, yet. The skeletons are of a man and a woman, in their forties I'd say; only an educated guess, you understand. They were both killed with a shotgun and they've been in the ground for at least a year, nearer two. Anything more is going to require a much more detailed examination, I'm afraid.' He went back to where his men were carefully sifting through the surrounding earth.

'Bollocks!' cursed Carmichael. 'It's not the de Kuipers. We know for a fact that they were active in Syria just a couple of months ago.' He scratched his head. 'So who the hell are these two? Any ideas, Dawes?'

'Actually, sir, I think I have. I believe we'll find that the man was a primary school teacher called Donald Draycott. He disappeared from the village very suddenly some time ago; everyone thought he'd left to take up a headship, somewhere up north.' Jack recalled Bugsy trying to trace the man to answer charges of false accounting. Having discovered that all activity on his tax, bank account and mobile phone had ceased abruptly two years ago, Malone decided he'd either legged it abroad to avoid arrest or he was dead. Now they knew.

'Didn't get very far, did he, poor sod?' observed Carmichael.

'We've found the woman's handbag, sir,' shouted one of the white-coated vultures, picking over the bones. He produced a cheap vinyl handbag – non-biodegradable. When they looked inside, the woman's driving licence was also intact. It was Patsy Tincknell.

'Dead people, six – police still nil,' announced Carlene at breakfast. 'Our clear-up rate ain't gettin' any better, is it?'

'Come on, Carlene, be fair. The first two were accidents and the Arabs self-destructed.'

'If you say so, Mr Jack.'

'All right, Sherlock, what's your masterly verdict on Donald and Patsy?' Malone buttered a slice of toast and piled on enough marmalade to last most normal people a week.

'Bleedin' obvious, innit?' said Carlene.

Rosemary, ever the romantic, paused for dramatic effect; her coffee cup poised awkwardly between her bandaged fingers and halfway to her lips. 'They were star-crossed lovers who fell out. In a fit of passion, Donald shot Patsy, then full of remorse, he turned the gun on himself.'

'Then some kind person wiv a shovel come along, decided they was makin' the place look untidy and buried 'em,' said Carlene.

'Oh, yes,' said Rosie, sheepishly. 'I'd forgotten that. So what did happen, then?'

'Like I said, it's obvious. They was both killed wiv a shotgun, right? And in the country, every bugger owns a shotgun and goes round blastin' off at the wildlife like a Yardie down Hoxton High Street.' Carlene wiped her mouth on her napkin. 'What we're lookin' for 'ere is someone wiv a shotgun *and* a motive for wantin' Mrs Tincknell and her boyfriend dead. Fink about it. Who was a real nasty bastard and treated his wife like a skivvy? Who beat 'er up if she answered back and went after 'er wiv a gun when 'e sussed she might be runnin' off? All togevver now . . .'

'Thomas Tincknell,' they chorused, obediently. All except Dick, who choked on a piece of crispy bacon.

'Surely not,' he said, eyes watering. 'This is a gentle Somerset village. Men here wouldn't settle marital infidelity with violence, they'd talk it through and come to an amicable agreement, as I'm sure Marcus will when we hand over the love letters Millie wrote to Simon.'

Carlene looked at him pityingly. 'Blimey, mate, you really did come down wiv the last shower, didn't ya?'

Rosie leaned towards Corrie. 'You see now why I wouldn't let him post them through the letterbox? He has absolutely no idea when it comes to emotional relationships.'

'I reckon Sherlock's right,' said Malone. 'Tincknell shot Draycott and Patsy in a jealous rage when he discovered they were leaving the village together. Patsy was his property and he wasn't about to let some other bloke take her. Then, he buried the bodies in the garden of Gibbet Cottage; maybe to implicate the de Kuipers but more likely because he needed to get rid of 'em smartish and he didn't dare bury 'em at Black Oak Farm because it'd be the first place the authorities would look.'

Jack agreed. 'Simon and Saskia were abroad much of the time so Tincknell would be able to creep into their garden, concealed by all the undergrowth, and bury the bodies at his leisure.'

'What riles me,' said Corrie, 'is that the murdering old scrote got away with it for two years and now he's dead and can't be brought to justice. Why didn't anyone report them missing at the time?'

'Like who?' asked Jack. 'Someone – almost certainly Tincknell – started a rumour that Draycott had left Lullington to go up north for a better job. Donald had no relatives, so when he disappeared, people simply believed it. When Patsy vanished at the same time, the villagers drew their own prurient conclusions. Tincknell, all indignant and self-righteous, would have wallowed in everyone's sympathy and then had to get a quick divorce. He could hardly claim to be widowed, could he? He married Dimpsy because he needed another farm labourer that he wouldn't have to pay.'

'I think I'm beginning to understand now,' said Dick. Carlene rolled her eyes skywards but said nothing. 'The de Kuipers somehow found out about Draycott and Patsy's affair and threatened to tell her husband unless they were given money. Because Draycott knew about Tincknell's violent temper, he paid up, but when he ran out of cash, he falsified the parish council's accounts in order to keep up the payments. I knew there had to be a good reason.'

'Well done, dear,' said Rosie, patting his sleeve.

'The coroner's going to want proof of all this,' said Malone.

'You've got Tincknell's shotgun; can't your forensics people prove it was the same one that killed Draycott and Mrs Tincknell?' asked Dick.

Jack shook his head. 'Unfortunately, ballistic fingerprinting doesn't work with shotguns, Dick. They fire cartridges and in most cases, the shot is inside a sleeve that prevents it from touching the barrel. Even if it did, the random movement of the shot wouldn't leave any consistent marks. We could examine the cartridge cases for firing-pin marks but we haven't got them. We don't even know for sure where the killings took place. I expect Tincknell caught the couple as they were about to run away. It's going to be difficult to prove anything, two years on.'

'Unless . . .' said Bugsy. They all looked at him expectantly. 'What about Old Mother Tincknell? She's still alive. I bet "her lovely Tommy" told her everything.'

'Very probably, but will she want to admit to us that he was a murderer, even though he's dead and can't be punished? She thought the world of him. My guess is that she won't tell us anything.'

But Jack's guess was wrong.

The Sea View Nursing Home mouldered in its own grounds on the distant fringes of Lullington Barrow. The name was somewhat misleading. Residents could, indeed, catch a glimpse of the sea if they were athletic enough to stagger into the day room and climb on to the sideboard, but since their average age was eighty-seven, few attempted it. The building was stark and ugly with barred windows and high perimeter walls. Had there been searchlights and a watch-tower, passers-by might easily have mistaken it for a prison. The residents frequently did.

Dawes and Malone had telephoned ahead and were expected. They parked the car in a marked-out space in the car park but ignored the ticket machine that demanded five quid on pain of being clamped. The two detectives strode up to the reinforced steel front door and knocked. Presently, they heard keys clanking, chains being removed and bolts sliding back. The matron, a plump, cheerful little body, eased open the door and immediately, three or four elderly residents in dressing gowns and carpet slippers shuffled towards freedom, shoving each other out of the way in their haste. Care assistants grabbed them and gently escorted them back to the day room.

'Inspector Dawes and Sergeant Malone?' They produced their warrants but the matron waved them away. 'Do come in, I've told Mrs Tincknell you're coming but I'm not sure she took it in. We've put her on the top floor because she isn't mobile so she doesn't need access to the downstairs facilities.' She took them up in the lift then bustled briskly down a long corridor of rooms, clustered very closely together. The two men had almost to jog to keep up with her. Eventually she stopped outside one of the doors and unlocked it with a key hanging from a bunch on her belt. 'We have to keep the doors locked,' explained Matron, 'because some of our residents get confused and tend to wander and we can't risk them falling down the stairs.'

Ethel Tincknell shared a tiny, box of a room with another elderly lady called Lavender, who was fast asleep on her back, mouth open and snoring loudly. Ethel lay in the other single bed, her vast twenty-stone body filling it to capacity, with the excess hanging over the sides.

'Wake up, Mrs Tincknell,' trilled the matron, archly. 'There are two handsome young men here to see you. Aren't you a lucky girl?'

'Bugger off!' said Ethel, without opening her eyes.

'Now, now, dear, that's not very nice, is it?' The matron turned and mouthed to Jack and Bugsy. 'I shouldn't stay too long. She could go at any time.'

'I 'eard that!'

The matron fetched them two chairs from the corridor then scurried out of the room.

'What do you two clowns want?' Ethel Tincknell recognized Dawes and Malone even before they introduced themselves and showed her their warrant cards. 'Are you 'ere to get me out of this dump? If not, you can sod off.' She turned her head away and studied the garish, flocked wallpaper; brown with nicotine from the days when inmates were allowed to smoke.

Dawes and Malone sat either side of her bed. 'We'd like to talk to you about your son,' began Dawes.

She looked at him, then, with beady, malicious eyes: 'My Tommy's dead. He were murdered by that little bitch what's living in my 'ome. You locked 'er up, yet? She deserves to 'ang from Lullington gibbet.'

'Did you know that Dimpsy is expecting your grandchild, Mrs Tincknell?' If Dawes had expected her to be pleased, he was disappointed. She almost spat with disgust.

'She never ought to be carryin' that runt! My Tommy tried to kick it out of 'er, more'n once.'

'How did you get along with Tommy's first wife, Patsy?' asked Malone.

It was like lighting the touch paper of a very large firework. Ethel hauled herself up to a sitting position and screamed at them. 'Don't talk to me about that dirty slut! Dropped 'er drawers for a skinny schoolteacher, didn't she? Married to my lovely Tommy but that weren't good enough for 'er. Oh no! She 'ad to open 'er legs for that scrawny piece o' piss!'

'I'm surprised your Tommy didn't do something about him,' said Malone. 'After all, it's humiliating for a man, isn't it? Finding out his wife's having it off with another bloke.'

Her coarse, ugly features twisted into a look of triumphant cunning. 'Oh, my Tommy put a stop to it, all right. Good and proper, 'e did. Don't 'ee worry about that. He put an end to their dirty little games.'

'But he didn't, though, did he, Mrs Tincknell?' taunted Dawes. 'Donald and Patsy ran away together to start a new life up north. The whole village knows that.'

'Only 'coz that's what my Tommy wanted 'em to think.'

Malone goaded her. 'But it's the truth, Ethel. You know it is. Donald Draycott got a first-class job as a headmaster, miles away from Somerset, and he took Patsy with him. I expect they've got a lovely home, not like that filthy hovel Patsy was living in with your Tommy. I bet she's really happy, now. Who knows, they might even have a baby and—'

It had the required effect. 'They're dead!' screeched Ethel, eyes bulging. 'They're not 'appy 'coz they're both rottin' in the sod. My Tommy put 'em there. He took his gun and 'e shot their bloody 'eads off!'

'Ooh my good Gawd!' Poor old Lavender, startled awake by the terrible revelation that she was sharing a room with the mother of a killer, sat bolt upright and farted ferociously.

Malone put his tie over his nose and went to open the window.

'Are you telling us that your Tommy murdered his wife, Patsy, and Donald Draycott?' asked Dawes.

'It weren't murder; it were 'is right! The dirty cow was tryin' to escape with 'er fancy man. My Tommy caught 'em and 'e put 'em down, like filthy beasts. 'Tiz the way o' country folk and I were proud of 'im.'

'What did he do with their bodies, Ethel?' asked Malone.

Her hysterical outburst had exhausted her and she sank back onto the pillows. 'Buried 'em . . . one night. Wheelbarrow. Incomers' woods.' She closed her eyes and Dawes knew they would get nothing more from her; but it was enough. Far from being reluctant to speak about it, as Dawes had first anticipated, she'd boasted about what 'her lovely Tommy' had done.

Back outside, Malone sucked in a deep lungful of fresh air. 'Blimey, Jack, I wonder what they give 'em to eat in there.'

'Lots of fibre to keep them regular. What was that other old lady's name again?'

'The one with the terrible wind? Lavender.' He grinned at the irony. 'Tell you what, Guv. If I ever end up like that, you can draw a weapon from the police armoury and shoot me.'

'Ditto.'

They walked across the car park; Dawes was immersed in troubling thoughts. He'd believed there was nothing left in Lullington Barrow to sicken him but he'd been wrong. What kind of morality did these people live by? How could they dismiss such behaviour as 'the way of country folk'? He thought so-called 'honour killings' belonged to a different, altogether more violent culture that was hopefully being eradicated.

'What a bleedin' liberty!' exclaimed Malone.

'I know, Bugsy. I'm having trouble squaring it with decent human behaviour, too. That evil old woman actually believed it was Tincknell's "right" to kill his wife and her lover.'

'I don't mean that!' exploded Malone. 'Our bloody car's been clamped!'

CHAPTER NINETEEN

Saturday night was two days before the full moon and decidedly chilly. The heatwave had abated and the drop in temperature was noticeable. So much so, that Liz Boobyer lit a cheerful, crackling log fire in the private, downstairs dining room where the supper was to take place, to make it 'cosier, for 'ee, m'dear'.

Rosie worried that 'cosy' was the last thing this occasion would turn out to be. It had seemed like such a simple idea in concept. You accidentally acquire a whole lot of very sensitive, confidential items belonging to your neighbours so you arrange a pleasant, social evening in order to hand everything back over a nice meal. Everyone goes home happy. That was the best scenario. The most likely one, however, was that several fights would break out, eyes would be blacked, marriages would founder and everyone would go home hating you. The de Kuipers were such a toxic pair; all sorts of horrors could emerge from their blackmail kit.

The first snag was the 'nice meal'. Corrie was the acknowledged food expert and she and Carlene consulted Liz Boobyer about the menu. The answer came without hesitation.

'Cold meat, salad and boiled potatoes.'

'Oh. I was rather hoping we might have something a bit more adventurous,' said Corrie.

Liz was offended. ''Tiz what I've put up for Lullington Harvest Supper, every year regular. No one's ever complained. I'm not a trained chef like you, Mrs Dawes, I'm a pub landlady. 'Tiz a busy job. I don't have time for fiddling with fancy food.'

'I'll do it,' volunteered Carlene, immediately. 'Just let me 'ave the run o' your kitchen. I'll do everything.'

'Oh.' Liz seemed mollified by that. 'All right, m'dear. If you're sure. Just let me know if you need anything.'

'What menu had you in mind, Carlene?' asked Corrie after Liz had gone back behind the bar where she was obviously more at home.

'What about Somerset pork? I could cook it in a cider sauce wiv them dauphinoise spuds you taught me to do. And maybe some posh veg. You always say use local ingredients where you can.'

'I think that's an excellent suggestion, Carlene. And what about strawberry cheesecake for dessert made with Cheddar strawberries and served with farmhouse clotted cream?'

'Then proper Cheddar cheese wiv oatcakes?'

Corrie pursed her lips. 'What about Edwina? She's vegan.'

'No problem,' said Carlene. 'I'll make her a noodle and soy bean salad with grilled tofu.'

Corrie was impressed. 'Well done! Where did you learn to make that?'

'From a vegan Japanese lady what used to live in the flat next door to us. That was before they took me mum away and I got put in a home.'

A brief cloud flickered across Carlene's relentlessly cheerful features and although Corrie desperately wanted to ask about the girl's past, she decided not to push it.

'I doubt if the village shop will have anything decent. Why don't we take a trip to Lowerbridge and buy everything fresh?'

They found a farmers' market which had everything they wanted and returned later that afternoon, confident that the food would be good even if the company was strained.

Everyone accepted the invitation so there were eleven of them around the table; Jack and Corrie, Dick and Rosemary, Marcus and Millie, Giles and Edwina, Peter and Jane and Bugsy, sitting hungrily with his napkin stuffed in his collar. It threatened to be an uncomfortable evening with everyone being painfully polite but suspecting they knew why they were there in this private room with the current owners of the de Kuipers' cottage and two detectives.

Most of the men, uncertain of the dress code, had come in sweaters or sports jackets. All except for Marcus who, predictably, wore a dinner jacket and, far from appearing out of kilter with the others, looked mouth-wateringly handsome and suave. However, anyone particularly observant would have noticed that the gold Rolex watch was missing and so were his diamond cufflinks. Jane wore a smart, emerald green trouser suit and Edwina had abandoned her perpetual jeans and shirt for a long black shift, reminiscent of the frock Mary Queen of Scots had worn at her execution. Oblivious of the drop in temperature, Millie burgeoned from a low-cut, neon pink, mini dress with a silk peony stuck down her cleavage. On her, it looked cheap but it had probably cost a fortune. She clung pathetically to Marcus's hand, throughout virtually the whole evening. Corrie and Rosie had opted for classic M&S dresses in unobtrusive shades of taupe and mushroom.

Carlene was almost unrecognizable in a neat black dress with a white apron and she had scraped back her magenta hair into a Croydon facelift, which was hidden under her white cap. She moved unobtrusively around the table, filling their glasses with white wine prior to serving the starter. She had high hopes of Corrie allowing her to serve at some of the posh 'Coriander's Cuisine' dinner parties, as well as cook and wash up, and this was a good opportunity to show she could do it.

'I'll have a pasty, double chips and baked beans, please, waitress,' quipped Malone.

Carlene whisked his napkin out of his collar where he'd tucked it and draped it across his lap. Then she bent over and whispered in his ear. 'Pasties come from Cornwall, not Somerset, Sergeant Bugsy, and you're not gettin' any chips and beans. Not tonight. Please don't show me up.'

Bugsy considered himself duly reprimanded and smiled. Best thing the guvnor's missus ever did, taking on Sherlock as an apprentice. It had changed the kid's life.

As if in need of Dutch courage, Giles took a long slug from the very dry white wine that was far from Premier Cru but the best that Hangman's Inn had been able to supply. As the sour acidity assaulted his palate, he disguised a slight grimace.

'Sorry, sir,' said Carlene, noticing. 'Some o' that cheap white plonk can really make you clench your buttocks. It ain't so bad if you 'ave it wiv the starter.' She hurried off to get it.

Initially, there was a little friendly small talk then the atmosphere became very tense, as if the neighbours knew they'd been called together for a reason and tonight there could be no more obfuscation. It had to be the truth. Peter glanced at Giles and Marcus before he spoke.

'We heard about the police digging up two bodies in your

woodland, Dick. It must be very upsetting for you both.'

'Yes, it is,' agreed Rosemary, 'but it would have been worse if we'd known the couple.'

'Donald Draycott and Patsy Tincknell,' observed Giles. 'We all wondered what had happened to them but I don't think any of us suspected Thomas Tincknell had killed them both. Not until Ethel confirmed it.'

'Good job he's dead,' said Edwina, shrewishly. 'Saves the expense of a trial and keeping him in prison to watch TV and read *The Sun* for the rest of his life. Well done, Titus.'

News travels like lightning in this village, thought Dawes. He wondered how much more of the recent developments were widely known. The villagers must have noticed the MI6 teams taking Gibbet Cottage apart and even though they'd been passed off as pest control officers, it was unlikely anyone had believed it, especially after Carmichael had called on them, telling them not to leave the area and asking about the de Kuipers. And the incident with the two Arabs was common knowledge, since many locals had been in Hangman's Inn when Carlene roared into the car park in the Cadillac with Corrie and Rosie in the back.

'Tell me, dear,' Jane asked Rosie, 'how are your poor fingers? What a ghastly experience. It must have been simply terrifying.'

Rosie held up her hands, still bandaged but only lightly now. 'It was. I'm getting through it with the help of my healing crystals and lots of lavender and tea tree oil.'

'And what about you, Corrie? Are you fully recovered?'

'Pretty much, except for a burning twinge in my shoulder if I try to look to the left.'

Carlene arrived with the starter and served everyone expertly, then stood back while they ate.

'What sort of fish is this, Sherlock?' asked Bugsy. 'And why hasn't it got batter round it?'

'I believe it's trout,' said Marcus.

Peter disagreed. 'No, it's salmon. Definitely salmon.'

'Actually, it's eel,' said Carlene, 'hot-smoked over beech and apple-wood which gives it that delicious and succulent flavour. I fink they catch 'em in the River Severn.'

Edwina, toying with a plain green salad, surreptitiously filched a piece from Giles's plate when she thought nobody was looking.

Marcus and Millie had said very little until now and neither had eaten much. The brittle atmosphere and banal nonsense about food had become too much for Marcus and he had to get things out in the open. 'Would I be right in thinking, Inspector Dawes, that the purpose of this evening is to discuss certain items that officers from the Intelligence Agency found in the deposit box that Dick dredged up from his pond?'

Several people spoke at once:

'We just wanted to return them,' said Rosie, hastily.

'No need to actually discuss anything, surely,' added Dick.

Millie and Edwina simply looked shocked and muttered exclamations of despair; Jane buried her face in her hands and Giles could almost feel the handcuffs snapping shut.

'Do we really have to do this?' asked Peter.

'No, Peter, no more prevarication; no more lies,' interrupted Marcus. 'This is the end of the line. Armageddon, apocalypse, the day of reckoning. Time we all came clean, old man, even if it does mean ruin for some of us.' He put down his knife and fork. 'You'll have guessed by now, Inspector, that Simon and Saskia had been extorting money from Peter, Giles and me and there's a strong possibility that other villagers have also been victims. We didn't discuss the details between ourselves but we knew we were all paying.'

'Me, too,' whispered Millie.

'And me,' confessed Edwina.

That the two wives had been victims, too, was obviously a surprise and the men would have bombarded them with questions but Corrie intervened.

'I simply can't believe that sensible, educated people like you would pay hush money to such parasites. It must be the malevolent influence that hangs over this nasty village like a hostile cloud.'

This meal's going well, thought Carlene, grimly. They've only had the starter and now, nobody's going to have any appetite left.

Even Dick with his complete lack of occasion realized that the time had come to produce the contents of the package and allow the neighbours to decide how they wanted to handle it. He had placed the items on a tea tray, for want of something better, and covered them, predictably, with a bar tea towel. Now, he put the tray on a side table.

'Perhaps . . .' he began awkwardly, dreading any kind of situation that might turn into an emotional scene, '. . . perhaps you'd care to take a look, one by one, and privately remove anything that belongs to you.' It was like some ghastly parlour game.

'Oh no,' said Giles, with gusto. 'Dammit, Dickie, Marcus is right. Just empty everything onto the table here in front of us and we'll sort it out together.'

'Well, if you're sure.'

They made a space in the middle of the table and Dick reluctantly slid the items into it, where they tumbled about amongst the condiments and wine glasses. For a while, the Gallows Green crowd just looked and nobody spoke. Jack had been silent until now but felt it was time to speak.

'I must caution you, I'm afraid, that if there's any evidence here of a crime having been committed, as a police officer I'm obliged to act on it.'

'Fair enough,' said Peter. 'We understand. Who wants to go first?'

'I will,' offered Marcus, 'because human salvation lies in the hands of the creatively maladjusted.'

'That's incredibly philosophical of you, Marcus, even if I don't quite understand the relevance,' said Corrie.

Marcus smiled. 'Not I, fair Coriander. It was Martin Luther King Junior who said it and I believe he meant that maladjusted creativity often brings the most radical solutions to long-term problems. In a very few moments, you'll discover how my maladjusted creativity brought the kind of radical solution that might well end with your husband and his sidekick clapping me in irons and leading me away.'

Millie gasped, 'No! I shan't let them,' and she clutched at Marcus, who gently disentangled her and picked up the CD bearing his name.

'I don't know precisely what's on here, Inspector, but Simon de Kuiper assured me he had copied enough evidence from my laptop to provide me with indefinite accommodation in one of Her Majesty's less salubrious hostels and I have no reason to doubt him.' He paused and took a steadying slug of wine. 'You see, the stock exchange tempts you to perform conjuring tricks with other people's money. I made some of it vanish then reappear in my own account to maintain a lifestyle that I could no longer support.'

'It's all my fault, isn't it?' sobbed Millie. 'It's because I'm so extravagant. Oh darling, can't you put the money back before any of the people find out?'

'That's what I've been doing for the last week, my angel, and I believe I've finally succeeded,' croaked Marcus, hoarse with the strain. 'It took every penny I could raise so there'll be no more high living or designer outfits or—'

Millie threw her arms around him. 'I don't care! I don't want you to go to prison!'

Marcus smiled ruefully. 'Sorry about the bloody nose, Dickie, old man. I was the intruder that you chased across your garden that night. I was searching for Simon's hidden stash, hoping to find this CD, and I whacked you with the rake so I could escape without being seen. I aimed at your chest but in the dark, I misjudged your height. I hope you'll forgive me.'

Dick managed a curt nod. In truth, he was more annoyed at the reference to his lack of height than by the clout on the nose.

Then Marcus offered the disk to Dawes. 'Here you are, Inspector. I'll come quietly.'

Jack made no attempt to take it. He knew he could probably charge Marcus with a number of offences, fraud and assault to name just two, but compared to the other, much worse crimes that had been committed in this village, he really couldn't see the point of pursuing it. Marcus had put the money back and Dick didn't seem inclined to press charges. Jack gestured at the CD. 'I fancy it's getting a little chilly in here, Marcus. Someone ought to put something on the fire.'

Marcus smiled his enigmatic smile and nodded grateful thanks to Jack. Then he tossed the CD into the flames and they watched it slowly twist and melt.

'Looks like it's my turn.' Giles picked up the photo of himself opening the tailgate of an articulated lorry with several crates of guns and ammunition clearly visible in the back. He passed it to Edwina. 'First, I owe you an explanation, Weena. I'm not a television producer any more; the BBC cancelled my contract a year ago due to cuts in the budget. I decided to try something completely different and I became a long-distance lorry driver. That's why you found the LGV qualification on my driving licence. Strangely, I rather enjoyed the freedom, being out on the road; my own boss. That was until Simon found out. He spotted me in Amsterdam, planted some of his filthy guns on my truck.

I had no idea they were there until I opened the tailgate and saw them. That was the moment he took that photo of me. Obviously, I made him unload them but when we got back to the UK, he threatened to report me to the authorities and give them the photograph if I didn't pay up. He said they'd never believe my story. I must have paid him thousands and then it got worse. He said I could be useful to him, smuggling arms for real. Then, miraculously, we managed to make the de Kuipers disappear but I had to find this photo so I let myself into Gibbet Cottage using the key under the flower pot. I knew Simon and Saskia used to hide things under the floorboards so I moved your furniture while you were out, Rosie, hoping to find it, then I couldn't remember where it had been to start with. I'm sorry it scared you. It was a rotten thing to do but I was desperate.'

'I knew it!' Rosemary squealed triumphantly. 'Didn't I tell you, Dick, that someone had broken in and messed up my Feng Shui and you kept insisting I was confused and forgetful.'

Dick was speechless. He could hardly believe the way the evening was developing.

Giles took Edwina's hand. 'I'm so sorry I lied to you, Weena. I accept our marriage is over, now. A lady of your breeding and principles won't want to share her life with a lorry driver who very nearly became a gunrunner, too. I know I have to let you go but I'll never stop loving you.' He pushed the photo across to Dawes, who glanced at Malone. He knew Bugsy was all for turning Giles over to the Spooks but Jack decided he deserved a second chance. After all, he hadn't actually *done* anything and you can't bang up a bloke for what he *might* have done. He raised an eyebrow at Malone.

'What do you think, Bugsy?'

'I think the fire's dying, Guv, and it's getting cold again.' He slid the photo back to Giles but Edwina picked it up and stared at it for a long time. Everyone held their breath, wondering how she'd react. She was such an uncompromising, judgemental person and this situation was exactly what Rosemary had feared – the termination of a good, if unconventional marriage right before their eyes.

Edwina stood up and walked slowly across to the fire. She knelt down and carefully poked the photograph into the centre of the logs and watched it curl up in the flames. Then she returned to her seat, picked up the photo of the man in overalls standing next to his lorry and holding the hand of a little girl. She handed it to Giles. Her face was ashen against the black dress but, like Mary Queen of Scots, she held her head high and proud.

'There's nothing wrong with being a lorry driver, Giles. It's an honest, decent occupation. That's a photo of me and my dad. He wasn't a diplomat; he was a lorry driver and a wonderful, loving man. I lied to you, Giles, and everyone else here, to make myself seem more important. And my real name is Edna, like it says on the back; Edwina was just another of my stupid affectations.'

Giles was astounded. Suddenly, he felt he didn't know this woman at all. 'But why, Weena? Why did you pretend?'

'My mother died when I was five. My father worked himself into an early grave bringing me up and putting me through university. Moments before he died, he kissed me and told me to make something of myself, to be someone who mattered, to win respect. So that's what I did. I invented a new identity, a different background. I even put *wi* in the middle of Edna, to remind me. Oh, my company is genuine all right; I worked hard to make sure it succeeded, but everything else about me is a pack of lies as Saskia very soon discovered. She all but bled me dry.' Edwina took a deep, shuddering breath and it was obvious the iron self-control was starting to crumble. 'To be honest, it's a huge relief to get it all out in the open.' She turned to Giles, very close to tears. 'If you'll still have me, I'll gladly live with a lorry driver if you can bear to live with a cheat.'

Giles couldn't speak; he simply took both her hands in his across the table. Jane and Rosie were filling up and surprisingly, so was Dick. He pulled out a hankie and blew his nose noisily. He hated all this soul-baring. He was a banker; he didn't do emotion and feelings. He'd expected everyone would surreptitiously take their belongings and slink back to their homes.

Corrie was still puzzled. 'Edwina, I don't understand why you paid Saskia. After all, what you did wasn't illegal, just a bit . . . well, phoney. I guess it might have been embarrassing to own up but I bet loads of people in top jobs have pretended to be something they're not.'

Edwina nodded sadly. 'If I'd only risked embarrassment, I'd have told Saskia where to go. But when I started my business, I applied for a very large loan. I got it because I lied on the application about my background and my rich, influential father. Saskia said I'd have to answer fraud charges and I'd lose the company and even go to prison if they found out I'd provided false securities against the loan.' She turned to Jack. 'What must I do now?'

Jack shrugged. 'Sorry, Edwina, I'm a murder detective. I don't know anything about company law. What about you, Sergeant?'

Bugsy grinned. 'Bugger all, boss.'

Edwina went to put the photo on the fire but Giles stopped her. 'Don't burn it, Weena. It's you and your dad. Wouldn't you like to keep it?'

She put it away in her handbag then pushed aside the mineral water she always drank and took a big gulp of Giles's wine.

With tears streaming down her face, Millie picked up the last item on the tray; a pathetic bundle of love letters. She held them out to Marcus but before she could explain, he took them from her and hurled them onto the fire where the flames quickly consumed them.

'Life's too short, my darling. Nothing matters now except that we're together.'

CHAPTER TWENTY

'I don't s'pose no one fancies any grub?' asked Carlene, desperately. 'If I keep it 'ot much longer, the pork'll be like shoe-leather.'

'Now that you mention it, my sweet Carlene,' gushed Marcus, 'I'm absolutely starving.'

'Me belly thinks me throat's been cut,' agreed Bugsy. 'Bring it on, Sherlock, love.'

With the harrowing disclosures safely over, everyone had regained their appetites. All except Peter and Jane who were no longer convinced that the birth certificate had gone up in smoke in the Browns' loft. It must have been in the deposit box with all the other things. They exchanged anxious glances but decided not to ask about it. Not until later when Peter could explain about the fire.

Carlene proudly served her Somerset pork and dauphinoise potatoes to vociferous acclaim and people tucked in with a keenness that nobody had felt an hour ago. But when she placed the soba noodle and soy bean salad with grilled tofu in front of Edwina, the woman's naturally glum face became even more lugubrious.

'Oh. Noodles, soy beans and tofu,' she said, without much enthusiasm.

'It's all right,' Carlene assured her, 'it's proper vegan. All of it. I checked.'

'Yes, thank you very much, Carlene. I can see you've taken a lot of trouble, but . . .'

Carlene waited. There was always a bloody 'but' with these picky eaters.

'Actually . . .' Edwina looked longingly at Giles's plate, 'I was rather hoping I might have some of the pork. It smells wonderful.'

Carlene grinned and whisked away her plate. 'No probs. I made loads. I'll get you some.'

'But Weena,' said Giles, confused, 'you always said you hated meat and despised the farmers who wrongfully collude in raising and killing animals for food.'

'Just another deception, I'm afraid. After you've gone to work in the morning, I make myself a bacon sandwich. And I eat sausages. And eggs.' They both laughed.

The meal was a resounding success with everyone eating so much, they could hardly move. All except Peter and Jane who refused dessert and only nibbled at the cheese like a couple of nervous mice fearing the snap of the trap. Corrie noticed and so did Carlene. They were both thinking about the birth certificate that was still lying safely hidden in Corrie's handbag. When Carlene went to the kitchen to fetch the coffee, Corrie followed her and nearly tripped over Ted Boobyer, who was lying comatose on the tiled floor.

'Dear me,' exclaimed Corrie. 'Whatever's happened to Mr Boobyer?'

Carlene stepped casually over him to fill the coffee pot. 'When I bent down to get the coffee out the cupboard, 'e put 'is 'and up my skirt, so I decked 'im.'

Corrie was horrified. 'But that's awful. I knew he was a sexual predator with young girls and I'm so sorry you found yourself alone with him. I should have been more vigilant.'

Carlene shrugged. 'No sweat, Mrs D. 'Appens all the time where I come from. 'Specially on Saturday nights when the pubs turn out. Don't worry about it.'

But Corrie did worry, even more than before. Carlene was living in appalling conditions in that hostel. And the girl was working so hard to save for a flat and make a future for herself. It made Corrie even more determined to do something about it and as soon as she could discuss it with Jack, she intended to help. But right now, she had to find a way to return the birth certificate to Peter and Jane.

'What you goin' to do wiv it, Mrs D? I mean, if you were Jane, you wouldn't want the world to know that yer son's dad was a famous gangster, would you? Even if 'e was dead.'

'No, I wouldn't. And it's a bit different to the other items because it involves the future of someone who isn't here; their son, Michael. That's why I didn't want Mr Brown to put it on the tray with the rest of the stuff. I'll slip it to her secretly when we go back in.'

Together, Corrie and Carlene carried in the coffee. Dick and Jack were dispensing liqueurs and the atmosphere was considerably less chilly now all the skeletons had been dragged from their cupboards and cremated.

As Corrie placed the dish of after-dinner mints and petits fours on the table, she dropped the certificate into Jane's lap. She was positive nobody saw, not even Jack and Bugsy, who spotted anything dodgy immediately. Jane's face lit up and she passed the document to Peter, under the table. He hesitated for several moments then whispered in Jane's ear. She nodded agreement. Peter took out his pipe and sucked at it, unlit. Like a baby's dummy, it provided comfort when he was faced with a nerve-wracking situation.

'Excuse me, everyone.' He cut through the buzz of conversation, which was mostly speculation about Simon and Saskia. 'The de Kuipers had dirt on many of the villagers, and I think you all know that included Jane and me. You'll be wondering why there was no evidence about us on the tray. Well, there was, but Mrs Dawes very kindly kept it out of sight because it has repercussions for someone else, someone very dear to us. It's this . . .' He put the certificate on the table.

'You really don't have to explain, Pete, old man,' said Giles. 'We three men shared the fact that we were all being blackmailed and needed to get rid of the de Kuipers but we avoided sharing all the unpleasant details. There wasn't any need.'

'No, but I think I owe Dick and Rosemary an explanation and Jane agrees that we should tell the truth, as you all have.'

'When I was seventeen,' began Jane, diffidently, 'I lived in the East End of London. It was a very colourful place in those days and although I was brought up very respectably by strict, religious parents, like most teenagers, I hankered after bright lights and excitement. I got into bad company and one night, I went with some rather unsuitable friends to a pub in the worst part of the district. While I was there, I met a man who obviously had a lot of money and commanded a great deal of respect on his manor. I was too young and naive to realize he was a notorious gang leader, into all sorts of violence and criminal activity. All I could see was a handsome, well-dressed, charismatic man who found me attractive and desirable; something no one else had ever done. I was flattered and infatuated, and well . . . to cut a long story short, I became pregnant. When my father found out, he disowned me and I had to leave home.'

'Jane, you don't have to tell us this, you really don't,' urged Edwina.

'Yes, I do, dear.' Jane patted Edwina's arm. 'Just before my eighteenth birthday, I gave birth to a beautiful little boy and I called him Michael. Foolishly, I thought his father would be thrilled. He allowed his name to be put on the birth certificate out of bravado because he had fathered a son, but after that, he completely lost interest in me. Worse than that, he told me I could live in one of his brothels. The other girls would help look after my son while I worked the streets to pay for our keep. I was horrified. I couldn't believe what was happening to me and I ran away to a different part of London. For a while, Michael and I lived in a disgusting bed-and-breakfast establishment paid for by Social Services. I feared for my life if Michael's father found us and if it hadn't been for my little boy, I might have ended it myself. But then I met Peter.' She looked at him lovingly. 'I'd gone into his tobacconist shop to buy sweets for Michael. Peter could tell immediately that I was at my wits' end and well . . . you know the rest. We became dear friends, fell in love and married. Peter adopted Michael and has always loved him as his own son. Even Michael doesn't know the identity of his real father.'

'So who is it?' asked Millie, bluntly. A question the others had tactfully avoided.

Jane opened up the certificate and spread it on the table where everyone could read the name. There were gasps. It may have been many years since this notorious man ruled the East End of London with protection rackets, prostitution and murder but his name remained synonymous with a vicious life of crime.

'I can see why you wouldn't want this to get out,' said Dawes. He could also see why Corrie and Carlene had furtively pocketed the certificate when all the items had first been spread out on the table in the pub. Corrie would have realized the potential repercussions and Carlene would have recognized the gangster's dynasty. 'This could mean the end of your son's career as a Cabinet Minister and any hopes he had of becoming the next Home Secretary. If the press got hold of it, it may even be the end of his work as an MP.'

'We know that, Inspector,' agreed Peter. 'That's why we were so desperate to get the certificate back from Simon and Saskia. And I'm afraid I'm guilty of a very stupid and reckless act of arson.' He turned to the Browns. 'Dick, when you mentioned that the de Kuipers had left behind tea chests full of documents in your attic, I was convinced that Michael's stolen certificate was in one of them. I went into your house to search while you were out playing golf and Rosemary was walking on the beach. I guessed you'd both be gone for some time. I must have put my smouldering pipe down on one of the chests of papers while I was rummaging about. I'm afraid it was I who carelessly started the fire then hastily put it out. Obviously, I shall pay for any damage and I'm immeasurably sorry. He fell silent, head bowed, and Jane put an arm around him.

Marcus swallowed hard. 'My God, Peter, what a story. You must have been worried out of your minds.'

Rosie leaned towards Dick and hissed in his ear. 'See? I told you the sun couldn't have ignited those papers. You and your Olympic flame theory!'

'But how did Simon and Saskia get all these things in the first place?' asked Corrie.

'They latched on to the fact that everyone in Lullington Barrow leaves a spare key under a plant pot in the garden,' said Marcus. 'They just walked in when we were out and took what they wanted. The same way we were able to get into Gibbet Cottage to look for our stuff. Pathetic, isn't it?'

Jack stood up. 'I think we all need a very large cognac,' he said, briskly. 'Then I want you to tell me how you *really* managed to get rid of the de Kuipers.'

While Jack was in the bar ordering the brandy, everyone took a much-needed breather. The three men were in a huddle, discussing how they would explain what had been an effective but complicated plan to get rid of the de Kuipers, thought up predominantly by Marcus who had been the brains behind much of the plot. Their wives, oblivious to any conspiracy, wondered what further shocks were in store and chatted about inconsequential things.

Malone went across to Carlene who was clearing plates from the side table. 'Oi, Sherlock; you got a driving licence?'

She hesitated, then answered cautiously but without actually lying; a trick that life had taught her during her seventeen years. 'Er . . . almost.'

'What's that supposed to mean?'

'I got the application form, but I 'aven't finished fillin' it out yet.'

'So you haven't got a licence and you haven't passed your test. How come you know how to drive? Mrs Dawes told me you drove that Cadillac from the cider mill to Hangman's Inn like Lewis Hamilton.'

'Did she? Ace!' Carlene looked proud for a brief moment then resumed a suitably demure expression. 'I may 'ave 'ad a little go in me mate's car. It was only once or twice . . .'

'Don't tell me any more or I'll have to nick you. Now, listen, Sherlock, here's what we're going to do. We'll get you a provisional licence and then I'll take you out in my motor and you can learn to drive it properly, not like a getaway car. Then you'll pass your test and you'll be legal. Okay?'

Carlene's eyes saucered. 'Would you really do that for me, Sergeant Bugsy?'

'I've said so, haven't I? Now scram while the boss gives these blokes the third degree.'

It was a quarter to three in the morning and they were back round the table with Dawes looking tough. Poor Millie was resting her head on Marcus's shoulder, her eyes almost closing. Jane had been in the ladies for some time and now her eyes were red and swollen from weeping; partly from relief and partly from the shame of having to relate her sad story to her neighbours. Edwina's eyes, normally sharp and piercing, seemed to have sunk further into her head with emotional exhaustion. Rosemary had taken out a tiny phial of camomile and lavender oil and was dabbing it, fretfully, on her temples.

Marcus appealed to Jack. 'Inspector, is it really necessary for the ladies to stay? It's very late and as you can see, they're stressed and exhausted. I promise you, they know very little of this matter, only that Simon and Saskia needed to leave Lullington Barrow fast and that our consortium facilitated that by buying Gibbet Cottage cheaply and for ready cash. They don't know why the de Kuipers had to leave in such a hurry and they certainly know nothing about the arms trafficking and other items that were found in the deposit box. Indeed, even Giles, Peter and I weren't aware of the full extent of the blackmail. Let the ladies go and we'll tell you everything we know.' Giles and Peter nodded agreement.

'Fair enough,' agreed Dawes.

'Actually, Jack, I could use some sleep, too,' said Dick, lamely. 'Will you need me at all?'

'I doubt it, Dick. I'll let you know in the morning if there's anything you can add. You go with the ladies and get some shut-eye.' What a wimp, thought Jack. In his place, I'd be desperate to know what had been going on in my house.

After they'd left, Corrie and Carlene remained resolutely in their seats. 'What about you, Carlene?' asked Jack. 'Don't you think you should go to bed?'

'No fanks, Mr Jack. I wanna know what those Arabs were up to. I've still got the cuts and bruises.'

Jack turned to Corrie. 'Don't even think about it,' she said, before he could speak. 'I've still got a dodgy shoulder and a bald spot.'

They were a small group round the table now: Marcus, Giles and Peter on one side of the table; Malone, Corrie and Carlene on the other, with Dawes at the head.

'Okay, gentlemen, tell me what happened?'

Marcus glanced at the other two, who nodded. 'I think I should explain, Inspector, since I was the main protagonist in ensuring the departure of our friends, Simon and Saskia, and I can assure you it was sheer coincidence that I was able to do it.' He refilled his glass from the bottle of cognac that Carlene had obtained from Boobyer after he had recovered consciousness. Ted had said nothing but simply handed it over under the watchful eye of Liz.

Marcus began in his smooth, persuasive voice. 'As we now know, the de Kuipers made a considerable amount of money in the black market arms trade, profiteering in particular from the Arab uprisings in the Middle East. From time to time, things got hot and they needed to hide out somewhere completely anonymous; they chose Lullington Barrow in order to appear like ordinary, Somerset villagers. They bought Gibbet Cottage, which had recently come up for sale following the death of the old lady who owned it, and they kept their heads down. Obviously, as "incomers" they were not made welcome. You've met some of the locals, Inspector, and they're not exactly friendly. Simon and Saskia were, it has to be said, intrinsically evil. They responded to the villagers' lack of hospitality by burgling their homes and taking confidential and sometimes incriminating information. Then they blackmailed them, mainly for sadistic amusement and petty cash. As you can imagine, this made a lot of people's lives a misery including ours, so Peter, Giles and I put our heads together to discuss the best way to get rid of them.'

'Not murder, though?' asked Corrie, anxiously. 'You never considered killing them?'

'No, my fragrant Coriander. Mind you, had we known they were putting the screws on Edwina and Millie as well as us, we might have sought a more robust solution. However, I digress. During one of the de Kuipers' sales trips to a repressed regime, they managed to get hold of that list of dissidents who were intent on overthrowing the dictator and were working within his government's own security forces; a very unsafe place to be. This list was a valuable and very dangerous document to have in their possession. Anonymously, they let it be known that someone had it and offered it to the highest bidder; either the revolutionaries or the government. They had no particular preference either way as they already traded arms with both sides and they had neither scruples nor conscience. At that point, they returned to Lullington, kept a low profile and waited for the bids to come in via their close Arab contacts. The next part is where the serendipity kicks in and it's rather complex. As you know, I grub a meagre living as a stockbroker and I have many wealthy clients including an Arab millionaire who lives in Dubai. We were at Eton and Oxford together. As it happens, he has a brother in government in a neighbouring country. This brother is one of the pro-democracy rebels plotting the downfall of the president and he told my client about the dangerous list he is on and the people who are offering it for sale. At this point, nobody in the Arab world knew exactly who or where the de Kuipers were. They were very adept at what they did and their aliases were myriad.'

Malone was beginning to see how the plot was forming but wondered how Marcus had made the connection between the arms dealers and his neighbours. He was about to find out.

'With the threat of exposure and the certain torture and execution of his brother, my Dubai client needed to realize some of his investments and send money to speed up the cause. As his stockbroker, he contacted me and explained why. During our business, he showed me a photo on his phone that had been taken secretly by his brother during one of the arms deals. Although the photo was badly out of focus, I was astounded when I recognized them immediately as Simon and Saskia, my next-door neighbours.'

'Did you tell him?' asked Dawes.

'Not at that point, no. I could see a way of getting rid of the de Kuipers once and for all and I wanted to talk it over with Giles and Peter, since they had a vested interest, too.'

'We were all in favour of shopping them to the Arabs and letting them take their chances,' agreed Giles.

'So you contacted your client in Dubai and told him the couple he was looking for were living in Gibbet Cottage under an assumed name and to send a couple of rebels to capture them and the list before the dictator found out and beat them to it?' said Malone, who was having trouble keeping up at gone three in the morning.

'Pretty much, Sergeant. Unfortunately, it didn't go quite according to plan. The de Kuipers were smarter than I gave them credit for and had built up an extensive network of informers, one of whom tipped them off that the rebels were on their way. They knew if they were caught, they'd be tortured and killed. They had to get out and fast, which was really the object of our plan. They knew they'd never be able to live in Gibbet Cottage again so they offered it to Peter, Giles and me for instant cash at a knock-down price, unaware that we had engineered the whole thing. That bit at least was true, Inspector.'

'So Simon sealed up the list and other paraphernalia in a metal deposit box as a kind of insurance if they were caught, then dumped it in the pond before they left?' said Dawes. Carmichael had been right; if they didn't have it on them, they had a chance of staying alive and coming back for it later.

'So it seems, but of course we didn't know that.'

'We thought they'd hidden it in the house somewhere,' said Peter.

'They told us that if we bought their house, they'd give our incriminating stuff back before they left, but of course, they never did,' added Giles. 'Then Dick and Rosie moved in almost immediately and we didn't get a chance to look properly while the cottage was empty.'

'I should emphasize, Inspector, that none of the ladies knew anything about our dealings with the Arabs; not before or after.'

'Well, Rosie and I certainly found out the hard way,' exclaimed Corrie. 'Those two goons were convinced that Rosie was Saskia de Kuiper and nothing we said would change their minds. They might have killed us if it hadn't been for Carlene.'

Marcus was contrite. 'I'm very sorry about that. We expected the Arabs to come in search of the de Kuipers but not that they'd kidnap the first blonde they saw.'

'They won't send more freedom fighters, will they?' asked Peter, anxiously.

'I doubt it,' said Dawes. 'The Intelligence Agency has a wide network of informants, too, and they'll be making it known that the key document is safely in their hands. Of course, we still don't know where the de Kuipers are and they'll be number one on the Arabs' hit list.'

CHAPTER TWENTY-ONE

Sunday morning and everyone was limp. To them, it was as if they'd been through a traumatic ordeal rather than a congenial supper with the neighbours. The alcohol had helped them cope the previous evening, but now, in the cold, sober light of day, they were relieved it was over. It had been exhausting but at the same time, cathartic.

Dawes and Malone still had some loose ends to tie up. One of these was to obtain a signed statement from Ethel Tincknell confirming that 'her lovely Tommy' had shot his first wife and her lover and that she had witnessed their dead bodies with their skulls shattered by his shotgun; the same gun that he had used to threaten and pursue Dimpsy when she ran off. The coroner would want rather more than hearsay from the two detectives and Ethel was too ill to be called to give evidence at the inquest. Jack telephoned the nursing home for an appointment and it was agreed that the two policemen could visit later that morning.

The Sea View Nursing Home was relatively quiet as the residents took a morning nap to build up their energy for the daily effort of eating lunch. Today, it was boiled cod and mash and the corridors reeked with the unappetizing odours of stale fish and lumpy potatoes. Last time cod featured on the menu, the matron had asked chef if he could manage to make the meal look a little less grey. He had responded by adding a dollop of puréed carrots to give it some colour. Today, it was puréed sprouts for a nice touch of green. The matron thought she'd better warn Mrs Tincknell about the impending visit and as she ascended in the rickety lift, she braced herself for the barrage of abuse that the old lady invariably hurled at her as soon as she opened the door. This time, however, there was silence. An eerie, ominous silence. She approached the bed with her usual brisk bonhomie.

'Wake up, Mrs Tincknell, those two nice gentlemen are coming back to see you this morning. They want you to sign something so we need to have you sitting up and taking notice, don't we?'

'You'm wasting yer time.' It was Lavender from the next bed. ''Er's gone. Croaked just after breakfast. Gurgled a couple o' times, screeched 'Tommy' then fell back on 'er pillow – dead as a doornail. Bloody good riddance if you asks me, what with 'er son bein' a murderer.' Lavender was perfectly calm and matter-of-fact about it.

The matron checked Ethel's pulse to make sure but the old girl was right. 'Why didn't you press your buzzer for assistance, dear?'

'Ain't workin'. 'Asn't worked for weeks.' Lavender brightened, suddenly. 'Can I 'ave 'er bed? The view's better from 'er window.'

The matron went back down to her office to call the undertakers. It was Sunday, so they'd take an age to come and in the unhealthy heat of the nursing home, rigor mortis was setting in rapidly – she could tell from the muscles in the old lady's face. They'd have the devil's own job lugging that great carcass down the corridor and into the lift, never mind after it had gone rock hard. And she'd better ring those two policemen. No point in a wasted journey.

Dawes and Malone were bracing themselves with strong coffee in the pub breakfast room before facing another visit to the Sea View Nursing Home. Corrie joined them, looking serious.

'Jack, Bugsy, I need to have a word and I don't want you to over-react and shout at me.'

'What? Us?' said Jack, feigning umbrage. 'Why would we do that?

'Besides,' added Bugsy, 'my head hurts too much to shout. What can we do for you, Mrs Dawes?'

'It's about Ted Boobyer and Danika.'

'I thought your mate in the Licensed Victuallers was dealing with that one,' said Jack. He explained to Bugsy. 'Boobyer's a sex pest who can't keep it in his pants and he's been taking liberties with Dani. He tried it on with Carlene but she knocked him cold.'

'Good old Sherlock,' grinned Bugsy. 'But why didn't Dani say something? We could have sorted him out, issued him with a warning.'

'I think it's gone way beyond just a warning, Bugsy. The reason Dani couldn't complain to the police is that . . . well, she shouldn't really be working here at all.'

'Why? Is she claiming benefit or something?'

'No . . .' Corrie hesitated, then it all came out in a torrent. 'She's an illegal immigrant. She and Aleksy are Albanian not Polish.'

'What?' shouted both men in unison.

'Now, don't start! You promised you wouldn't shout. I couldn't tell you before because I needed to get my facts straight. And besides, there were too many other things going on like having my shoulder dislocated and my hair torn out.'

'Oh bloody hell!' said Jack. 'And Boobyer found out and made Dani have sex with him.'

'Worse than that. Boobyer is responsible for smuggling her in. He arranged the forged papers and took all her savings to pay for them. Now he says it wasn't enough and she has to work for peanuts and he makes her have sex with other men in the village. He did it before in London and got two years in the Scrubs and a ten grand fine. Now he's back to his old tricks here in Lullington where he thinks he won't be discovered.'

'The bastard!' Malone jumped up. 'Shall I go and drag him in here, Guv? He needs teaching a lesson before we arrest him.'

'But what about Danika and Aleksy?' protested Corrie. 'She supports elderly parents in Albania with the little money she has left after Boobyer has taken his cut.'

'Aah.' Bugsy sat down again. 'How d'you want to handle it, Jack?'

'Well, we can't get round the fact that she's here illegally. We have to nick Boobyer and she's bound to be deported when the authorities find out about her.'

Bugsy was thoughtful, then: 'Not necessarily. Tell you what, Guv. Don't let's do anything yet. I've got some mates in the Border Control Agency – we were having a jar down my local a couple of weeks back. They were telling me that the most recent Home Office estimate suggests there could be between 300,000 and 600,000 unauthorized migrants in Britain. The government admits it's impossible to be more accurate. They generally fill jobs considered too dirty or too dangerous by UK nationals. It's a vast hidden army of illegals making sure that offices and homes are cleaned, streets are swept and drinks are served in pubs like this one. If they get caught, they face deportation. But according to a new study, an amnesty on their status could be worth up to six billion to the economy in taxes as opposed to the potential five billion cost of finding and deporting 'em. My mates reckon they've got more than enough on their hands policing the borders and removing the newly arrived, failed asylum seekers. It's just not practical to expect them to go round the country to villages like Lullington, detaining and deporting up to half a million people. It just isn't going to happen. Give me a chance to have a word tomorrow and maybe I can spin it so that Dani gets included in an amnesty.'

'Bugsy, do you really think you could fix it?' asked Corrie.

'Well, it's worth a try. What do you say, boss?'

'If you can find a way for her to stay in the UK legally, I'm all for it. In the meantime, call your mates in Border Control and tell them to come and pick up Boobyer. This will be his second offence so they'll throw away the key this time.'

Corrie hoped so. 'I'm assuming that as Dani's forged papers were in the de Kuipers stash, they were putting the pressure on Boobyer as well. What an enterprising couple! They never missed a trick.'

'Right!' Dawes stood up. 'Come on, Sergeant, we've put it off long enough. Get your notebook out and let's get down to the nursing home and take a statement from Ethel.'

Malone grumbled under his breath. 'Never mind a notebook; you need a ruddy gas mask in that place. I don't know which smells worse; the food or the farts.'

Just as they got outside, both their mobiles rang.

'Bloody Garwood,' said Dawes, looking at the name that had flashed up on his screen.

'Smelly nursing home,' said Malone, peering at his.

They strolled to different ends of the car park to take the calls.

'Good morning, sir,' said Dawes, brightly. 'You're surely not working on this sunny Sunday morning? Shouldn't you be in church with Mrs Garwood about this time?'

Garwood was even more irascible than usual. His bowels were still badly affected by the business with MI6 and the Foreign Secretary, and he hadn't dared stray far enough from the facilities to go to church. 'Don't sound so blasted cheerful, Inspector, I'm not in a good mood. For a start, it isn't sunny here, it's chucking it down. And Mrs Garwood is holding one of her church coffee mornings. The damn house is full of cackling females stuffing their faces with your wife's gateaux.'

'But Corrie's here with me, sir.'

'I know that. Cynthia always keeps a dozen of 'em in the freezer. Anyway, never mind bloody cake, the chief constable of Somerset's been on, complaining that the body count has shot up since you and

Malone got there. More stiffs in that tiny village in two weeks than in the last fifty years, he says, and now his patch is crawling with Intelligence Agents. The Foreign Secretary's private office has been chewing his ear off about letting arms traffickers operate under his nose and he doesn't bloody well like it!'

'There haven't been *that* many bodies, sir.'

'How many are we talking about, man?'

'Er . . . six, if you count the farmer, the priest and the two Arabs.'

'That's only four.'

'Aah, yes. The Spooks dug up a couple more in my brother-in-law's garden.'

'What! No, don't tell me the details; the less I know about it, the better. I'll read the report when you get back. What the devil is it about you, Dawes? As soon as you left, it was quiet as the grave in the Murder Squad. Not a single incident. Send you to a quiet country village and they start dropping like flies. If I didn't know better, I'd say you did it on purpose to extend your holiday.'

'It hasn't been much of a holiday, sir. In fact, it's been pretty harrowing, what with—'

'Don't tell me your troubles, Inspector; I've got enough of my own. Just get it all sorted and get back here as soon as you can.' He slammed down the phone.

Malone waited until the Inspector had finished. 'What did the old windbag want, Guv?'

'Nothing much. I think he just wanted to give someone a bollocking and it's usually me. What did the matron want?'

'We aren't going to get our signed statement. Ethel Tincknell snuffed it this morning. They're waiting for the meat wagon to come and take her away and I must say I don't envy them. I hope they send more than two assistants or it'll be hernias all round.'

'Oh bloody wonderful,' said Dawes. 'Another body. That makes seven and I daresay I'll get the blame for her, as well.'

'It wasn't our fault, Guv, it was natural causes.'

'Depends how you look at it, Bugsy. If we hadn't arrived in Lullington Barrow stirring things up, the old girl might have gone on living happily with her "lovely Tommy" on Black Oak Farm for another ten years.'

'Yeah, and the pair of 'em making Dimpsy's life a living hell.'

'That's a point,' said Dawes. 'I guess Dimpsy owns the whole place now; lock, livestock and cider barrel. I doubt if the nursing home will have let her know. It'll be down to us.'

'I've always hated being the copper who has to notify the next of kin that their loved one's dead. Somehow, though, I don't think this next of kin's going to be too upset, do you?'

They found Dimpsy in the fields, harvesting the wheat. She was driving an ancient Massey Ferguson tractor that looked like it belonged in an agricultural museum. It had none of the modern safety requirements such as a cab or rollover protection; in fact, nothing to prevent it from overturning at all. Dimpsy was bouncing along at an alarming rate and for a pregnant woman, Dawes considered her severely at risk. How typical of Tincknell to persist with old, dangerous machinery rather than invest in some new equipment. But then, he never had to drive it, so why should he waste his money? A new wife was cheaper than a new tractor.

The two men caught up with Dimpsy as she slowed down to turn the corner. 'Could you come down from there, please, Mrs Tincknell? We need to speak to you.'

'Sorry,' she shouted back. 'Can't stop. Gotta get this wheat in afore the rain comes and rots it.'

'Dimpsy, your mother-in-law's dead!' bellowed Malone. It wasn't how he usually delivered bad news but it had the required effect. Dimpsy pulled up and climbed carefully down. Malone took her elbow to steady her and she smiled at him.

'Thanks.' He wasn't sure if she was thanking him for the help or the good news.

'Did the Tincknells have any other relatives, Dimpsy?' asked Jack.

'No, just me. I'm the only one left, now. Me and my baby.'

'Dimpsy, love, did you know we found Thomas's first wife buried in the woodland next to Gallows Green?' asked Malone.

'Yes, Mrs O'Dowd told me.'

Word of mouth travels faster than email in this village, thought Jack. 'Thomas shot her, Dimpsy. And Donald Draycott, the schoolmaster. I'm very sorry.'

'Me too,' she said. 'I liked Mr Draycott. He taught me to read and write when I were little. Then 'e just went away. Now I knows why.

Thomas were a very bad man, weren't 'e?'

'Yes, I'm afraid he was. Maybe it was for the best that Titus stopped him or we don't know what he might have done.'

Dimpsy looked at him, her black eyes shrewd and piercing. 'I'm not simple, Inspector, whatever folk say. I know Thomas would have killed me too, soon enough. Me and my baby. He nearly did it that time I ran off, but he were too drunk to aim straight.'

'What will you do now, Dimpsy?' asked Malone. 'You surely don't intend to carry on running this farm on your own and with a child to bring up?'

She smiled. 'Oh no, Sergeant, I won't do that. Don't 'ee worry about us.' She put her hands lovingly on her skinny belly that was now showing slight signs of swelling. 'We'll be all right now.'

Dimpsy Tincknell watched the two policemen stroll away across the golden field in the sunshine. Once they were out of sight, she abandoned the tractor and walked slowly back to the farmhouse. She stood in the middle of the kitchen, hands on her hips, and let the news slowly sink in. They were alone now, just the two of them, her and Primrose. The hospital people had told her that her baby was a girl when Doctor Brimble took her for a scan. They'd even given her a picture. She'd decided to call her daughter Primrose because it was her favourite flower.

Suddenly, she smiled. A broad, triumphant smile. Then she fetched a chair and placed it beside the blackened kitchen range. Holding on to the towel rail to steady herself, she climbed carefully on to the splintered wooden seat, testing it to make sure it would take her weight. It wouldn't do to fall and hurt herself now, after everything she'd been through; the cuts and bruises, the broken bones, and worse, the abject misery and shame of being treated like a retarded slave. There was an old bread oven in the wall behind the cooker, long abandoned and bricked up; or so it seemed. Dimpsy knew better. She had hidden outside in the yard and peeped through the cracked, grimy window-pane as Thomas climbed on to the range, took several bricks out of the wall and extracted a large tin. She had watched him stuff it with money on many occasions, wondering how the old miser could plead poverty and scrounge drinks in the pub when he had all that cash put by. Old Ethel had often hinted at 'Tommy's nest egg' and taunted Dimpsy that she'd 'never get 'er thievin' 'ands on it.' Well, she'd see about that. Ethel and Thomas were both dead. Burning in hell, where they belonged.

Dimpsy reached in and pulled out the tin. Then she placed it carefully on the range while she climbed down. The lid was warped and took a bit of loosening but Dimpsy was strong; farm labouring was hefty work. She wrenched at it and the lid finally flew off, skittering away across the filthy quarry tiles, followed by thick bundles of fifty-pound notes. More money than Dimpsy had seen in her whole life. She sat on the floor and picked up handfuls of it, tossing the notes into the air with delight. For the first time in her life, she was rich! But not half as rich as she was going to be after she'd sold Black Oak Farm and all the surrounding land. She knew Thomas hadn't left a will; the very thought of leaving anything to anybody was more than he could bear. And now the old woman was dead, too, there was only one rightful owner – Dimpsy! She got up, put all the money tidily back in the tin and went to telephone a solicitor to act for her and Primrose.

CHAPTER TWENTY-TWO

'What do you think will happen to Dimpsy?' It was late on Sunday night and Hangman's Inn was in darkness. Corrie couldn't sleep for the country noises; foxes barking to each other, the night call of a startled pheasant, yokels tottering unsteadily home and cursing as they walked into the maypole on Gallows Green. Jack couldn't sleep either but not because of the country sounds or for worrying about Dimpsy. He had far weightier things on his mind. It was time he and Bugsy returned to the Met but there were still questions that needed answers here in Lullington. Ted Boobyer was still on the loose and Operation Blondie was ongoing.

'I shouldn't worry, sweetheart. Dimpsy's a lot smarter than the folk around here give her credit for. She'll manage much better than you think.'

'Yes, but she's expecting a baby, Jack. Do you think she'll cope with bringing up a child all on her own on that ghastly farm?' Corrie flicked on the light and reached for the glass of Merlot that she'd had the foresight to collect from the bar on her way to bed. Her consumption of alcohol had soared since they came to Lullington Barrow. 'It's barely habitable. The roof and windows leak and the poor little mite's lungs will be full of coal dust and fumes after a week or two in that kitchen. The range is straight out of the ark and a health hazard.'

Jack pinched her glass and gulped quickly. 'What makes you think she'll stay on at Black Oak Farm?'

'Where else would she go? Even when she tried to run away, she ended up coming back. She doesn't know anywhere else but Lullington Barrow.'

'If you believe her version of events, she only came back because a drunken Tincknell caught her and stuck his shotgun in her belly. She was scared for her baby. She's free now. She can go wherever she pleases and I should be very surprised if she stays on that farm. Too many miserable memories. She'll want to bring up her child in a happy, cheerful place, not a dark hovel that's falling down around her ears. You wait and see.'

'I hope you're right. Do you think I should go and see her? Make sure she knows what she's doing and what help she can get?'

'I've got a better idea. Why not send Carlene to see her? She's a young woman who's been through the mill of life and come out the other side more or less intact. I believe Dimpsy will identify better with Carlene.'

'You're right. That's an excellent idea, darling.'

'I do have them, sometimes, you know.'

Corrie swiped back her Merlot and finished the last dregs. 'So what's keeping you awake?'

'Hard to explain. I know there's nothing to stop us from going home now. I've already had Garwood on the phone, moaning that it's time Bugsy and I were back at the MIT but I still have this uneasy feeling of a job half-finished. The de Kuipers are still out there somewhere and they're a dangerous, violent couple with no conscience at all.'

'I know, darling. You're never happy unless everything's completely explained and all the villains are safely banged up. But in this case, you have to leave Simon and Saskia to Carmichael. Arms trafficking isn't really your line of business. Think of it in a more positive light. Since we arrived in this poisonous village, you've solved the mysterious disappearance of Donald Draycott and Patsy Tincknell and identified their murderer, who's now dead himself, along with his evil mother. Then there's the disgusting but dead Father John who'd been getting away with abuse for years, thanks to a collusive bishop, who'll soon have some very difficult questions to answer in a civil court. And he'll be without the protection of his hierarchy, who will no doubt deny all responsibility and hang him out to dry. Dimpsy Tincknell now has a half-decent chance of making a happy life for herself and her baby and with any luck, Bugsy will have straightened things out for Danika and Aleksy and put Ted Boobyer safely behind bars yet again. That sounds like a pretty good result for a couple of weeks when you were supposed to be on holiday.'

Jack grinned. 'You're right as usual. But our Carlene would still say the statistics were "dead people seven – police nil". She still believes the two accidental deaths weren't accidental at all and I have to admit, she was right about Tincknell killing his wife and her lover.'

Corrie yawned. 'Didn't Carlene make a great job of serving dinner on Saturday?'

'She sure did; she's a natural. And I hardly recognized her all scrubbed up like that.'

'It was her way of showing me how much she wants to succeed in catering and I've an idea about how we could help her. We need to discuss it first but it'll wait until we get home.' She lay down and, aided by the soothing effects of the Merlot, was asleep in seconds.

Five o'clock on Monday morning and up in their room, Danika and Aleksy were frantically packing their meagre belongings. Dani spoke urgently to her son in Albanian, telling him to hurry because they could no longer stay. Just after dawn, she had woken suddenly, unsure why. Her room was next to the back stairs and she heard it again; footsteps creeping down the creaky wooden staircase. They were the staff stairs and normally, only she and Leksy used them. Moments later, she heard the back door of the inn open and close. She jumped out of bed and ran to the window. In the early half-light, she saw Ted Boobyer loading suitcases into the back of his car. He glanced furtively up at the windows and she dodged back behind the curtains. Satisfied that he hadn't been spotted, he climbed into the driver's seat, closed the door as quietly as possible and drove swiftly away.

Dani had always known this day would come; the day that the authorities would close in on Boobyer and his racket. When the two policemen from London had arrived at Hangman's Inn, she had become anxious, thinking they had come for her, but they rapidly became involved in other crimes and appeared to ignore her. Then Mrs Dawes had approached her and had known everything. She'd promised that Mr Boobyer would be arrested and that she would see if she could make things easier, but now Dani was watching him escape and knew that she and Leksy would be left behind to take the blame. They had to get away before that happened; maybe to Bristol or Birmingham, a big city where they could lose themselves among all the other foreigners and find work. She had thought of doing this before, but Mr Boobyer had threatened to come after her and hurt Leksy. But now he'd left and so must she.

*

Later, at breakfast, Dawes, Malone, Corrie and Carlene sat at their usual table waiting for Danika to bring their coffee. After some ten minutes, Carlene got up.

'I'll go and see what's keepin' Dani.'

There was no need. Seconds later, a furious Liz Boobyer rushed into the room, still in her dressing gown and clearly in a state. She stopped at their table, leaning on it for support and gasping for breath.

'He's gone! The bastard's run off and left me!'

'Sit down, Liz, and tell us what's happened.' Corrie pulled a chair out for her.

'I knew he were up to summat, the swine; always got a bit o' skirt on the go, but this time, he's really for it. 'Tiz the end for 'im when they catches up with 'im.' She turned to Jack. 'Tell me what you wants to know, Inspector Dawes and I'll give 'ee all the evidence you need to put the bugger away for life! I just found where he'd hidden it, down the cellar, behind the barrels.'

Carlene disappeared off to the kitchen to make coffee and cook breakfast. Danika was nowhere to be seen and it looked like it was going to be a long job. Mrs D, Mr Jack and Sergeant Bugsy would want some grub at the end of it. While she was pushing bacon and eggs around the hotplate, something outside caught her eye. A taxi had drawn up and the driver was waiting with his engine running. That's a bit random, thought Carlene. Boobyer had already legged it, his wife was in the dining room with the others and there weren't any more guests at Hangman's Inn. Who would've called a cab? Then she saw Dani scurrying past the window dragging a bag with one hand and Leksy with the other. Carlene's only thought was that she had to stop her. This wasn't the way out; running off to what could end up being a worse hell than the one the poor cow had already been through. Carlene had total faith in Mrs D and if she said it had to be sorted out the proper, legal way, then she believed her.

Carlene dropped her egg slice and nipped out the side door, just in time to waylay Dani and Leksy before they reached the taxi.

'Stop! Don't do it, love. You'll just make fings worse for yourselves. The little lad deserves better than a life on the run. I should know; I've been there. Come back wiv me and we'll talk to Mr Jack and Sergeant Bugsy. It'll be okay, I know it will. But not if you scarper.'

Dani glanced at the distance to the taxi and wondered if she should run for it. Then her spirit failed, her chin dropped and she knew Carlene was right. They had become quite friendly, cooking together in the kitchen and now, Aleksy ran to Carlene and buried his face in her apron. She put her arms around him and waited. Realizing the sad inevitability of her position, Dani dismissed the cab driver and he roared off, muttering imprecations about 'bleedin' foreigners what can't make their minds up'. Carlene, Dani and Leksy walked slowly back to the inn where blue smoke was drifting out of the kitchen door.

'Bloody 'ell!' shrieked Carlene, breaking into a sprint. 'I've only left the flippin' eggs and bacon on the 'otplate!'

Police Constable Fizzah (call me Fizz) Chowdhry had been sent from Portishead to Lullington Barrow as a temporary replacement for the disgraced Gilbert Chedzey. She was young, bright and enthusiastic. The effect on the village couldn't have been more traumatic if they'd sent Xena the Warrior Princess. The shocked locals slouched around the public bar of Hangman's Inn in their grimy dungarees and bemoaned the loss of good old Gilbert. 'What be the world comin' to?' they asked each other. The problem that the villagers had with PC Chowdhry wasn't so much that she was a woman – although that was quite bad enough. It wasn't even the fact that she was 'well . . . you knows what I mean . . . 'er's foreign, innur?' Their real concern was that she insisted on doing her job properly and got 'real comical' when folk objected. Constable Chedzey had never demanded they clean up the road when their dilapidated old tractor-trailers had deposited a trail of cow muck all through the village. Old Gilbert hadn't gone round checking their knackered vehicles for daft things like tax discs and MOTs and asking to see shotgun licences. ''Tiz all right and proper to fine the "incomers" but not folk what's lived 'ere all their lives.' And what business was it of hers if they put red diesel in their cars, slaughtered and ate their own beasts and sold untreated milk. 'Bloody meddlin', that's what I calls it!'

But her worst transgression in the eyes of the locals was when she arrested their friendly pub landlord, Ted Boobyer. As soon as Liz had shopped her husband to Inspector Dawes and told of his attempted getaway, Malone had telephoned the police station and told PC Chowdhry to get after him, fast. His route would take him out of the village and right past the police station on the southern perimeter of Lullington and from there, onto the M5. Chowdhry had taken off in the powerful BMW 5 Series pursuit car that she'd brought with her from Bristol, blues and twos screaming. Soon, backup from Taunton joined her and at least six police cars were speeding down the motorway towards Devon and the Cornish coast, which was Boobyer's intended escape route abroad.

In the event, the additional resources proved to be overkill. Boobyer's station wagon was no match for the BMW and in less than twenty minutes, PC Chowdhry had him boxed in on the hard shoulder. She hauled him out of the vehicle, none too gently, cautioned him and snapped on the handcuffs. He was driven back to Lullington Barrow, protesting his innocence and outrage all the way. Chowdhry finally silenced him by telling him Inspector Dawes and Sergeant Malone from the Met were on their way to the police station to question him.

When they got there, Boobyer was sitting on a bunk in the police cell, noisily slurping down the cup of tea that the newly assigned PC Chowdhry had brought for him. He had a rather prominent nose that stuck out above the mug and a large Adam's apple that bobbed up and down as he swallowed. He looked somehow thinner and scrawnier than when he'd been throwing his weight around with young women in Hangman's Inn. Being banged up, even if only briefly, did that to a man.

The rattling of keys from outside heralded the advent of Inspector Dawes, who strode in and stood there, his eyes narrowed and angry. Boobyer's Adam's apple clunked up and down more rapidly as he gulped, leapt to his feet and blurted out his wounded innocence before Dawes could get a single word out.

'I don't know under what laws you think you can hold me here, Dawes! I've done nothing. This stupid policewoman wouldn't listen to a word I said and I shall be suing for wrongful arrest. The whole thing is a nightmare; completely unreal. I'm numb. I feel nothing.'

'You'll feel a sharp pain in the goolies in a minute,' snapped Malone, 'and it'll be real all right.'

'Please – I hate violence.'

'You didn't seem to hate it when you were sexually assaulting those young foreign women that you've been smuggling in illegally.'

'You can't prove any of that.'

'On the contrary, Danika has told us everything,' bluffed Malone.

'She'd say anything to save her own skin. I took her on in good faith. I had no idea she was in the country illegally. You've no evidence. It's her word against mine.'

Dawes's lip curled with disgust. 'That's where you're wrong. Your wife has finally had enough of your criminal activities. She's handed over everything; forged papers, the names of your contacts abroad, copies of your bank statements showing the regular payments—'

'The bitch!' roared Boobyer. 'I should have dumped the ugly cow years ago and got the hell out of Lullington Barrow.'

'Yes, you probably should,' agreed Dawes. 'What you're going to do now is make a full statement confessing to everything you've done since your last spell in prison. Then you'll be handed over to officers from the Border Control Agency who are very anxious to speak to you and the people you've been working with.' Dawes turned on his heels and marched out.

'Well done, Constable Chowdhry,' said Dawes. 'That was a good piece of pursuit work.'

'You're not planning on staying in Lullington Barrow, are you?' asked Malone.

'No fear, Sarge. They want me to clean up this place then I'm off, back to the city. It'd drive me barmy living here among all these yokels. They don't even speak proper English.'

When Dawes and Malone returned to Hangman's Inn, Liz Boobyer was serving behind the bar as if nothing had happened. She certainly showed no signs of regret that her husband was in custody and would remain so for many years. She was aware that she might be charged as an accessory but was sticking firmly to her story that she believed her husband had been going straight since his release from the Scrubs and it was only after he'd left her that she discovered evidence in the cellar that he'd been up to his old tricks. There was every chance that Danika would confirm her story since Liz had taken no part in Boobyer's transactions with her and would have cheerfully gelded him with the pub's ice pick had she found out about the sexual abuse and pimping. She nodded to Dawes and Malone as they came in and indicated that they should go through to the lounge bar where Dani was sitting quietly with her hands in her lap and her head bowed. Corrie and Carlene sat with her and Rosemary had come from her room bringing some soothing sachets of rose and flax, which she passed round.

Expecting the worst, Dani had sent Leksy off to school with Jeremy as usual. They would soon break up for the long summer holiday and it was during this time that she suspected they would be deported back to Albania. Leksy was a bright child and his education had improved immensely in the UK. Now, with the prospect of no job and little money, she feared for his future. Her deeply superstitious nature told her that God had punished them for breaking the law; a belief that had been supported by the death of Father John and the sea's destruction of St Mary's Church of the Blessed Virgin. She had gone to the ruins and knelt there, praying for forgiveness, but God was unyielding. Now, she must suffer whatever punishment He chose to mete out through His servants: Inspector Dawes and Sergeant Malone. She almost trembled as they approached; Jack and Bugsy almost trembled at the daunting army of female Mafia waiting for them.

'Good news, ladies,' said Malone quickly, pre-empting the first strike. 'My colleagues in Border Control have looked at Danika's circumstances and they're pretty sure it will be possible for her to stay. Apparently, there are a lot of poor devils who've been working here for years and it's taken the authorities so long to try and sort out their deportation that they've decided to invoke an amnesty, if only because it'll be cheaper. They think Danika can be included. Mind you, there'll be a good deal of negotiating and form-filling to be done, there always is, but it's going to be all right.'

Corrie, Carlene and even prim Rosie cheered. Dani still looked scared and confused. 'What, please, is amnesty? I do not understand. Are we to be sent back to Albania?'

'No, love,' said Bugsy. 'You'll be able to stay here and work legally.'

'No strings and no massive deductions from your wages,' said Corrie.

'No looking over your shoulder all the time,' added Rosie.

'And no manky old bloke making you 'ave sex wiv 'im and 'is mates or else 'e'll blow the whistle,' said Carlene, getting right to the crux of the matter, as ever.

Dani's face lit up like a light bulb as she finally took in what they were saying. 'This is miracle, yes? God has answered my prayers.'

'I think Carlene's point had more influence on the government's decision than God,' said Malone. 'You were being systematically abused by Ted Boobyer and his mates.'

Danika was defensive. 'I did it for Aleksy. I had to protect him even though I hated it.'

'The wicked irony of it,' observed Dawes, 'is that the poor little lad was doing something similar to protect you.'

Dani frowned. 'What was Leksy doing? I don't understand.'

Rosie found it almost impossible to believe that a mother wouldn't know that her child was being abused but the facts confirmed that it happened more often than she wanted to imagine. 'Aleksy was being sexually abused by Father John. He put up with it because the priest threatened you with eternal damnation; excommunication from the faith that was so precious to you.'

Dani jumped up. 'No! That's a lie! Father John was a holy man, a saint; he would never do that. He heard my confession, gave me the blessed sacrament, he was . . .' She looked around at their faces and saw that it was true. She sank back into her seat and buried her face in her hands, sobbing over and over again: '*Fëmijën tim të varfër.*' My poor baby.

CHAPTER TWENTY-THREE

With Boobyer safely behind bars and facing a long stretch, and Danika and Aleksy's futures potentially more settled, Corrie was looking forward to going home. It was hard to recall that initially, she'd only come to Lullington Barrow to cater Rosie's housewarming barbecue and enjoy a few days' holiday with Jack. A lot had happened since then; some of it pretty hair-raising. She'd been away from Coriander's Cuisine far longer than she'd intended and she and Carlene would have a lot of catching up to do with existing orders and new business. And she had a proposition to put to Carlene; one that she hoped would be taken up with enthusiasm, if not wild euphoria. Although it was hard to predict with Carlene. Her harsh young life had been so full of neglect and disappointment; it was almost as if she found it hard to accept good fortune in case it was snatched away again. Corrie would have to handle her with great sensitivity and maybe even a bit of affection. Goodness knows, she'd had precious little of that in the past.

Inspector Dawes was also anxious to get back home to the Met although he still had a niggling sense of a job not quite finished. It was the blasted de Kuiper situation. If Carmichael's contacts were right, Simon and Saskia were still out there somewhere, getting away with lucrative arms trafficking that was supporting terrorism and repression in several countries. Following the appearance of the two Arabs in Lullington Barrow, albeit briefly, Carmichael and the heads of his organization were still convinced that the de Kuipers would turn up, sooner or later, to collect their valuable stash from the pond where Simon had left it. Operation Blondie was still in place and although there were operatives concealed in every available nook and cranny, to the average passer-by, Gibbet Cottage seemed deserted. Dawes thought he'd pay one last visit for an update before heading for home the next day.

Carmichael was speaking urgently on his mobile as usual. Jack started to walk away but he motioned for him to wait. He was obviously talking to the boss.

'Yes, sir, I understand. Looks like we might be able to wrap this one up pretty soon. Yes, we'll stay vigilant, sir. Full red-alert threat level for the time being. I understand.' He snapped off the phone and spoke to Dawes.

'We've just received intelligence from our undercover agents in the Middle East that Simon de Kuiper has been picked up on the border between Syria and Turkey. He's being 'interrogated' by the Turks. I'll leave you to imagine what that's like.'

Dawes winced. 'What about Saskia? Have they captured her, too?'

'It seems not. The smart money is on her having escaped disguised in a *burka* during the fight when her husband and his Arab accomplices were taken.'

'So is that the end of Operation Blondie?' Dawes wanted to know.

Carmichael shook his head. 'Not yet. They seem to think Saskia will head straight back to Gibbet Cottage to pick up the list of dissidents in order to bargain for her husband's life.'

'She doesn't know it's already in western possession?'

'No. How could she? As far as she's concerned, it's still in the sludge at the bottom of the soakaway. One thing's for sure, she won't hang about. She'll want to get back here as soon as possible while there's still some of Simon left to save. My orders are to maintain the surveillance operation until she turns up and then grab her. She still has a great deal of useful information that we'd like to get our hands on.'

Dawes was thoughtful. 'How secure are your communications?'

'Very secure. Why do you ask?'

'No reason, really. It just occurred to me that Saskia de Kuiper is only safe as long as the Arabs don't know you've already found what they're after. Once they find that out, they've no reason to keep her or her husband alive as they have nothing to barter with. Is there a chance that someone might tip them off?'

Carmichael shrugged. 'You can't be sure of anything in this game.'

Carlene was ambivalent about visiting Dimpsy Tincknell – or she would have been if she'd known what the word meant. On the one hand, if Mrs D and Mr Jack thought it was the right thing to do and it would help, then obviously she would go. On the other hand, her previous visits to Black Oak Farm had filled her with gloom and heart-rending pity. There had been times in Carlene's life when she believed she must be the unhappiest wretch on the planet. Meeting Dimpsy and seeing the appalling circumstances of her existence had made her appreciate the irritating old adage that there's always someone worse off than you. Now, Dimpsy was pregnant and there would be another unfortunate little soul living in that filthy, godforsaken place.

As she crossed the yard and headed for the kitchen door, she had a weird feeling that something had changed. She knew that the deaths of Thomas and his mother must have had a massive impact on Dimpsy, never mind the knowledge that her husband was a murderer, but it was more than that. The whole atmosphere of the place was different, more positive, somehow, but she couldn't quite put her finger on why. Even the scrawny chickens looked bright-eyed, pecking and scratching around; free range now, not cooped up and half-starved in a rusty pen. The cows were grazing contentedly in the fields, no longer fearful of a sudden, bad-tempered wallop with a spade. There was no sign of Dimpsy in the yard so Carlene knocked tentatively at the kitchen door. On her last visit, the old panels had been rotten with slats missing and she'd have had reservations about knocking on it at all. The door was still shabby but someone had attempted to mend it with some lengths of wood and now, it was much sturdier and even weather-proof. When it finally creaked open and Dimpsy stood there, Carlene was rendered speechless for the first time ever.

Dimpsy had been shopping in the city with some of Tincknell's 'nest egg'. Her hair, previously unkempt and invariably tangled with bits of straw had been cut and styled. The baggy, faded dungarees had been replaced by a pair of smart designer jeans and her bright pink hoodie bore the logo of a fashion house so expensive that Carlene could only dream about wearing their clothes. But the biggest change was in Dimpsy herself. She was relaxed and confident and she had carefully applied some subtle make-up. Her eyes, so often bruised and swollen, were now accentuated with smoky pearl shadow and pink lipstick emphasized a smile instead of a split lip. She reached out for Carlene's hand and pulled her inside.

'Hello. I remember you – you're Carlene. You were there when those policemen questioned me and you stopped 'em from bein' bullies.

I were grateful. Would you like some tea? I got cake, too.'

So far, Carlene hadn't spoken, just nodded and smiled. She was stunned by the change in this young woman who, in truth, was only a few years older than herself. Never mind a makeover, this was a bloody miracle! She looked around the kitchen while Dimpsy busied herself making tea. It was very much cleaner than on her first visit and Carlene noticed that Dimpsy had acquired an electric kettle and a microwave oven instead of battling constantly to generate some heat from the ancient range. These were items of 'foreign new-fangled trash', the purchase of which Tincknell would never have countenanced had he been alive. 'That range were good enough for Mother and her mother afore 'er, so 'tiz good enough for 'ee!'

When they were seated at the scrubbed pine table with mugs of tea and slices of a splendid homemade Victoria sponge, Carlene thought she'd better ask some of the questions that Mrs D had suggested, to make sure Dimpsy was okay, but she was beginning to think her visit was unnecessary. Dimpsy looked great, like a different person.

'How you gettin' on then, what wiv you bein' pregnant an' all? You got any plans? This is awesome cake, by the way; couldn't do better meself.'

Dimpsy beamed at the praise, which was a new experience for her, having, like Carlene, spent most of her life being told she was soft in the head and therefore useless. 'Thanks.' She put her hands lovingly on the slight swell beneath her jeans. 'Me and Primrose are doin' fine. Doctor Brimble reckons she'll be born just afore Candlemas.' She looked around her with distaste. ''Course, we won't be livin' here then.'

Carlene helped herself to more cake. 'You finkin' of movin'? Don't blame ya, love. This is no place to bring up a kid.'

'My solicitors are dealin' with everythin',' declared Dimpsy, proudly. 'They've sorted out all the legal stuff and they say that the farm and all the land's mine and I can do what I like with it, so I'm sellin' the lot. I've been offered a good price by developers and they're goin' to build houses here for nice, gentle folk. I'm glad o' that. I shall come and watch when they pull it all down.'

Dimpsy became thoughtful, smiling to herself. How Thomas and Ethel would have hated that. How furious Thomas would have been to watch the total demolition of the farmhouse he'd lived in all his life, and his father and grandfather before him. She almost wished that he and his horrible mother were still alive to see it. But that was daft because if they were, it wouldn't be happening. They'd lived like filthy pigs, wallowing in their own muck for years and years and never wanting anything to change. But now it was over and the end of the Tincknells for ever, because Dimpsy already had plans to change her name after she left. She had no intention of baby Primrose being called Tincknell; a constant reminder of her violent, cruel father.

'That's real mega gear you're wearin',' said Carlene admiringly. 'Them jeans are to die for.' She pulled a rueful face. 'Sorry, love, bad choice of words. I shouldn't 'ave mentioned dying, not when you've just lost your 'usband.' She paused, then: 'Mind you, some people might say old Titus did you a bit of a favour, like.'

'Titus did Thomas a favour, too,' returned Dimpsy.

'How d'you work that one out?'

'Thomas always boasted that he'd been born here on this farm and he wanted to die here, like his father and grandfather afore him. If the police had locked 'im up for them two murders, he'd have died in prison, like as not. Titus just gave him his wish. 'Tiz more'n he deserved, to my mind. I'd 'ave liked to see 'im rot in jail.'

Dimpsy looked Carlene frankly in the eye, defying any challenge to that view. It was in that moment that Carlene was absolutely certain her initial gut feeling had been right and that Dimpsy had trapped Tincknell in Titus's pen on purpose, knowing the beast would kill him. The story about him being drunk and accidentally falling into the bull pen after climbing a ladder to mend a leak in the roof had, to Carlene, been an implausible and convenient one, but impossible to disprove. For a few defining moments, the two stared at each other in silence. Despite their different backgrounds – gritty city and crude country – they were not poles apart. Both young women were significantly smarter than people realized. Pity, mused Carlene, that people judged you on biased assumptions rather than letting you prove what you could actually achieve. Not Mr Jack and Mrs D, though. They'd given her the benefit of the doubt and she was not about to let them down. But right now, she needed the answer to a vital question.

'Not bein' funny or nuffink, Dimpsy, but it *was* an accident, I s'pose?' asked Carlene, cautiously. 'To be honest wiv ya, I wouldn't blame ya if you'd, like, helped him on his way. He was a wicked, murderin' old bastard, pardon my French.'

'Don't really matter now, do it?' said Dimpsy, shortly. 'Thomas believed in the old country ways. The right to take the law into his own hands. That's why he killed Patsy and Mr Draycott. Thomas were cruel to Titus and Titus got his own back. It were old country justice and that's an end to it.' She stood up. 'Thanks for comin' to see me; it's been nice chattin' but I gotta get on now. The lorry's comin' to take the cows to the abattoir for slaughter and I still 'ave to wring the hens' necks.'

Outside in the yard, they shook hands formally. 'Bye, Dimpsy, and good luck wiv the baby,' said Carlene. 'Don't 'spect we'll meet again, 'coz I'm goin' 'ome soon.'

'Thanks. We're goin' to be fine, now. I hopes you 'ave a safe journey.' As Carlene walked away, Dimpsy called after her. 'By the way, my name ain't Dimpsy, it's Holly. I were born on Christmas Day, see. I ain't goin' to be called Dimpsy no more, not by anyone.' She waved and went indoors.

As Carlene strolled back to Hangman's Inn, her mind was in turmoil. Until now, life's vicissitudes and the best way to deal with them had always been pretty straightforward; grim and often violent, but straightforward. She'd had few choices, most of them associated with simple survival. But she recognized that this was a much trickier situation that needed careful handling. She was quite certain that Dimpsy, who was now Holly – a much nicer name – had contrived an ingenious way of disposing of a vindictive, vicious husband without taking the blame. She'd all but admitted it. But on the other hand, Tincknell had cold-bloodedly taken his shotgun and murdered two people, believing it was his right. He had been quite capable of killing Dimpsy, too, if she displeased him sufficiently. It was only because she was strong and robust that he hadn't already beaten her to death. But did that make it right for Dimpsy to get rid of him? It was what posh, educated people would call an ethical dilemma and it was all to do with principles. Carlene had never been able to afford the luxury of principles. Added to which, Dimpsy was expecting a baby, a little girl. With the father dead, there were no other relatives able to look after her. Dimpsy's parents, the Puddys, were already overcrowded with unwanted kids. So if Dimpsy went to jail, the child would be put into care. Another poor, innocent little bugger at the mercy of Social

Services and all the horrors that went with it. Now that was something Carlene knew *all* about and it made up her mind.

Inspector Dawes, Sergeant Malone and Corrie were having lunch in the dining room when Carlene returned.

'Whatcha, Sherlock!' called Malone. 'Want some fish and chips?'

'No fanks, Sergeant Bugsy, I'm not very 'ungry.'

'How was Dimpsy?' asked Corrie. 'Do you think she's going to cope all right when the baby comes?'

Carlene sat down on the empty chair at their table. Corrie poured her a cup of tea because she looked like she could do with it.

'Oh yeah, she'll cope all right. She's got it all worked out. She's selling up and movin' away. Buying a nice, clean little bungalow by the sea for herself and baby Primrose. She'll be well off and happy for the first time in her life.' Corrie thought Carlene sounded wistful and not a little envious.

'Do you still believe Dimpsy trapped Tincknell in the bull pen on purpose?' asked Jack.

Carlene hesitated, but only for a heartbeat. 'No, Mr Jack. I got that all wrong. She ain't smart enough to 'ave planned it. And she ain't called Dimpsy no more. Her real name's Holly. Dimpsy was just a nasty nickname given to her by nasty people.' She looked across at Corrie with an expression that Corrie found hard to interpret. 'Can we go 'ome, tomorrer, Mrs D? I don't like the countryside much.'

CHAPTER TWENTY-FOUR

Next morning, having convinced himself that his work in Lullington Barrow was finally over, Inspector Dawes was helping Corrie to pack. The aim was to return to London straight after breakfast and before the traffic had built up.

'Whenever I go away anywhere, I always seem to have more stuff to take home than I came with, even when I haven't bought anything,' said Corrie. 'Isn't it funny?'

'Hilarious,' wheezed Jack, sitting down hard on her suitcase. 'I suppose it couldn't have anything to do with those two huge hairy sweaters that your sister gave you.'

'Dick bought them for her birthday but they're the wrong size; much too big for her. They fit me perfectly, though.'

'The black one comes down to your knees and the sleeves drag on the floor. It makes you look like King Kong.'

'Thanks. You'd think if you'd lived with someone as long as Dick has lived with Rosie, you'd know what size they were.'

'Dick wouldn't. He's a twerp.'

'I know, but we have to cut him some slack. He's had some really nasty experiences recently. I mean, you're a murder detective; your life is one long nasty experience. Dick's a banker and he's not used to it. You have to feel a bit sorry for him.'

'No, I don't. Only a twenty-four carat plonker would buy a house in a toxic village like Lullington Barrow from a couple of blackmailing, gun-toting shysters on the run from the Arabs. Any normal bloke would have done some checks then bought a house in Milton Keynes or Stratford-on-Avon.'

'That's not really fair. It's easy to be wise with hindsight. Dick had no way of knowing the previous owners were criminals and you have to admit, the property was an amazing bargain. Imagine having that huge garden with your own private woodland and a beautiful, lush green lawn—'

'... which has a couple of bodies buried under it. Never mind the friendly neighbours who take it in turns to break in, set fire to your attic and welt you with a garden implement in the middle of the night.' He fastened the bulging suitcase. 'Is this the lot?'

'No, hang on a minute, I forgot my golf shoes.' She pursed her lips. 'Blast! They're still at the golf club. I put them in Rosie's locker. Well, I'm not going home without them, they cost a fortune. I'll nip down and get them. See you at breakfast, darling.'

The sun, already fierce, scorched down out of a cloudless sky as Corrie took the short cut down the lane that ran along the back of Gallows Green. When she arrived, Lullington Barrow golf links had just opened for business and a scattering of early morning golfers strolled out towards the first tee. It looked tempting in the sunshine with the seashore as a backdrop. The tide was in, no longer wild and angry, just white-tipped, gentle waves. Corrie paused to enjoy the view then hurried away to the ladies' changing room to fetch her shoes. Jack, Bugsy and Carlene would be waiting for her, anxious to make an early start before the motorway became clogged with holidaymakers, crawling back home to the city.

On the way out, Corrie spotted Bridget O'Dowd behind the bar of the clubhouse. As usual, when Mrs O'Dowd was cleaning, the room reeked of metal polish, furniture wax and bleach. Corrie thought she'd just pop in and say cheerio to her. The woman was an entertaining character and after all, she'd just lost Father John with whom she must have developed a close relationship, having been his housekeeper for many years. She wondered how much Mrs O'Dowd had known about the priest's proclivities and whether loyalty and her Catholic faith had compelled her to stay silent. If she hadn't known about it before his death, she obviously knew now; it was all over the village despite the bishop's vociferous rebuttals. Corrie decided to tread carefully.

'Mrs O'Dowd, I've come to say goodbye. We're going back home this morning.'

Mrs O'Dowd looked up briefly; then satisfied it wasn't anyone important, she continued polishing furiously. It was Marcus's hole-in-one golf trophy mounted on the heavy green Connemara marble that was so much admired by the old Irish cleaner.

''Bye,' she mumbled. She didn't exactly say 'and bloody good riddance' but it was inherent in her manner and written on her face. But she was only one member of the Lullington Barrow community who would be glad to see the back of the Metropolitan Policemen and their associates.

Any prudent person would have walked away then, but not Corrie. She could never leave well alone. 'I . . . er . . . I just wanted to say that Father John's death must have been a terrible shock for you and I'm sorry for that.' Corrie carefully avoided saying she was sorry he was dead because she wasn't. If she'd been the kind of person who believed in acts of God, then the avenging golf ball had been a timely and well-aimed one. 'I expect you'd developed great fondness and respect for him over the years.'

Bridget O'Dowd put down the trophy and her sharp eyes raked the deserted bar to ensure that they were alone and out of earshot of any eavesdroppers. Then she fixed Corrie with a glare that would have stunned a marauding Black and Tan at fifty paces. When she spoke, it was in a hoarse, blood-chilling whisper that barely concealed the underlying venom.

'Father John was a pompous, canting old hypocrite. He didn't worship God; he thought he **was** God. He strutted about this village in a homemade halo, preying on the helpless and innocent for his own wicked pleasures. The man was a monster, and someone . . .' she picked up the trophy, '. . . had to put a stop to him.' Outburst over, Bridget took a cloth, soaked it well in bleach and rubbed hard at the golf ball that surmounted the plinth.

Corrie gulped. The message, whilst not spelled out in words of one syllable, had been unequivocal. There was nothing more to say. Corrie gathered up her bag and golf shoes and strode swiftly out. Glancing up, Mrs O'Dowd watched her hurry cross the terrace and out through the wrought-iron gates.

As Corrie walked slowly back down the lane, facts from Father John's death that had previously seemed irrelevant now flitted around her brain like demented butterflies. Try as she might, she couldn't dismiss them so she considered each one, logically. Fact one; the forensic findings determined that death had resulted from a fractured skull; blunt force trauma caused by a small and extremely hard round object. Fact two; a golf ball covered in the priest's blood had been conveniently discovered in the grass near the body. Fact three; faint traces of the same blood had been identified in the soil sample that Bugsy took from beneath the sacrarium, so Father John could have been killed in the sacristy and his body moved later. Corrie reckoned it was pretty widely known that undiluted household bleach such as Mrs O'Dowd used to clean the golf ball trophy can denature cells, making any DNA results inconclusive. And why, she wondered, would the housekeeper leave a hot Indian curry for Father John's supper when, at the barbecue, she had prevented him from eating anything spicy because it made him 'fart like an old Labrador'? Why? Because she knew he wouldn't be alive to eat it. And finally, there was Carlene's total conviction that someone had 'lamped the old perv'.

Corrie didn't believe for a moment that the killing had been pre-meditated; rather that it was conceived and carried out spontaneously. Mrs O'Dowd must have been taking Marcus's trophy home to polish it when she discovered Father John sexually abusing Aleksy in the sacristy and she'd decided to put a stop to him, once and for all. She had taken the trophy from her capacious bag and simply bashed him over the head with it. The indentation in his skull made by the ball mounted on the marble plinth would have been virtually impossible to distinguish from an airborne one, hit by a golfer. She had been aided during the night by the freak tide that had breached the crumbling wall around St Mary's. The raging sea water had surged through the church, cleansing the sacristy where the old priest had met his death and effectively sweeping away any evidence that might have remained. Of course, Bridget couldn't have anticipated such a natural disaster occurring at exactly the right time and that, thought Corrie, might cause people who were so inclined to wonder again about the possibility of an Act of God. God wasn't usually so obliging.

Although she didn't know it, Corrie was wrestling with an ethical dilemma similar to the one Carlene had faced after her meeting with Dimpsy Tincknell, now Holly Puddy. Her quandary was whether it's acceptable for someone to take the law into their own hands and bump off a human being simply because he was a total bastard and didn't deserve a place on the planet. By the time Corrie reached Hangman's Inn, she had unknowingly come to the same conclusion as Carlene; she would say nothing about what she had found out and she was satisfied she could live with that decision. The only thing that bothered her was that the locals would say of such rough justice: 'Aarrh, 'tiz the old country ways, innur?' It was definitely time to go home!

Jack and Corrie said goodbye to Dick and Rosie after breakfast. With Operation Blondie still in force at Gibbet Cottage, it seemed they would be unable to return home for some time.

'It's been lovely seeing you both and young Jeremy, despite the unfortunate chain of events. You must come and stay with us,' invited Corrie, trying not to look at Jack.

Dawes was quick to respond. 'Don't be daft, Corrie. Dick and Rosie are country folk now and probably not keen to spend time wallowing about in the city filth and pollution that you and I live in, never mind all the crime and violence.'

Dick recognized that this was what he'd said to Jack when they first arrived and despite being an insensitive twit, the irony wasn't lost on him. He shuffled his feet, stared down at them, then glanced at Rosie, who nodded. Dick cleared his throat, several times.

'Actually, Rosie and I have decided that we may have made a slight error of judgement in moving to the countryside.'

'Oh, for goodness sake, Dick!' Rosie interrupted impatiently. 'The truth is, we made a terrible mistake. It wasn't at all what we expected. We'd hoped for a safe, gentle place to bring up Jerry but it's turned out to be simply ghastly; a positive nightmare. We've put Gibbet Cottage back on the market at a bargain price for a quick sale. We're hoping to move out as soon as Mr Carmichael and his team tell us it's all clear.'

Corrie flashed Jack a look that said 'I told you so' but she didn't say it. 'I'm glad, Rosie. I'm sure you'll be much happier away from Lullington Barrow. Have you had any thoughts about where you'll go?'

'We're going to live near Lex and his mum.' Jeremy had burst in, arm in arm with Aleksy, who was beaming widely.

'We don't know exactly where, yet,' confirmed Rosie, 'but as Jerry and Lexy have become such close friends, we've said we'll try to arrange for them to go to the same school. It'll help them both to settle and give them a little stability after all the moving about and the . . . er . . . unpleasant things that have happened.'

'I think that's a smashing idea,' said Corrie, giving both boys a hug. 'Parents underestimate what an upheaval it is for children, moving house and changing schools. It can make them feel insecure for the rest of their lives.'

'S'right, Mrs D,' agreed Carlene, deadpan. 'I was never in the same school more than six months before they slung me out. That's why I'm such a quiet, shy person; too scared to say nuffink out loud or make a show of meself.'

'Me, too, Sherlock,' said Bugsy. 'I blame all those nuns and monks for me ending up picking over dead bodies for a living. Too sensitive and emotional, that's my problem. People take advantage of me.'

Dawes grinned. 'Come on, you two; let's get going before you have us all in tears.'

It was while they were loading up the van that Carlene spotted it; something black flapping from the gibbet up on Gallows Hill. There hadn't been anything there when she'd climbed the hill on the day she rescued Mrs D and her sister. She couldn't quite make it out so she shielded her eyes from the sun, the better to see it. Gradually, her dazzled gaze made out a dummy of some sort, hanging by its neck from the noose. Now, why would someone do that? This place is seriously mingin' and the yokels are a sad bunch of sickos, she thought. She was about to turn away when she noticed the dummy had long blonde hair, blowing in the breeze. She swallowed hard. It couldn't be, could it? Bloody hell, what if it was? It was too 'orrible to even imagine and she looked away, quickly. But she couldn't leave without telling someone. She tugged at Malone's sleeve.

'Sergeant Bugsy, what d'you fink that is, up there on Gallows Hill? It ain't a body, is it?'

Bugsy put down the heavy suitcase that he was about to stash in the back of the van. 'What are you up to now, Sherlock?' He, too, shielded his eyes from the sun and looked to where she was pointing. 'I hope you're not winding me up because . . .' He gulped as the shredded *burka* and yellow hair came into focus. 'Holy shit!' He walked over to Dawes who was wrestling with a pile of Corrie's catering containers and spoke quietly in his ear. 'Jack, unless I'm badly mistaken and I hope to God I am, I think we just found Saskia de Kuiper.'

Carmichael and his men got her down. She was naked under the *burka* and it was clear she had been subjected to a prolonged and savage assault before she was hanged. They weren't sure how long she'd been swinging there but it was long enough for the crows to have pecked her eyes out. The *burka* had been ripped to ribbons.

'That,' said Carmichael, 'would have been their rage that such a woman would dare to wear an item of clothing sacred to the Muslim faith, especially as a disguise in order to escape. And you were right, Jack. Our communications weren't as secure as we thought. Saskia de Kuiper was only safe as long as the Arabs didn't find out we'd already seized the list that they were after. Once they knew that, she was as good as dead. Someone on the inside tipped them off. Probably the same person who let the Arabs know where they were hiding out originally.'

Inspector Dawes recalled Marcus's story about his wealthy client in Dubai and his freedom-fighting brother in Syria. The Arab network was far-reaching, fanatical and ruthless. The de Kuipers had been involved in a very dangerous business. It had only been a matter of time before they were caught and eliminated. The villagers were deeply shocked; especially Edgar Brimble who had been called to examine Saskia's violated body and pronounce life extinct. As a country doctor, he had witnessed many dreadful injuries from farm machinery and the like, but nothing as brutal and pitiless as this. His face was ashen as the young woman's mutilated body was taken away.

'What I don't understand,' said Corrie, sickened by the terrible turn of events, 'is how these men were able to get into the UK to carry out this awful execution. I know Bugsy's Border Control mates reckon our coast is more porous than we think, but surely Arab assassins can't just come and go without attracting suspicion?'

'That's just it, Mrs Dawes,' said Carmichael, 'they can. For example, those two men who kidnapped you and your sister were British. They were born in Wolverhampton and held British passports. We were able to trace and identify them after we took their bodies away.'

Corrie was astounded. 'But that's impossible! They can't have been British; they were fanatical Arabs with beards and everything. They claimed to be the avenging Sword of Islam, spawned in war-torn Kabul, not Wolverhampton. They said that the Holy Jihad to wreak vengeance on the enemies of Allah had been nurtured in their beloved country. Surely they didn't mean the West Midlands.'

Carmichael's expression was even grimmer than usual. 'They

may have been born here but they'll have been trained and radical-
ized abroad and they'll have many relatives living there. Even though
they're technically British, to them, the revolution is still theirs and
they're just as committed to the cause as the terrorists in the Middle
East who trained them.'

Corrie swallowed hard. 'That's the scariest thing I've ever heard.
You tell yourself you're relatively safe from terrorism here in the UK
and all the fighting and violence is happening somewhere else, a long
way off. But that isn't true any longer, is it?'

Jack put his arm around her. 'Come on, sweetheart, let's go home.'

CHAPTER TWENTY-FIVE

Many tourists had chosen to remain in the West Country while the weather held, so the motorway traffic to London was moving along briskly. Even so, the journey home was long and tedious. The atmosphere in Corrie's van was sombre with everyone immersed in their own dark thoughts about the recent, shocking events. It was Carlene, squashed in the back between Bugsy and a pile of trestle tables, who broke the heavy silence and lifted their flagging spirits.

'Who wants to play *Spot The Crime?*'

'Pardon?' said Jack. Carlene never ceased to surprise him and he wondered what was coming next.

'People reckon it's, like, more legit out in the sticks, right? And I guess it is, mostly, but not where we've just been. I was wonderin' how many crimes we cracked while we was there, 'coz we're a real mint team. Ain't that right?'

Nobody answered. Carlene sighed. 'Say "Yes, Carlene".'

'Yes, Carlene,' they chorused, obediently.

'So, I'll start, shall I?' She began to count on her fingers. 'Murder – Saskia de Kuiper, obviously. Then there's Donald Draycott and Patsy Tincknell. And the two Arabs what kidnapped Mrs D and Mrs Brown. Kidnap's a crime, ain't it?'

'Yeah, and the violence that went with it. But their deaths were more of an execution and a suicide than murder,' corrected Bugsy.

'Okay, if ya wanna be picky. 'Course, some of us still have our doubts about how that old priest carked it.'

'An accident,' said Corrie swiftly. 'Father John's death was an accident, like Thomas Tincknell's. But you can add wife-beating resulting in actual bodily harm and child abuse to your list. I daresay the bishop's guilty of something too; covering up a crime?'

'You're forgetting blackmail,' offered Jack. He'd got the hang of it, now. It was like playing *I Spy* to while away a long car journey, only considerably more macabre. 'As well as illegal arms trafficking, Simon and Saskia were putting the screws on most of the village, just for amusement. Then, breaking and entering by the neighbours looking for the blackmail evidence and assault by Marcus on Dick with a garden rake.'

'What about fraud and false accounting?' asked Corrie, cautiously overtaking an old man in a Bentley doing thirty miles an hour in the centre lane. 'Both Marcus and Donald Draycott were guilty of those.'

'I don't fink we should count Marcus as a criminal,' declared Carlene.

'Why not?'

'"Coz he was dead sorry and he put everyfink right in the end. And he's well fit,' she muttered, under her breath.

'I doubt if that last bit would stand up in court, Sherlock,' grinned Bugsy.

'Ted Boobyer for sexual harassment and importing and employing illegal immigrants,' said Corrie, with feeling. She still recalled the look of shame and fear on Danika's face.

'Accepting bribes,' added Malone. 'Doctor Brimble for taking a backhander on the planning committee of the parish council, but it was only the once and they're not going to follow it up because he's a damn good GP. Then there's that piece of pond life, Gilbert Chedzey. Some copper he turned out to be, Guv, despite your brother-in-law thinking the sun shone out of his . . . er . . . orifice.'

'Conspiracy to murder and collusion,' said Jack. 'Ethel Tincknell for concealing the shootings that her son committed.'

'Failure to report a death and illegal disposal of a body,' said Malone. 'Dimpsy Tincknell – I mean, Holly Puddy. But I doubt she'll have charges to answer.'

'Arson. Peter set fire to Dick and Rosie's attic. But not deliberately, though,' Corrie said.

'Perverting the course of justice,' yelled Bugsy, 'and that includes just about everyone. How many crimes is that, Sherlock?'

'Dunno. I give up countin' after ten. It's a bleedin' lot, though, for a coupla weeks in a manky little village. And there was me, thinking Hackney was the capital of crime. Huh! It'll almost be a relief to get 'ome, although I'm not looking forward to going back to the hostel. My room in Hangman's Inn was real cool – and there was a lock on the door.' It was clear from the sudden change in her mood that she was unhappy about returning to the halfway house.

Corrie was even more convinced that her plans for Carlene were the right ones. She'd tell her as soon as they got home and she'd had a chance to discuss it with Jack but she knew he'd be in favour.

Carlene edged away from Malone and wrinkled her nose. 'Not bein' funny, Sergeant Bugsy, but that suit's clappin'. Reckon it's time you got a new one, to be honest wiv ya.'

Malone feigned indignation. 'There's nothing wrong with this suit; I've only had it twenty years, there's loads of wear left in it.'

Carlene was undaunted. 'It stinks somefink 'orrible. Reckon it's all the manky food and old fag-ends you stuff in the pockets. And it don't fit ya no more. Reminds me of the old geezer who sleeps in a cardboard box on the steps of my hostel. No offence, like.'

'None taken,' grinned Bugsy. He fished in his jacket pocket, pulled out a smelly, half-eaten pork pie of uncertain vintage and bit into it.

'Are there really people sleeping in boxes outside where you live?' asked Corrie, even more disturbed by this revelation than the potential food poisoning Bugsy was risking.

'Yeah, but they don't do no 'arm. Mostly, they're pissed or out o' their skulls on crack.'

That does it, decided Corrie. It was no place for a young woman trying to go straight.

Detective Chief Superintendent George Garwood repositioned his blotting pad to dead centre on his highly polished, mahogany desk and took a deep, steadying breath. Now that the threat of an international arms dispute between the UK, NATO and the Middle East had been averted, he could at least sleep properly again but his bowels had not yet returned to normal. Whisky helped. He opened his drawer, took out the bottle of Glenfiddich and poured himself a dram.

Thankfully, the Foreign Secretary had declared himself satisfied that the situation in Lullington Barrow had been brought under control but that wasn't enough for Garwood. He had demanded a full report from Inspector Dawes on everything that had taken place. What the blazes did the man think he was playing at, getting mixed up with Arab revolutionaries and repressed regimes, never mind kidnap and torture? He was a murder detective with the Metropolitan Police; he had no business interfering in matters of national security. They had special operatives for that; experts in their field for whom, happily, Garwood wasn't responsible and whose cock-ups wouldn't ruin his chances of promotion. Added to which, it seemed that Mrs Dawes had very selfishly managed to dislocate her shoulder. Larking about, no doubt. Cynthia was giving him earache, panicking that Corrie might not be able to cater a very important dinner party they were giving next Saturday evening. Garwood had instructed his secretary to send for Dawes and Malone because he wanted to speak to them urgently. My God, he would give them such a bollocking!

While he waited, he pulled his in-tray towards him. Since Dawes and Malone had returned, there seemed to be an awful lot of overtime claim forms for him to sign. He was tugging the cap from his gold-plated fountain pen – a present from Cynthia – when the telephone rang. It was the commander.

'Sir Barnaby, how very nice to hear from you.' Garwood snapped to attention in his chair, back ramrod straight, and eased down his silver-buttoned tunic to its usual immaculate smoothness. 'Excellent round of golf yesterday if I may say so, sir. Sheer genius the way you blasted out of that bunker at the fourteenth.' The commander had cheated, of course, and they both knew it. They also knew that Garwood would never dare say so. He remained with the phone clamped firmly to his ear for several minutes. As he listened, his expression changed from obsequious to suitably grave. 'Yes, sir, I agree. Very nasty business. Arms trafficking and Arabs running riot in a peaceful little Somerset village? It beggars belief. Matter of fact, Mrs Garwood and I have a country cottage in Cornwall but nothing of that nature has ever occurred. I shall, of course, be conducting a rigorous de-brief with Inspector Dawes. When I allowed him to stay and assist the anti-terrorist team, I had no idea that his handling of the situation would be so . . .' he paused as the commander spoke again, '. . . outstanding. Yes, Sir Barnaby, that's just what I was about to say. First-rate piece of work. Head of MI6 said that, did he? Very decent of him. And the Chief Constable of Avon and Somerset? Well, that's most gratifying. Yes, of course I shall pass on your appreciation to Dawes and Malone and thank you very much, sir.'

Garwood put the phone down and took a deep breath. Christ

Almighty, he'd very nearly put his foot right in it. Another minute and he'd have made a complete idiot of himself. Bloody Jack Dawes, he'd done it again, hadn't he? Put Garwood at a disadvantage; made him feel inferior. He'd dearly love to have the blasted man transferred but he couldn't afford to do that because most of the successful clear-up results of the MIT were down to Dawes, and the commander knew it. He had already mentally rehearsed the conversation he'd intended to have with Dawes but now he'd have to review it. But before he could gather his wits, the door banged open and Malone slouched in, carrying a bacon roll balanced on top of an overflowing mug of tea. He dumped the roll on Garwood's highly polished desk and took a swig of his tea, sloshing some on Garwood's very expensive carpet.

'Inspector Dawes is just coming, sir. Got held up on the phone to the "funny buggers" . . . er . . . someone from the Intelligence Agency, I believe he said. But he won't be long.'

Garwood screwed up his face with distaste as the smell of bacon permeated his carefully air-conditioned office. He looked Malone up and down. The man was a mess – fat and balding, unshaven, the same crumpled suit with the lapels stained with food. Hadn't he got anything else to wear?

There was a tap on the door and Dawes strode in. 'Sorry about that, sir. Mr Carmichael from Intelligence wanted to speak to me. Here's the report on the Lullington Barrow cases that you asked for.' He placed a thick file on the desk in front of Garwood. 'Quite a lengthy document, I'm afraid, and knowing how meticulous you are, I expect you'll want more detail—'

A curt chop of the hand sliced him off short. 'Never mind,' said Garwood through clenched teeth. 'I don't have time to de-brief you now, Inspector; I'll read it at home, tonight.'

'Mr Carmichael said you had some feedback for me from MI6 and the Chief Constable of Avon and Somerset, sir. Apparently, the commander was going to ring you.'

The chief superintendent's angry glower bounced harmlessly off Dawes's expression of utter innocence. Garwood hadn't intended to pass on their comments and Dawes knew it but the bloody man always seemed able to wrong-foot him. 'Well done,' he said, grudgingly. 'Now get back to work.'

As the two men trooped out and closed the door behind them,

Garwood took off his glasses and pinched his nose. Suddenly, he felt very tired.

'Well, I don't know about you but I think Lullington Barrow should serve as a cautionary tale for anyone who has ever dreamt of swapping city life for a more peaceful existence in the country.' Corrie was putting on her Winnie-the-Pooh pyjamas and looking forward to a good night's sleep now she was back home in her own bed in Kings Richington.

Jack eased the cork from a bottle of rather good champagne and caught the rising bubbles expertly in a flute. 'Too bloody right, darling. What a green and desperate land!' He passed her a foaming glass.

'For me, the worst aspect of village life is the infestation of gossip, malice and spite that seems to endure for generations. Even if you discount the Arab dimension, the rest of it was pretty ghastly.'

'And the scariest part is that nobody wanted anything to change from that chocolate-box delusion.'

'I've just spoken to Rosie on the phone. She says after we left, *For Sale* signs sprang up all over Gallows Green like mushrooms on a dewy morning.'

'Is she okay, your sister?' asked Jack. 'She had a pretty rotten time of it.'

'Oh yes. She's tougher than she looks. A few whiffs of lavender and a cup of camomile tea and she'll be good as new.' Corrie sipped her bubbly. 'Mmm . . . Bolly . . . yum.' She smacked her lips as the nutty finish caressed her palate. 'Jack, I need to talk to you about Carlene.'

When Corrie had rented the catering unit on the industrial estate, it had come with a fully-fitted bedsit above. It was this accommodation that Corrie wanted to offer Carlene but as Jack had helped to finance it, it was only right that he should be consulted. After all, his job meant he was in constant contact with villains and recidivists and he might still see Carlene as a risk, although of course, Corrie knew she wasn't. But before she could put her proposition to him, Jack launched into a spontaneous eulogy of his own.

'She's doing so well, isn't she?' exclaimed Jack. 'I can't believe how much she's progressed since you took her on. She isn't a lost cause, like that dopey social worker kept insisting; she just needed to get stuck into a decent job with someone who believed in her. After that, she just blossomed. Some of her deductions about the crimes in Lullington

Barrow were masterly; the girl has a brain. Tell you what, though. I think we need to get her out of that hostel; it's full of the kind of people she's trying to avoid and it can't be easy for her.' He took a long slurp of Bolly. 'What about that bedsit over your catering unit? It's fully furnished and lying empty. You've been meaning to let it for ages. I know it's small and she'd be "living over the shop", as it were, but Carlene might prefer it to sleeping with one eye open because there's no lock on her door. What d'you think? Shall we ask her?'

Corrie smiled at Jack and was reminded for the umpteenth time why she had married him. 'Darling, that's a brilliant idea. Why didn't I think of it?'

CHAPTER TWENTY-SIX

Corrie returned to a lucrative backlog of catering orders. The heatwave had abated and the smart set of Kings Richington had tired of fiddling with pool-side barbecues and regained their enthusiasm for upmarket party food. She had assured a distressed Cynthia Garwood that her dislocated shoulder would not affect her ability to cater the very important dinner party which was to include several senior Metropolitan Police officers. It was this meal – goat's cheese soufflés, slow-roasted Tuscan pork with garlic mash and George's favourite, chocolate marquise – that she and Carlene were busy preparing in the catering unit.

'How do you feel about serving this one as well as helping to cook it?' asked Corrie. 'We could get you the proper clothes; dress and apron and things.'

Carlene was thrilled. 'Blimey, Mrs D, d'you really fink I could do it? There'll be posh coppers there wiv their WAGs and everyfink.'

'That doesn't matter. Look how well you coped with that meal in Lullington Barrow. The atmosphere was dreadful. A few self-important policemen can't be any worse than that.' Corrie hesitated. 'We might have to change your appearance just a wee bit, though.'

'You mean the colour of me 'air and the studs through me eyebrows and fings?'

'Yes. Is that a problem?'

'No . . . it's just that I don't have much room in the hostel and it's all a bit scuzzy for gettin' meself done up proper, the way I'd like. But I can manage, I know I can.'

Corrie was aware that Carlene had never been upstairs to the bedsit and thought this might be a good time to show her.

'Come with me, a minute, Carlene. Mr Jack and I have had an idea about your living conditions and we'd like your opinion.'

They trooped up the stairs and Corrie unlocked the door. The bedsit was small, as Jack had pointed out, but it was clean and bright and Corrie had decorated it with cheerful fabrics and good furniture. They went in and stood in the middle of the room.

'Well? What do you think?' asked Corrie. 'Could you be comfortable here? It would be great for me, having you so close to the business and at least it would be private and all yours. Don't worry about the rent; we'll arrange something along with your wages.'

Carlene said nothing. She just stood and looked around her at the spotless kitchen area and a tiny fridge where she could keep food without it being nicked while she was out; the separate bathroom that nobody else would use and leave the bog mingin'; the clean, bright duvet on the bed that matched the cheery curtains and cosy cushions on the sofa. There was even a small TV on the wall that Jack had installed. To Carlene, with her background of care homes, bail hostels and halfway houses, it was a palace. She stood and looked but could say nothing. Then big tears began to roll slowly down her cheeks. She didn't weep or sob – there were just floods of tears that she seemed unable to control. The last time she'd cried had been when the authorities came to take her mum and had dragged a small Carlene away, prising her fingers from her mother's skirts, where she clung desperately. She'd promised herself then that she'd never cry about anything, ever again. But this was different and she couldn't help herself.

Corrie looked at her and was horrified. She'd obviously got the situation completely wrong. Maybe Carlene valued her independence in the hostel more than she and Jack had thought and didn't want to give it up. Maybe she saw this as a step too far that would bring her too close to Corrie. After all, she wasn't a relation or anything, just her boss, and Carlene had never been close to anybody; she'd never been given the chance. She had no way of knowing how fond Corrie had become of her and the growing respect that Jack had for her determination and intelligence. Corrie was never usually lost for words but now she thrashed about for a way of recovering the situation and restoring their happy, working relationship.

'Look, Carlene, I'm so sorry if I've upset you. I don't really understand young people. You see, I've never had any of my own, sadly. It's just that Mr Jack and I thought you'd like your own place. If we've made a mistake, it wasn't intentional. Just forget I said anything.'

Still unable to speak, Carlene walked slowly across to Corrie, put both arms around her and hugged her so tightly she could hardly breathe. Then they both wept.

Carlene celebrated what she saw as her unbelievable good fortune by holding a bedsit-warming party. She had cooked the same meal that she was to serve at the Garwood's function, by way of a rehearsal and to prove to Corrie that she could do it. Corrie, Jack and Bugsy were squashed around her tiny dining table while Carlene served them.

'So what's this, then, Sherlock? You taken a vow of conformity or something? I hardly recognized you without the purple barnet and all the metal in your face.'

'And I hardly recognized you in that wicked new suit, Sergeant Bugsy. Now try not to chuck your grub down it or put fag-ends in the pockets.'

Bugsy pursed his lips. 'I'll have you know, young Sherlock, that since you told me I stink, I've given up smoking.'

Corrie and Jack looked at each other incredulously. Bugsy – a fag-free zone?

'You certainly look different, Carlene.' Jack had been stunned when he first arrived. The tormented magenta hair had gone, replaced by a shiny chestnut bob beneath a spotless white cap. All the studs in her ears, eyebrows and lips had been removed and she wore a smart black dress with an apron over it. Even her shoes were different; no longer did she teeter on impossible wedges but walked confidently in fashionable but more suitable pumps. This, thought, Corrie, is Carlene's Damascene moment and she's making the most of it.

'Mrs D's teaching me to speak proper and I'm starting part-time study at catering college next week,' said Carlene proudly, while they devoured her magnificent soufflés.

'It's always good to have some qualifications,' said Corrie.

'And Sergeant Bugsy's teaching me to drive, so when I've passed my test, Mrs D says I can do deliveries in the van.' A fleeting frown crossed her face. 'Sometimes, I fink – I mean, think – this is all a dream and I'll wake up back in my room in the hostel.'

'Don't be daft, Sherlock, course you won't,' said Bugsy, giving her a playful shove. 'And I may have given up smoking but I haven't given up eating. Where's my pork and mash?'

If the meal at Hangman's Inn had been the worst dinner party ever, this one was undoubtedly the best. They ate till they couldn't move, laughed till they cried and drank more wine than was good for them, necessitating the need for taxis home. As they were preparing to leave, Carlene said, 'Can I ask you something, Mr Jack? Something to do with the law and justice and stuff?'

'Dear me, this sounds very heavy. What do you want to know?'

She hesitated slightly. 'Is it always wrong not to tell the police everything you know?' She was thinking of Dimpsy Tincknell, her unborn baby and her virtual admission that she'd trapped her husband in the pen, knowing Titus would kill him. It had been weighing heavily on her conscience. 'I mean, if it wouldn't help anyone to know everything, might even make things worse for someone, do you still have to tell? Even if it doesn't seem right?'

Corrie thought of Bridget O'Dowd and her confession that she'd 'put a stop' to Father John. That, surely, came under the same rules and Corrie had said nothing. Jack and Bugsy were thinking about the priest's blood that was present in the soil sample from beneath the sacrarium. They, too, had decided not to pursue it and had kept the information to themselves.

'What I need to know,' said Carlene, 'is whether it's always right to insist on justice if weak people suffer as a result?'

Jack hesitated and Corrie wondered what he'd say. She knew he had a strong sense of truth and integrity, which is what made him such a committed policeman. But unlike many coppers, he also had strong feelings about the rights of human beings.

'What I've learned as a policeman, Carlene,' said Jack, 'is that for the sake of compassion and humanity, it's sometimes necessary to jam a stick in the wheels of justice. Does that answer your question?'

She beamed happily. 'Yes, thanks.'

Once the 'incomers' had left, the villagers of Lullington Barrow settled back into their indolent, rustic routines. It was a lazy, Sunday afternoon, and the regulars were once more comfortably installed in their usual chairs in Hangman's Inn, playing crib and dominoes and putting the world back to rights. 'Course, it wasn't quite the same without good old Ted Boobyer behind the bar, pulling pints of Lullington Gold, but his missus was coping all right. Pity about old Ted. They blamed that flashy young foreign trollop. Once you start letting

oreigners in, you'm asking for trouble, they told each other. Shame
bout old Bert Chedzey, too. Lost his job and his pension, thanks to
hey comical buggers from up London. Old Bert were a bloody good
opper; knew when to look the other way and didn't keep asking damn
ool questions. Not like that PC Chowdhry, forever poking her nose in.
Another foreigner, see. 'Tiz always the same. Their collective verdict
on the grisly fate of Saskia de Kuiper was that 'tiz no more'n she
deserved, sellin' guns and the like to murderin' Arabs. Next thing, they
oreigners'll be wantin' to live in peaceful villages among decent folk'.

The houses on Gallows Green were all empty now. On the market
or silly money. Probably be sold to more rich 'incomers'. Well, they'd
oon show the buggers they weren't welcome. Don't 'ee fret about that.
This village don't need change; 'tiz fine just like it is.

'Where be they goin' to on a Sunday?' An old farmer in overalls and
gumboots had got up to stagger to the gents. As he passed the window,
he'd spotted a convoy of heavy machinery and diggers, trundling up
the main road through the village.

'They'm only passin' through, innum?' suggested another man,
standing up to look.

'No, they aren't passing through.' A smartly dressed young woman
who had been sipping orange juice, unnoticed, in one of the snug
booths now stood up and walked confidently into the public bar.
They're on their way to Black Oak Farm.'

Everyone in the bar turned to look at her. 'Dimpsy? Dimpsy
Tincknell? What be you doin' in 'ere, girl? An' all done up like a
Cursmas tree.'

'My name is Holly Puddy, now, but don't exhaust your simple
brains trying to remember it; I shall only be staying long enough to
watch the bulldozers flatten the farm, ready for the contractors to
move in on Monday.'

They looked at each alarmed. 'Contractors? What be you talkin'
bout, you silly mare?'

She smiled. 'The contractors who'll be building new housing estates
on the site of Black Oak Farm.'

The old yokels relaxed then. They laughed and nudged each other.
She'm soft in the 'ead, young Dimpsy, allus was,' they chuckled.
Houses? 'Tiz a load o' bullshit. Black Oak Farm has been in the
Tincknell family for years. 'Tiz farm land for beasts, not buildings.

Allus will be. All right, Thomas did away with Patsy and that school-teacher but you can't blame 'im for that, can 'ee? What else was 'e meant to do? Let 'em get away with carryin' on behind 'is back? But they can't take his farmland for building, even though he is dead and gone. They can't do that.'

'Actually, they can.' Edgar Brimble had said nothing until now but felt it was time for both Holly and Lullington to move on. 'I've seen the plans and the county council have approved them. There'll be three very extensive estates of semi-detached dwellings with a main road running through, and at the end of that road – a massive Tesco superstore.'

'What?' shrieked the old girl who ran the village shop. 'I'll be ruined!'

'And me!' said the old bloke who ran a filthy old garage and petrol station.

'Soon,' continued the doctor, 'the "incomers" as you call them will be swarming all over this village. They'll almost certainly outnumber the locals. The new properties are to house the overspill of workers from cities like Bath and Bristol. They'll be commuting by car and train and who knows, they may even drag you lot into the twenty-first century.' He held his arm out to Holly. 'Come along, Ms Puddy. Let's go and watch the bulldozers.'

After they'd left, a stunned silence fell over Hangman's Inn. Then, one by one, the villagers got up and shambled out. Liz Boobyer threw a tea towel over the pumps.